HEADSTONE CITY

"A beautiful and perversely funny sort of crime novel: a hard-boiled hallucination.... *Headstone City* gives you the distinctive shiver good horror writing—all good writing—provides: the certainty that the writer's own ghosts are in it."
　　　　　　　　　　　　—*New York Times Book Review*

"Alternately funny, sad and thrilling... A stellar supernatural crime novel... Piccirilli plays cleverly with his hero's paranormal ability, keeping the reader guessing—and jumping—by blurring distinctions between the living and the dead."　　　　　—*Publishers Weekly* (starred review)

"A tense and sometimes sorrowful yarn with just enough supernatural elements to lift it above more typical crime fiction fare. Subtle and masterful."　　　　—*Rue Morgue*

"A seamless and wholly believable blend of the supernatural with hard-boiled noir. Razor-sharp characterization as the dead and the damned play out their violent destinies in a modern-day Dante's *Inferno*."
　　　　　　　　　　—Bill Pronzini, author of *Mourners*

"Fuses flesh-crawling creepiness... with muscular hard-boiled fiction... A keeper."　　　　　　—*Fangoria*

"Piccirilli subverts familiar mob story clichés with sly, dark humor.... A quintessential Tom Piccirilli novel about a man trying to deal with the considerable weight of the past so he can move on to a meaningful future."
　　　　　　　　　　　　　　　　　—*Locus*

A Choir of Ill
Children

"Riotous, surprising, and marvelously gruesome."
—Stewart O'Nan

"Will appeal both to genre fans and to readers of Flannery O'Connor and even of William Faulkner. James Lee Burke and Harry Crews devotees should also take note."
—*Publishers Weekly*

"Disturbing and compelling."   —*Rocky Mountain News*

"A narrative puzzle as intellectually challenging as it is slap-your-knee entertaining...There is as much poet as popular entertainer in Piccirilli's approach."   —*Cemetery Dance*

"Beautifully written, ingeniously plotted, richly atmospheric...Piccirilli is one of the few living authors who can mingle with the masters of the genre."
—Thomas Ligotti

"Lyrical, ghastly, first-class horror."   —*Kirkus Reviews*

"A marvelous fable about family, responsibility, and owning up to your nightmares."   —*SF Site*

"Better start revising your favorite author list—Piccirilli deserves to be at the top."   —*Book Lovers*

"Brilliant. Surprises abound on every page, and every one of its characters is unforgettable and sublimely imagined."   —*Flesh & Blood Magazine*

"Piccirilli is a master of the snapshot, of the slice of life—he plunges you headlong into various worlds, makes his points, then ushers you out, leaving you to reflect on what you've experienced."   —*Hellnotes*

"Tom Piccirilli writes with a razor for his pen. *A Choir of Ill Children* is both deeply disturbing and completely compelling."
          —Christopher Golden, author of *Wildwood Road*

"A resonant, powerful, lyrical, and disturbing piece of work."   —Simon Clark, author of *Stranger*

"*A Choir of Ill Children* is spellbinding. Piccirilli writes like lightning, illuminating a dark landscape of wonders."
          —Douglas Clegg, author of *The Hour Before Dark*

"An eerie, turbulent book that pushes at the boundaries of reality and horror fiction alike. This has the same paranoid energy as Philip K. Dick at his best."
          —Ed Gorman, author of *The Day the Music Died*

"Deep, daring, and stunningly original...A macabre work of art."   —Edward Lee, author of *City Infernal*

"*A Choir of Ill Children* is effing brilliant—Carson McCullers by way of William S. Burroughs....A powerful meditation on isolation, pointless anger, and familial obligation."   —Gary A. Braunbeck, author of *In Silent Graves*

"If Victor Frankenstein had stitched together pieces of Flannery O'Connor, Stewart O'Nan and James Lee Burke, his creature might have risen from the slab to write *November Mourns*.... Piccirilli manages, like the best magic realists, to create landscapes pulsing with otherworldliness.... This is a place you find yourself wanting to experience for yourself." —*Colorado Daily Camera*

"Tom Piccirilli is the master of the Southern gothic, quietly building horror where the chills grow with increasing strangeness.... When he is done, the uneasy horrors of Moon Run Hollow are in your bones." —*Denver Post*

"Tantalizes with hints of awesome mysteries that defy complete understanding." —*Publishers Weekly*

"Few can match Piccirilli's skill with words.... *November Mourns* is dark, ambiguous, strange, and sometimes surprisingly sweet. The taint in the land brings William Faulkner to mind, while the taint in the people is pure Flannery O'Connor." —*Locus*

"A novel by Tom Piccirilli will take you places you've never been before.... Beautifully written, *November Mourns* mesmerizes from the start and never lets up." —*Talebones*

"A kaleidoscope of memorably bizarre and wonderfully realized characters... *November Mourns* is a literary arrow... fired with a deft hand and a keen eye." —*Cemetery Dance*

"Tom Piccirilli breaks genre form with a potent brew of poetry and atmosphere to concoct his unique brand of shudder-inducing, highly literate horror."

—*Rue Morgue*

Also by Tom Piccirilli

NOVELS

Headstone City

November Mourns

A Choir of Ill Children

Coffin Blues

Grave Men

A Lower Deep

The Night Class

The Deceased

Hexes

Sorrow's Crown

The Dead Past

Shards

Dark Father

COLLECTIONS

The Devil's Wire

Mean Sheep

Waiting My Turn to Go Under the Knife (poetry)

This Cape Is Red Because I've Been Bleeding (poetry)

A Student of Hell (poetry)

Deep Into That Darkness Peering

The Dog Syndrome & Other Sick Puppies

Pentacle

NONFICTION

Welcome to Hell

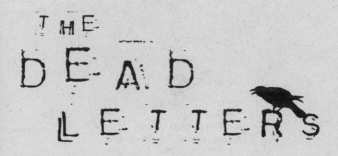

THE DEAD LETTERS

TOM PICCIRILLI

BANTAM BOOKS

THE DEAD LETTERS
A Bantam Book / October 2006

Published by Bantam Dell
A Division of Random House, Inc.
New York, New York

Bantam Books and the rooster colophon are trademarks of
Random House, Inc.

ISBN-10: 0-553-38407-4
ISBN-13: 978-0-553-38407-9

Printed in the United States of America
Published simultaneously in Canada

www.bantamdell.com

OPM   10 9 8 7 6 5 4 3 2 1

For Michelle & Patrick Lussier

ACKNOWLEDGMENTS

A big thanks go out to the following folks for their support and encouragement: T. M. Wright, Ed Gorman, Dallas & Lee, Matt Schwartz, Gerard Houarner, Adam Meyer, Keene for all the groovy comics, Jack Barbera, and Dean Koontz.

As always, special thanks to my editor Caitlin Alexander.

Love makes your soul crawl out from its hiding place.
— ZORA NEALE HURSTON

THE DEAD LETTERS

PART I

TESTAMENT OF YA'AL

ONE

Killjoy wrote:

Words are not as adequate as teeth.

Incisors are incapable of lying. If I pressed them into wax or paper or fish or flesh you would know my meaning, the constraints of form, and every trivial fact there is to be found, distinguished in its context, beyond the obvious. Words are deficient, even impractical, when attempting to convey the substance of true (modest) self. Deed is definition. We are restricted by mind and voice but not in action, wouldn't you agree? That we can never completely express that which is within. That sometimes the very act of feeling isn't enough to encompass all there is to feel. Frenzy is trying to explain your behaviors to yourself. I suspect I have yet a long way to go at the art of becoming human.

Remember Schlagelford's great treatise on the fear of non-existence. He spent some thirty-seven years of his adult life with his left hand clamped to his left thigh (trouserless, of course). Despite his grip cutting off all circulation in that leg until it withered, blackened, and eventually had to be amputated *(and the hand, no more than a frozen talon, had grown useless, and continued to squeeze the phantom limb),* at which point he gripped his right thigh with his right hand and had to write his last major work, The Season of Femoral, *with quill champed between adequate teeth, still he was content.*

Satisfied in his knowledge of personal existence in a world without enough promise or structure.

Do you ever feel that way, Whitt?

There are orange sneakers on the gelded man in the corner.

Which do you prefer? Writing or biting?

The season of femoral begins again.

Do your hands shake?

The mama cultist told Eddie Whitt about the dead ballerina, a god named Mucus-Thorn-In-Brain, and the starving baby that had been stolen out of the back room.

She and her two lumbering middle-aged sons smiled at him. Whitt tried to smile back but the muscles in his jaw were so tight that he barely managed a grimace. It got like that sometimes, when he was forced to hold himself in check. Luckily these people were so caught up in their own mania that they hardly even noticed him while they prattled on incessantly. They gave him a cup of herbal tea that smelled like turpentine and he left it on the scratched table in front of him.

Except for the murders, they were about the same as any other cult members he'd met. Considering his narrow range of interests and social obligations, he'd actually met more than his share. Whatever the hell a man's share of cultists should be in this world.

The woman, Mrs. Prott, who introduced herself as the High Priestess of the Cosmic Knot, spoke with near-hysterical excitement about a new god being born in the back of her son Merwin's heart. Merwin, who had awful surgical scars covering his forehead, grinned stupidly and petted his chest like he was stroking a luscious woman's hair.

The other son, Franklin, was blind and kept flexing his hands like he wanted to leap out of his chair and tear something to pieces.

Whitt feigned interest in Mrs. Prott's sermon and looked at her star charts, notes, magazine articles, and photographs of the multitude of people who played some role in her ever-widening tale of religion, murder, and secret government experiments. She kept tapping a spot between her eyes, saying they'd shot her there and her brain had leaked out, which was why she sometimes got mixed up. Whenever she said the word "government," Merwin would stop stroking his invisible lover's hair and thump his head.

This house had been the dumping ground for members of the group for years. Whitt got up and wandered around while the woman talked, rifling through stacks of newspapers dating back three, four years. He saw himself on the front page of more than one, laid out mostly in the open, as if waiting for him.

A metal shelf unit held two dozen upside-down mason jars, each sealed with contact cement and sprinkled with a handful of salt. Words, possibly names, were scrawled in black marker on old yellow masking tape: *Hogarth. Pedantry. Airsiez. Colby. Terminus. Kinnick. Insensate. Testament of Ya'al. Ussel. Dr. Dispensations. O'Mundanity.*

She kept on preaching. It threw him off a bit, this lady's willingness to discuss such matters so openly, in her strange manner, as though she were telling only basic, incontrovertible truths. Speaking in a happily lilting voice, like she was overjoyed to find someone who actually had interest in her life, no matter why. Whitt nodded like an idiot and she nodded back. Was it only loneliness that drove people to such extreme acts?

"And she came to you for help," he said, sitting down again, trying to keep Mama on topic. "The ballerina."

"For the truth, yes. And for love. Everyone, always in such need of love. You see, she also had quite the nervous disposition. Emotionally she'd been tormented by her parents, who never responded to her with affection of any kind. They merely drove her ever more forcefully toward the perfection of her dancing. Into the arms of boys. That's what the child was. A symbol of her desperation."

"And you murdered her," Whitt said.

Telling it while fluttering her hand at him as if he were absurd, so silly. "What do you mean? Who?"

Whitt forced his breath out in a stream that blew ripples across the stinking tea. He remembered to make the effort to smile again. "The ballerina."

Head eased back, Franklin rolled his blank eyes up and let out a guffaw. It came from down low in his belly and the depths of his hate. Whitt wanted to hear what the guy's voice sounded like, but so far Franklin refused to make any comment beyond that sick laughter. If any trouble started, Whitt would take out the blind guy before anybody else.

Mrs. Prott said, "Oh yes, that one. The dancer."

The first thing you saw when you looked at Mama Prott was the jiggle of turkey neck. Even when she wasn't turning her head, that neck still flapped, vibrating with her breathing, always catching your attention. Whitt couldn't get over it.

The woman was boiling with gaiety, heavy and earthen. She was someone you wanted to hug, really. Her expensive, chic clothing was mismatched and too tight. He figured she'd stolen them from ladies with taste in order to pretend she had some fashion sense herself. Lots of jewelry, most of it fake, but some pieces worth more than this shit hole's entire mortgage. She wore men's wedding bands on both thumbs.

Franklin's hands opening and closing in perfect timing to Whitt's pulse.

Mrs. Prott smiling, her teeth dark and crooked.

"Well, no one actually killed her. You cannot destroy that which is *obdurate. Insensible.* You can only transform it. She wasn't human." Doing the fluttery finger thing again. "She was *other,* and the purifying light of Mucus-Thorn-In-Brain struck her down when she tried to steal my breath one morning."

"I see," Whitt said.

"She climbed on top of me while I slept and tried to kiss me so she could steal the soulwind from my lungs. You can't call it murder to set right the karmic cosmic wheel again."

"I thought it was a knot."

"A knot that spins and spins like a wheel across the great ecclesiastical galaxy."

"Okay," Whitt said. "So what happened to her?"

"The only way to defend ourselves from a soulthief is to stab it thrice in the heart, with the point of the blade aiming north. Then the throat must be cut so its evil incantations will dribble to the floor instead of being raised to the cosmic masters. This is the transformation that must take place. Conversion. Reformation. Then the genitals must be removed or the seed may infect another vessel and give birth even in its dying throes."

"Dying throes," Whitt repeated.

"And we wouldn't want that. We could not bear that."

"No, we could not."

"More tea?"

"Please."

That blank gaze of the blind man landed on Whitt. Franklin's fists were grasping nothing. The other brother had his hand on his chest. Whitt whispered, "Government, government," and watched Merwin clunk his thatched head twice.

Mama Prott handed Whitt a series of graphs and charts that had been modified from the zodiac. Strange uses of cabalistic symbols, Teutonic characters, numerology, and scatterings of nonsensical pseudosexual terms, with an emphasis on bodily fluids and naughty bits. Phlegm in Hair. Whore's Bait. Orifice Eye. Mucus Desisting the Efforts of Knee. Failure of Urethra. The handwriting so crimped that it would take hours to decipher it all.

Pulling out one particular sheet, stained with pinkish fluid, "Here, here it is," she said, "proof that the girl was other. That the Sect of Purification and Consummation acted in protection of all the earth and humanity."

"So you're a branch of a larger—" What should he call this thing she believed in? He didn't think she'd take offense at the word "cult," but calling this a cult lent it too much credence. "—persuasion."

"Yes. We have nineteen more members back at the other house, where the majority of our communicants live, and where we hold our official ceremonies."

"Which house would that be?" he asked.

Pointing at the far wall, the mis-sized rings on her fingers jingling slightly. "The one on Carver Way, where most of the important rituals are held. This one here, we use it only every so often, to store our belongings. You're very lucky to have found us here this morning."

"Yes," he said.

It took another half hour of finagling, but Whitt finally got the ballerina's name out of her: Grace Kinnick. It was one of the names on the jars. What did the Protts think they had in there? Captured souls?

"And the child?"

"Stolen. That's why we need your help. The beget... the offspring...of the soulthief is still in its genuine form. It can be dealt with now. Sent back into the celestial continuum where it can once again rejoin with the great astral identiform."

"Sure."

"We have to have the child before midnight Friday night. You said you know who has it now?"

"That's right, it's with a friend of mine who works for social services," Whitt lied. He grinned at Merwin. "A government agency."

Merwin rapped himself in the head again, looking scared that somebody from the Pentagon might come take away more of his brain. And Whitt sitting here making a game of it. He had to have a little fun so he didn't go wild and start crossing the hard line, becoming what everyone told him he'd become.

"Oh, it's dangerous to have the beget loose like this," Mrs. Prott warbled, the neck going gangbusters. "Magic circles must be precipitated, the proper guiding influences invoked before the evisceration and following rituals."

Whitt said, "So the baby is *other*. Genuine. It's blood-tainted. And must be struck down by Mucus-Thorn-In-Brain. And returned to the cosmic knot."

She broke into a delighted squeal that went on for too long. "Yes, exactly. Oh, you are adept. A true sensitive. You have the gift, do you realize that? I've never seen an aura quite like yours. You're exceptionally dark and very powerful."

"How often have you done this?" he asked. "Purified these . . . evils."

"Oh, we don't keep accounts of such things. This is a spiritual war we fight. There are many casualties sprawled across both sides of the veil."

"Fourteen," Franklin said, a wet chuckle easing from his chest. "The ballerina was number fourteen."

That voice, obscenely joyful, yet frothing with its hate. Whitt shifted to the edge of the chair in case he had to dive. Thinking that maybe now Franklin was about to use those hands. "What do you mean?"

"The ballerina was number fourteen," Franklin repeated. "The baby, it would've been fifteen."

Mama Prott smiled at her boy. Whitt thought about the dead, probably buried in the yard, hidden in the house. He stared at the spot between her eyes, where she said they'd shot her and her brains had leaked out, and wondered if he could drop, roll aside, draw his .32, spring to his feet, and hit the target, the way he'd been practicing.

"So, Mr. Whitt, can you help us retrieve the off-spring?"

"Yes," he said. "I consider it my reverent duty."

"Glorious! We'll be holding services this afternoon at the other house."

"On Carver Way."

"Yes. Please join us so we can sanctify and protect you from harm. You'll never regret your initiation into that which is Mucus-Thorn-In-Brain and the clarity and peace you'll feel afterwards. We'll brighten your aura yet."

That thick neck wobbling. The blind guy glaring. The other one grinning, his scars thick and shining like leeches.

"I look forward to it," Whitt said.

He drove off, parked around the corner near a sump that doubled as a dump site, and waited until the woman and her sons left in their SUV with out-of-state plates. More stolen goods. Spoils of the dead. He returned to the house with a pickax, shovel, and flashlight and stepped in through the broken back door that had been tied shut with the elastic from an old brassiere.

He left the tools on the stoop while he searched the house for any other squirrelly cultists who might be hiding under a bed somewhere. Except there weren't any beds. The three upstairs rooms looked poisonous, toxic, the old paint peeling in strips and the plaster gouged by fingernails. He found bullet holes and dried spatters that could've been any of the bodily fluids the Protts seemed to groove on so much.

Whitt grabbed his tools again and looked for the cellar door. He found it hidden behind the metal shelving stacked with all the upside-down jars of trapped souls.

The old stupidity and lack of control overwhelmed him for a minute. He took great pleasure in smashing the glass containers and releasing Hogarth and Ussel and Airsiez and the rest. He held on to the jar with the ballerina in it and pressed it to the side of his head, knowing how insane it looked but feeling an urgency to will her to peace, if he could. You never knew what you could do when you put your mind to it. Finally he hurled the container against the wall with the rest of them and went into the basement to dig.

The body was in the corner of the dirt floor about three feet down, missing its genitals and wearing orange sneakers, just like Killjoy had said.

TWO

Brunkowski kept him waiting so long on the wooden bench outside his office that Whitt fell asleep seated next to a sixty-year-old Latino pimp. You'd think a pimp, even one from Nassau County, might be insulted by that. Yank a straight razor out of his back pocket and get to work with it, but the guy didn't seem to mind. In fact he shifted a little so Whitt's head fit comfortably into the crook of his arm. The pimp wore a chocolate silk suit and looked more like a Wall Street trader. Whitt lay there against the guy's shoulder dreaming of a playground covered with crows.

When his three whores were released on bail, the pimp gently woke Whitt and disentangled himself. The trio of white girls wearing transparent plastic blouses and thongs cackled, but the pimp said nothing. You could meet another member of the brotherhood of pain in a form and fashion you'd never guess possible.

Brunk finally opened his office door in a furious blur of motion and waved him in. Whitt approached, still feeling the pimp's warmth against him, and the cool glass of the jar where Grace Kinnick's stolen soul had been imprisoned. The smell of salt and turpentine. He couldn't get the words "Testament of Ya'al" out of his head.

Whitt checked his watch. He'd been waiting on the bench for almost five hours, and his legs and neck were stiff. His lower back burned from digging in the Protts' cellar. He had to stop relying on the pistol so much and get back into the gym.

He sat and Brunk hovered over him making a cranky face, leaning back against a huge, scarred wooden desk. It was the man's security blanket, that desk, a lot more so than the .45 in a shoulder holster currently slung over the corner of a filing cabinet. The gun had to be empty, hanging there just to tempt some perp into making a grab for it and adding an additional five years to any sentence.

Sergeant Chuck Brunkowski of the Nassau County PD cultivated a dangerous throwback to the forties appearance, always keeping his shirtsleeves rolled and his tie only loosely knotted. Disheveled like he'd just spent thirty hours straight cracking a case, working to protect his city. You walked in and you usually found him leaning over his desk, fists on his blotter so you could see the muscles in his corded forearms, his shirt too tight across the hunched, powerful shoulders. A man with a burden who wanted you to always know you were only adding to it.

"How'd you know about it?" Brunk asked without preamble.

"He told me."

Tonguing the inside of his top lip, thrusting it forward, Brunk nodded. "You're still in contact."

"Yes."

"You could be charged with obstruction."

"Again with obstruction? It would never hold up."

"Detained as a material witness."

"Go the fuck ahead."

It got Brunk posturing and glaring again, like he wanted to melt Whitt in his seat, but he couldn't quite pull it off with that hair. Just a weird little tuft on his head that he tried to comb back but it wouldn't go. It puffed up depending on air currents. Whitt sometimes had a ball trying to breathe just hard enough through his nose to cause the thing to move. You had to make your own fun when you were stuck in police stations as often as Whitt had been the past few years.

"You're an idiot," Brunk said. "You take no precautions. You ruin evidence. And just because that sociopath likes to chat with you on the nature of the universe doesn't mean he's your friend. In case you've forgotten—"

Look at this, look what he's about to say next.

Whitt snapped his chin up and eyed Brunkowski, thinking, So maybe this is it, maybe here is where we finally throw down.

But Brunk's voice faded. Gruff as the prick might be

on occasion, even he didn't have it in him to cross that line and finish his sentence. *In case you've forgotten, he murdered your daughter.*

Maybe later, when they got closer to Killjoy.

Brunkowski no longer mattered to him. Five years ago Whitt had sat hinged on every word Brunk, the commissioner, and the feds had said to him, believing them wholeheartedly, desperate to hold on to any sliver of hope that his sorrow might eventually lift, that the sledge of vengeance would come down. Brunk had explained what the cops would do, how they would catch the killer, shoving his fists into the blotter and swearing that justice would soon be "meted." Fucking guy, saying a word like that. Whitt should've known it was all shit right then. Instead, he'd gone home and lain in the dark, filled with a jittery confidence in the law. Forensic science. FBI profiling.

Now when the police spoke it was like they were only determined children trying to explain themselves to a patronizing adult.

Brunk settled into his seat, ready to talk man-to-man, the way he liked to have a conversation, so long as he had the upper hand.

"Okay, so how did he get back in touch with you?"

"More letters."

"And you didn't alert us. Or the feds."

"That's pointless. You can't catch him. The feebs can't either. You've got dozens of pages of his notes and nothing ever came of it. Thousands of man-hours.

Nassau County. Suffolk. Queens. The NYPD. You've wasted five years."

"The more information we have, the closer we can get."

"You ought to be ashamed even bringing it up."

Brunk enjoyed being on the edge, balancing on the point of it. Trying to go over and not go over. Glaring at Whitt, trying to get him to wither. "Okay, so what brought you to that house?"

"He wrote that I'd find somebody with orange sneakers dead in there."

"So he's been watching those people for a while. That's how he got the baby away before the Protts could kill it."

"Yes. But don't bother canvassing the area. The neighborhood's going through an urban renewal but it hasn't hit that corner yet. The other houses are mostly empty except for a few transient squatters."

"You've been watching too."

"I wanted to make sure I wasn't stepping into a trap."

"You were hoping you would. You were hoping he would be there."

"He's too sharp for that."

Brunkowski didn't push it. "Thanks for calling us in. We've got the three Protts in a holding cell, along with a dozen of their followers. Everyone in the D.A.'s office is killing themselves getting the right warrants, but so far it's running pretty smoothly. These fuckers are all nuts. Knots and wheels and the cosmos. There's a lot of stories we have to comb through."

"You can't ignore a tip saying there's a body in a basement. Especially after you find it. What've you got on Grace Kinnick, the ballerina?"

"Nothing yet. How did you get the Protts to open up about the murders?"

"I didn't say a word," Whitt admitted. "She just vomited everything out. It's her way, I think. She's been doing it for years. I walked in and told her I had some information on the baby Killjoy took from her. Said I wanted to join her group. It was the last word I spoke for twenty minutes while she spouted. Disgorged. Who's working her in the box?"

"The commissioner's got his own people on it."

"Should've been you. All you'd have to do is take notes on cosmic knots and soulwinds and mucus desisting the efforts of knee."

Brunk frowned so hard that his eyebrows overlapped. "The hell is that anyway?"

"I don't know, but don't get too close to her. She likes to cut off the fun organs."

"I've met a few like that in my day."

"Dated a few too, I bet."

A tight smile sliced open Brunk's face. "Think she does it herself? No wonder her kids are crazy then. Imagine being potty trained by a mommy who's always carrying a pair of scissors."

"The blind one is dangerous, I think. I bet he did some naughty things to the victims too. Franklin's probably the killing arm. The other mutilation is probably postmortem."

"They're all dangerous, including the other followers. A lot of them have files for serious criminal activity. A bunch of degenerates, every one of them, down to the last. We'll try to tie as many of them into the murders as possible."

"You found more bodies already?"

"Remains of two other recent kills in that same basement, even closer to the surface than the guy with orange sneakers."

"I missed them."

"They were under a bunch of trash in a corner. And an earlier kill in the other house, tucked away on a shelf in the basement, wrapped in plastic bags. His goodies were gone too. There was a label on his forehead that said 'The Unspeakable Ten Thousand Eight Names.' We just started checking the yard. We're going full throttle on this, the feebs are already on the scene. We'll be breaking up the concrete of the driveways, the patios, the whole works. As soon as I'm done with you, I'll be heading back over there."

They were moving so fast because Killjoy was back in the picture. They didn't want him to start solving all their cold cases now. There'd already been enough ridicule of the police, and Whitt did what he could to keep the media attention coming back to it. The commissioner hated Whitt's guts, but that was all right too. Let him take the credit for this one if he wanted. Whitt didn't mind, but he wondered if Killjoy might.

"Who did Killjoy give the baby to?" Whitt asked.

"The McConnellys."

Whitt remembered them vividly. First from the news and then in his brief interview with them about a year ago, when he'd mentioned the possibility of this happening. A child being delivered to them in the night. Bill McConnelly had thrown a wild left hook in his frustration. It was a move Whitt could've easily avoided, but he'd taken it in his gut. Sometimes he enjoyed pain, especially from those who were like him. Who had suffered a similar fate.

"Social services has the kid now," Brunkowski said. "Picked him up a few days ago."

"The mother's dead. Grace Kinnick's body is probably in that house someplace. They were calling her the ballerina. There probably won't be a father, or a family. Killjoy only wants a child that's alone in the world, one in desperate trouble. The McConnellys never had another kid after their son was murdered."

"You keeping tabs on them?"

"She can't come to full term anymore. They tried adopting but it's not working out for them."

Standing and hitting his position, fists on the desktop, Brunk leaned all the way over so he could really put the stony glower on Whitt. "You suggesting they just be allowed to keep this supposed ballerina's baby?"

"Yes. Did they willingly turn the child over?"

"No. A busybody neighbor saw them playing with the baby inside."

"She saw inside?"

"She's got a telescope. She's *that* kind of a nosy neighbor."

"Christ."

"She kept up with the papers, thought she knew what had happened, and called the precinct. The McConnellys hid the kid and denied everything, but it eventually came out. After the baby was taken away, McConnelly went crazy, drove his car over the neighbor's lawn and crashed into the front of her house. Parked in her living room, ran over her telescope. He's out on bail. The busybody moved in with her sister in Peoria."

Whitt said nothing, imagining what he'd do differently this time if Killjoy gave him a second changeling child, meant to replace the daughter he'd killed.

Brunk settled back into his chair. "You still believe he's trying to set the scales back in balance?"

"He can never do it, but yes, I think it's what he's attempting. Was the baby really starving?"

"If he was, the McConnellys fattened him up just fine. They had him for over a week. Kid's healthy."

"He won't stay that way for long if he goes through the system. You know that."

"What are you, a socialist reformer now?"

Whitt said, "Give the kid to the McConnellys."

"Nobody will allow it. The commissioner, the mayor, the feds, social services, none of them will let it happen. It'll seem too much like giving Killjoy what he wants."

"It'll serve the greater purpose."

Brunkowski drew his chin back and his features slackened, shifting, showing some glee, as he clutched his stomach and let out such a harsh bark of laughter, disgusting in its context, that Whitt felt as if he'd been slapped.

"You son of a bitch," Whitt said and got to his feet.

Brunk stood and centered himself. "You want to try me?"

"Yeah."

"You sure?"

"Yeah!"

He really did want to try sparring with the sergeant and see if the man was as tough as he always acted. He was in the mood for pain or retribution, one or the other, perhaps both, so he couldn't lose no matter how it turned out.

"You take a few martial arts courses, work out a little, practice with a pipsqueak .32, and now you think you can roll through anybody?"

Whitt said nothing. He'd changed more than Brunkowski was giving him credit for, but that was to be expected. He'd learned that men purposefully un-derestimated that which they feared. The more the cop tried to put him in his place, the more satisfaction Whitt gained from it. Somehow that was important at the moment, in the face of more deaths, more stolen babies.

Whitt turned to leave, the Testament of Ya'al still looming too large in his thoughts. He saw a fiery scroll unfurling from an ancient bloody sea, with all the Unspeakable Ten Thousand Eight Names on it, and his own was among them.

"What are you going to do, if you ever find Killjoy?" Brunk asked. "How are you going to feel during that face-to-face?"

A dozen incomplete answers rifled through Whitt's mind, but none of them felt right enough to say aloud. He opened his mouth twice to answer but the words wouldn't come, and they weren't for Brunkowski anyway.

Whitt left. He felt eager and feverish and horny, and he thought about the three whores cackling at him, mocking him. For two hundred bucks they'd moan his praises and let him do whatever he wanted—meting out his own justice—and they would do to him what-ever he asked for, except perhaps kiss him. You had no choice but to make do.

* * *

Perhaps it is merely a chemical deficiency or genetic hiccup, this failure on my part (assuming, of course, that it is a failure, but let's not quibble, shall we? We are gentlemen). A pair of misfiring neurons in the frontal lobe. An electrical pulse that cannot make the microscopic leap. Is there an atomic structure to the soul?

Let us recall the tenets of Kripotkin's threefold concept of Frailty and Want: What do I desire? How do I fulfill that desire? And to what extent am I willing to go to fulfill such desire?

At this point of his life—remember that the Perpetua-Genus Revolution had just occurred, and he was then rejected by all his former peers, even his own patron Madam Batisse (this is after that appalling dinner with the czar's niece and being caught with that underage chambermaid on the steps of the great Tolstoy Museum)—his mind had become keyed to proverb and theory, deciphering what the rest of mankind had been born knowing.

The irony being, of course, that although he created such tenets, he could not act on his own needs whatsoever. He could not define that which he wanted or how to achieve it. He could never give a value to these questions in his own life.

What courage Kripotkin showed in his willingness to entrust his own frame of perception to the points of view of others! Imagine, if you can, how open he was to the will of everyone else around him: the czar; the czar's niece; Madam Batisse; the underage chambermaid, her rather large and buoyant breasts nicknamed by him "Port de Bras" (the *left) and "Jumbo Titty" (the right); Tolstoy; and the benefactors and visitors and janitors of the great Tolstoy Museum.*

Have you ever pressed your mouth to a dying child's wounds, Whitt?

Would you like to?

THREE

Smelling of sour milk, Freddy Fruggman gave Whitt an open-armed half hug, led him across the set of his latest commercial and said, "How do I handle this sort of shit? You got any ideas?"

It looked like they were pushing some kind of high-tech floor mop. The set had been dressed with disco lights and different types of flooring material, a couple of girls on rollerblades wearing bikinis, a guy dressed like a priest—or, knowing Freddy's penchant for cinema verité, maybe it actually *was* a priest—and a little toy sailboat that was supposed to float on a carefully constructed stream of water bisecting the set. Whitt couldn't figure out any of it and gave up trying.

The place was frantic, everybody wandering around speaking morosely on their cell phones and going out of their way not to look at Freddy. Either that or glaring at the back of his head. Whitt had never seen so many eyes silently asking for his help, begging him to come back into the fold, correct the devastating mistakes, fix the traumatic errors, smooth and grease the process, regain all the lost beauty. It had been four years since he'd been on a set, but they all remembered him. He had a sudden rush of gratuitous conceit, a swelling warmth of generous power, the way he used to have back when he was directing. Sometimes he missed it.

"What the hell happened?" Whitt asked. "The Catholic Church coming down on you?"

"Nah, it has nothing to do with this shoot. We broke for lunch, so now they all have time to fret. Look at them, nobody's even eating."

Freddy was a fat guy who, through some misfortune of nature, had a head way too small for his body. Almost everybody had to give him at least a second glance. The first time you took in the three hundred pounds, the next you stared at that teeny head capping his neck.

He lumbered toward his chair, the crew parting before him and the actors backing away toward the far corners, the bikini chicks rollerblading off. Freddy didn't notice. He slugged down an oversized styrofoam cup of mocha café with at least one container of turned creamer in it. Whitt spotted a couple of company lawyers huddled by the back door, plotting, preparing to advance.

Freddy shut his eyes and relaxed, swallowing more

coffee. Whitt had always wished he could find the kind
of calm within himself that Freddy Fruggman possessed. It made him a wild-card genius about half the
time, a mostly freakyass clown the other half. But his
commercials sold product and the ad execs loved him
so long as things didn't go over budget and nobody was
suing.

So somebody must be suing. The buzz in the air had
a serious edge to it. Freddy opened his eyes and appeared very sleepy, like a ten-minute power nap would
put him back on top. "A real storm a' shit. We're getting slapped with lawsuits all over. So far, nearly thirty
of them."

"Jesus Christ, for what?"

"The hovercraft thing."

Whitt had to think about that for a minute. "You
mean the hovercart? The new scooter-wheelchair?"

"Yeah, supposedly makes the elderly more mobile
than any other kind of electric wheelchair out of there.
They say right in their ads you can take it over any terrain. Makes an old person feel like a kid again, fully
functional all around the house, zips up hills, across ice,
on vacation—"

Even without the specifics yet, Whitt was starting to
get the picture. "Oh man."

"Their last commercial had a bunch of these elderly
folks playing football. On the fuckin' field, zooming
around, throwing lateral passes, cracking into one

another like bumper cars. All these gray, dusty faces smiling, showing off their blue dentures. So I took fifty of them up into the Rockies."

"The Rocky Mountains?"

Taking another deep swig, staring over Whitt's shoulder at the suits congregating there, "Yeah," Freddy said.

"The mountains themselves. You took fifty geriatrics up into the mountains."

"Most of them could get around pretty much okay, even without the chair. Well, there were a few paraplegics. And I think there were two quads among them. They were the nicest of them all."

Whitt allowed that to pass. "And what did you do with these people?"

"Let them go."

"You let them go."

"Yeah."

"What the hell does that mean?"

"You know, let them just go zooming along on their hovercarts. Across the snow and the rocks a little. Cavorting. Not too near the cliffs, but sorta close enough that they could look down. I wanted to get them gazing at all that natural beauty, you know? They seemed to enjoy it. For a while anyhow. Then they're all complaining about the cold and how they're getting stuck in the mud. It's not my fault the machinery is for shit. The hovercart is supposed to keep zipping them around through all kinds of weather."

"You let them go."

"Yeah. A few of them passed out from the altitude, and there were some nosebleeds. A couple of old ladies were crying about their civil rights, and then they all wanted to go home. Suddenly they've all got rheumatism and arthritis, meanwhile on camera they're playing fuckin' football."

Sometimes you had to speak very clearly to Freddy, quietly without any emotion, so he wouldn't get distracted from the words. He didn't have an easy time being a genius, the fifty percent of the time that he was one.

"Freddy," Whitt said, "couldn't you have accomplished the same thing if you just hired actors who could play the parts of disabled elderly folks?"

"I prefer realism."

"Yeah, sure, but—"

"The viewers, they can sense lies."

"Yeah, but letting quadriplegics loose in the Rockies!"

"Only two were quads, I told you. The rest were mostly just old and could walk if they wanted to, the pains in the ass. They could've gotten out of the mud if they'd tried hard enough. But they'd rather bellyache about it."

The strength and rigidity of Freddy's presence beneath all his flesh resolved and clarified the world around him, brought it into focus. The way a dark figure in a snowscape painting conveyed mood and texture. He was grounded in life, spiked to it, a statue on the plain.

Five years ago, standing beside Whitt at Sarah's funeral, Freddy had been a second-rate actor, a low-budget virtuoso, and Whitt's best friend since their freshman year in college. Best man at his wedding.

Shortly after Whitt left advertising, Freddy hit it big with a surreal, postmodernistic thirty-second clip about shaving cream that somehow propelled him to mysterious cultural icon. He rode the wave of celebrity without accomplishment, and never let anybody shake his worldview. Whitt still didn't know what that worldview might be, but he realized it was unshakable.

Freddy had also been Sarah's godfather. He'd cried harder during the funeral than Whitt had ever seen anybody cry before. Much harder than he or even Karen had, groaning until Whitt could no longer feel the depth of his own anguish anymore. He'd been forced to console Freddy as they'd lowered the coffin into the ground.

Whitt still had a few issues about that, but you had to prioritize the levels of frenzy and desperation always building up around you.

Karen had been tranqued that afternoon, put under suicide watch, and despite Freddy's mass and density holding him, Whitt thought it might be extremely easy for him to follow his baby girl into the ground. He should've been under suicide watch himself, but all the mourners were watching Karen instead. She fainted three times during the service, but wouldn't leave.

He still wondered why he hadn't pitched himself in, or sat in his car with the engine on and the garage door down until the deed was done. He'd made a relatively long list of ways to take a powder, but no other method quite appealed to him as much as that. Maybe because he could listen to the radio as he faded from the fight. That morning of the funeral, he'd sat in the car for about fifteen minutes, listening to an oldies station and murmuring doo-wops under his fading breath, the smoke growing thicker around him until he started to cough, before he'd finally turned the key and shut the engine off. He still didn't know why.

But he'd been there at the graveside, alive when his child wasn't, tossing in the roses as he'd been expected to do, shaking hands with people he barely recognized. Hearing his name repeated over and over in varying degrees of urgency, but rarely responding.

Karen's dad, Mike Bowman, had stood on the other side of the grave, watching with mild annoyance as if he felt Whitt had done something just a little off, something just not right. Bounced a twenty-dollar check or missed mowing a patch of lawn. Making that kind of face.

Like you didn't have enough to think about with your daughter dead in the ground and your wife trying to chew through her own wrists, biting the backs of her hands down to the bone. Now you've got to have this guy—who was the father your own father never was—staring at you like you didn't quite pass the test, couldn't join the club, son.

Thinking back on it, that's when the real hunt for Killjoy had begun. At that moment, with Mike's dissatisfied expression. All the rest of it had followed effortlessly and naturally from there.

Freddy breathed another gust of sour milk into Whitt's face and nearly made him gag. "So how do I handle this shit?"

"Did you finish the hovercart commercial?"

"Of course. And it's damn good too."

"Anybody seriously injured?"

"Nah. They just needed some oxygen because of the altitude sickness. They got a little muddy, some of them."

"Then you'll be okay."

"Even with all these lawsuits?"

"The elderly have better things to do with their remaining time than be stuck in a courtroom with a case like this that'll drag out for years. The insurance company will settle cheap with most of them. Give them free electric wheelchairs. Crumb cakes and coffeemakers. A bonus paycheck."

"The quads want monkeys," Freddy said. "Can you believe it?"

"What?"

"You hold some kind of laser pen in your teeth and you point it at things, and trained monkeys go and get it for you. You want breakfast, you laser the toaster and the monkeys put the bread in for you."

"Just give them whatever they want."

"And then what, the monkeys bite somebody and I get sued for that?"

"Get them very calm, nice monkeys."

"Indentured slavery is what it is, forcing a lower life-form to make the goddamn toast for you."

The tiny teeth in the small mouth of the teeny face kept going, but Whitt quit listening when he heard Killjoy's name mentioned somewhere on set. He turned his head to listen—sounded like one of the lighting crew—and the guy immediately shut up, realizing he'd spoken too loudly.

Everybody scared to talk and not to talk, always dancing around Whitt now that he'd become this new person, taken on a different identity. Not a cop, not a servant of the Constitution, but an operator without a name. Someone who chased a killer and found babies swapped out, in the wrong places. The man with the dead kid and the crazy wife, funded by the rich father-in-law. Boiled down, it sounded ridiculous.

Whitt stood waiting for someone to say hello and nobody even came close enough to try it, for fear he might actually talk to them.

"You're making the papers again," Freddy said, as if he'd heard the name, too. "You trying to lure him out?"

"He's luring me out."

"You have to use that against him."

"Yes, but I don't know how."

"Still getting the letters?"

"Yeah."

"You should burn them."

"I should do a lot of things."

Freddy's demeanor shifted subtly, but Whitt felt it like a cloud passing over the sun. Their gazes met and Whitt waited. The suits in the corner were gone now, to compensate whoever needed to be paid off, and the lunch break was nearly over. Freddy would need to get back to work. Whitt could sense the new vibe working through his friend.

"What?" he asked.

"Don't listen to them . . . the journalists with their articles. I see how the tide has turned the last couple years. They've forgotten what it was like back then. Now, the way they rally, it's like Killjoy's a hero. Saving babies."

"What the media do or say has no influence on me," Whitt told him.

"Good. I'm sick of them switching it around. He's stealing kids from abusive families and crazy cults, and leaving them with the parents of the kids—"

Freddy couldn't say it, and his barrel chest shook with a deep, despondent breath. Like he might break into a sob any second. Jesus, Whitt didn't know what he'd do if he ever saw Freddy crying like that again.

Whitt finished the sentence for him. "The kids he murdered."

"So they're sweet on him."

"I wouldn't say that."

"Close enough."

Whitt didn't trust himself to reply. The media had begun to romanticize the outlaw figure of Killjoy, now that he was apparently trying to do some good in the world. Freddy was right, they'd mostly forgotten about the children he'd murdered a few years back. Now they could focus on the bizarre twist, the changeling kids kidnapped from the abusers and molesters and funny folks like the Protts. It made for more interesting stories, the Channel Five news team all smiling and cracking cutie pie jokes when they mentioned Killjoy's name now.

"I'm sorry, I shouldn't have brought it up."

"It's all right."

The first assistant director called for Mr. Fruggman, and Freddy heaved himself out of his chair toward the bikinis, the priest, the sailboat, and the mops. The disco ball started up and gleaming flashes passed over Freddy's face.

"And after this you'll go see Mike?" he asked.

Whitt had been planning on it, but he didn't know how Freddy knew. "What makes you say that?"

"You don't even realize it, do you? You're walking your pattern."

"Say again?"

"First you deal with Killjoy and the kids. Then that Sergeant Brunkowski. Then you come into Queens, stop in here to recoup for a while, listen to my asshole troubles. Then you head to the north shore of the Island and have a sit-down with Mike. Then you hop across the Whitestone Bridge and you drive upstate to Garden Falls and visit Karen. Then you come all the way back home and you're primed to deal with the killer again. If he's watching you, he'll know it."

Freddy wandered off and left Whitt there.

He didn't move for a while. He wondered how bad it would be, paralyzed and stuck in a hovercart, laser pen between his teeth, waiting for a monkey to make his toast.

FOUR

So if Whitt did have a pattern, maybe he should shake it up a little. If Killjoy was watching, then perhaps it would throw him off, as much as you could throw a lunatic off your trail.

But then he realized, No, you don't play it that way. You change the pattern only when you're ready. Only after the trap is set.

If Whitt had decided to stay in the garage with the car running that morning, listening to quiet music as he left through the big door, it would've been Mike who found the body and been forced to deal with it. Clearing out the carbon monoxide, opening the car windows, and giving Whitt's corpse that same expression of disapproval. Mike probably would've left him there for a while and gone outside to have a smoke.

Like Freddy Fruggman, Mike Bowman had a way of influencing the world by the very strength of his bearing. You could feel it as soon as you got within about twenty feet of the man, how the force of gravity around you would shift, drawing you toward Mike. Whitt could sense it even now, waiting here on the man's front stoop, the hair on the back of his neck starting to stand. It wasn't a sign of weakness, he thought. Mike Bowman could rattle damn near anyone.

He'd been embraced by Mike exactly twice. On his wedding day to Karen, and at Sarah's funeral. Both times he'd been apprehensive, knowing if Mike ever decided to do it, the man could crush Whitt in his arms in only a few seconds.

Now that Whitt had shed some pounds and built up his muscle tone, practiced a few street moves, learned to flush out the fear, he thought Mike would have to work for it a little.

"Hello, Eddie," Mike Bowman said, when the door opened. "Please come in." Karen had always asked Whitt to call him "Dad" even though that was impossible. A son only calls one man dad, to the end of time.

Mike was an ex-Marine who'd seen action in various conflicts they didn't explain much in school. Steel-gray hair still kept short, with just the slightest flair of curl up front. The brutal power inside him leaked out around the edges of his eyes, in the way he prowled across the carpet.

Whitt followed his father-in-law inside and could almost feel how the air heated up as the man cut through it, moving easily and with the assurance of an animal.

It was easy to forget that Mike was an advertising

magnate because you just couldn't wrap your head around the fact that this person could work in such a mundane occupation. Even if he did own the largest independent company in the country and went to war with the competition every day, brawling over millions of bucks a year.

But that was the draw for him. Always under pressure, forever fighting to protect his home ground, consistently being underestimated as an oaf without insight. Mike had won over some enormous clients from the major firms, not for the money but because it satisfied him to beat the bigger guns down.

They sat in the den. The chairs were placed directly opposite each other, not on an angle the way they were shown in the British libraries that appeared in the period plays on *Masterpiece Theater*. No, when you sat across from a man in this house, you looked him straight in the eye.

Mike poured two glasses of scotch from the server between them. No ice, no water. He leaned forward and handed one drink to Whitt. When their fingers touched Whitt felt his father-in-law's distress even though Mike showed nothing in his face.

"What is it?" Whitt asked.

Mike sipped, then said, "You're getting more reckless, Eddie."

That was it, for about a minute. He let the comment hang in the room. Whitt shifted and the liquor lapped loudly in his glass. "Say again?"

"You're directly involving yourself in matters now."

"That was the whole point of this undertaking."

"Not to such an extent."

"No?"

"It's dangerous. Foolhardy."

Whitt snorted. Yeah, he supposed you could call chasing after the serial killer who murdered your five-year-old daughter a little foolhardy. Yeah, maybe.

Mike had to work up to it in his own way. The man wanted to speak his piece and nothing would dissuade him. Whitt downed half the scotch, hardly tasting it. He sat back deeper in the chair, lit a cigarette even though Mike didn't allow smoking in the house. You had to take your victories wherever you could.

"Please put that out," Mike said.

Whitt did. You took your failures when they were handed to you, too.

"This new media attention he's receiving now, Eddie. It's inspiring him to work faster."

"It's not because of the press."

"What then?"

Whitt finished the scotch, reached for the bottle, and filled his glass again. He glanced at Mike and watched the man knock back his drink as well, now pushing the empty glass forward. Whitt poured him another.

The vagaries and nuances of manhood grew heavier in the room. Under the gaze of an older, larger man who wasn't your father but might as well have been, you had to be alert and stand ready. Each action was under regard and being critiqued.

If he drank the second scotch too quickly, Mike would think he was growing undisciplined, wanting to get drunk, and judge him on it. If he didn't sip it at all, Mike would believe Whitt to be wasting good scotch, a sin in its own right.

You had to be careful how you sat, the angle of your chin, the masculinity you exuded, the emission of a complete sense of personal control. It was fucking tough.

Sometimes the best thing you could do was wait and let the father figure finally get around to putting himself in your hands, for whatever reason and to whatever end. Whitt knew it was coming.

Mike stared off to his left, at an empty wall. That's what anybody else would see, this tough guy just watching the wall, in his zone. But Whitt knew Mike saw deeper than that, into the next room. Where framed photos of his family, all of them gone from him now in one way or another, rested on shelves. His deceased wife, his murdered granddaughter, his insane daughter. Even his younger self, smiling into the camera, nobody covered in mud or blood. Whitt could never get over those pictures where Mike was grinning happily, looking like a hipster, a wiseass loose with a joke, not yet clashing with life or himself.

"Eddie?"

Sometimes the way they said your name, it made your skin want to crawl off your bones.

Mike swung his gaze from the wall and pinned Whitt with the usual bayoneting glare.

"Yes?"

"I want to read his letters."

So that was it. The man finally wanted to step into the ring. "No, Mike. It's not a good idea."

"You think I can't handle it?"

"You can, but you shouldn't."

"Why not?"

"The reason you back me is because I'm the point man on this." Whitt was sort of proud to get in some military lingo there.

Mike threw back the second scotch and looked at the glass, judging himself the way he would anybody else. A tinge of regret worked across his empty eyes. "Is that why you think I take care of you?"

"Listen—"

"You're my son-in-law, the father of my only grand-daughter. You're my family." He spoke quietly, but the effort to do so was leaving him breathless. Saying it like he wanted to blame Whitt that there was nobody left to love. "I've lost as much as you, Eddie. I'll do anything I can to even the score."

The clichéd comment didn't sit well in the room, and Mike seemed to want to take his words back. But since they were already out there, Whitt followed up.

"That's just it, we can never make it right again. We can only try to stop it."

"I want those letters."

His legs tensed, readying himself to leap out of the chair to grab Whitt's throat. A moment ago the man had been saying how they were family, and now he was ready to smack his son-in-law around the room. You never really knew what the hell you were doing when you were dealing with emotions this blunt.

Whitt had the .32 on him and wondered, if it came down to it, would he shoot Karen's father, even to save himself? He took the time to line up the target, right between the man's eyes, and figured he had his answer.

"You just said I was making a mistake by involving myself too directly. Now you want to do the same?"

The contradiction forced a furrow deep into Mike's ashen brow but nothing was going to stop him. He was as hard and immutable as stone, even when he knew he was wrong. "Yes."

Whitt decided to allow it. Let Mike make his attempt at comprehending what couldn't be understood.

Besides, he wanted to see how far the tough Marine could go with this, how much he could take, sitting there thinking his son-in-law was the weakling, incapable of following through to the end.

How petty Whitt was to do this to the old man, simply because the conflicts between all sons and fathers eventually brought you to this line.

"Okay," Whitt said. "I have them in the car."

"You have them with you?"

"Sure."

"But—" Mike drew himself another drink, slugged the scotch down, and wiped his mouth with the back of his hand, a muscle trembling a staccato in the thick-callused web between thumb and forefinger. "Aren't you afraid he'll try to get them?"

"Why would he do that? He sent them to me. About half are copies, the feebs have those originals."

"Feebs?"

"The FBI. The rest I never showed them."

Whitt stood, the holster at the small of his back creaking as he did so, and went to his car.

He opened the trunk and for an instant saw the stroller in there, the dollhouse, and Karen's picnic basket. She'd actually had a wicker picnic basket she'd fill with wine, cheese and crackers, the baby's bottle when Sarah was small, and later, peanut butter, always peanut butter. A real picnic basket. Whitt still couldn't believe it. He'd once had a life where his wife had fed him on a large blanket laid out under the sun, while their child giggled and rolled across the grass.

A sound like ten thousand twitching wasps worked its way up his throat and he champed his teeth down on it. Reaching for the sides of the trunk, images of his happiness wafted past like steam. Whitt grabbed hold of the frame and his body tightened and spasmed, shaking the entire car until the shocks grunted.

It wasn't enough. He leaned in and caught the bottom of the open trunk in his mouth, gnawing the metal, moaning his anguish against it as the breeze swirled his hair across his eyes. The fillings in his back teeth buckled and crumbled against his gums. He'd had to replace them before. The cold, harsh taste of the metal slid like burned oil across his tongue.

The car thumped up and down, shocks squealing now, while all his screams were compressed into a sickly mewl. His locked muscles broiled and ignited his mind. A flash of brilliant molten pain filled him and then slowly receded until he regained control and could let go. He straightened and spit out shards of tooth and filling. He wiped tears from his face and glanced around the street, hoping nobody had seen. A postman down the block gaped and shivered in the sun, his mailbag bouncing across his hip.

Whitt thumbed blood from the corners of his mouth. He lifted his files with the Killjoy letters out of the trunk and brought them inside. He sat, and let the folders drop on the serving table with the solidity of bone. Liquor bottles chimed like a deranged kid plinking the high end keys of a piano.

"My God," Mike said. "So many of them."

"Thirty-one, starting just after Sarah was killed."

"All of these letters and the feds couldn't do anything?"

"He didn't mail them all. Two he left on my

windshield. Another two were handed to me in restaurants by waitresses as I was paying my bill."

Whitt watched his father-in-law tense at that. It was so easy to blame somebody else and think you could be smarter than the killer, catch him quickly, hardly breaking a sweat. So close, in the same restaurant, and *you let him get away?*

Mike spoke but Whitt tuned him out, knowing the words without hearing them. Why not plant a camcorder in your car if the guy was leaving letters under your wipers? Be more wary? Stand alert, chase him down. Get a description, memorize every face in every diner you ever ate in, so you could play the scenes back at night, do a fade-in, close-up on some dude in the corner, spot the glue of a false beard smudged under the left earlobe, and make your move. Jump on the Killjoy.

But it had been five years. He met Mike's eyes and thought, Could you do it, old man? Could you set a camcorder up to record for twenty-four hours every day for half a decade? Could you change the tapes eight times a day? It would take you a lifetime to record them and another lifetime to watch them. Would you sit there and stare out the window, watching an empty street as the remainder of your life dwindled and the hate set you adrift? Could you recall every face you met on the road each day? Hoping for the one moment when the man who butchered your kid came along?

"There's blood in your mouth, Eddie."

Mike slumped back in his chair. He couldn't do it and perhaps even realized it now. That was hard time. It would be worse than jail. The inactivity, the absurd waste of your life. Your nerve endings would fry out, no matter how much of a man you were.

The tic in Mike's hand grew steadily worse as he leaned forward and reached for the top file. He opened it as if expecting a great wash of noise to burst forth.

Whitt poured himself another scotch, a triple, sat with his knees crossed, and watched the old man's face as he began to read, features shifting through the scope of a normal person's understanding and tolerance, and then struggling toward that covenant of agony that lay beyond.

The first ghost I ever met was my own.

Let me explain. When Killjoy was a boy, no more than four, though he remembered each detail with excruciating clarity, on a night filled with his mother's crying and the sound of his baby sister hitting the floor, his father slipped into his bedroom and stood at the foot of the bed humming.

The sweet smell of beer and whiskey bloomed in the air as the moonlight against the bedsheets faded. Young'un Killjoy turned over and saw his pa in silhouette before the window, looking abominable, monstrous with dangling arms, his chin tilted. His pa, his daddy, he pulled out his snub-nosed .38 and pressed it to Killjoy's upper lip and said, "I'm doing you a favor, son. This world is nothing but work and waste and pain. Especially for anyone who's got some conjure blood in them."

Daddy had already murdered Ma and Sissy in the other room with his bare hands, although his hands had no blood on them.

His father lay on the bed and tucked his arm around Young'un Killjoy. The barrel tilted against his temple but Daddy's finger never left the trigger.

In the morning, when the men from town broke in the front door and came scrambling into the house through every window, Daddy grinned at his young'un and said, "I hope God's got a better plan for you than he had for me, son."

The boy Killjoy had understood the force of his father's will, but could not acknowledge it even when Daddy pressed the gun under his own chin and pulled the trigger and shot himself. It was the first time Killjoy had ever tasted blood.

Humble beginnings whence we come, with the strangers pressing our faces to their chests to avoid seeing the remnants of Mother and Sissy on the rug, leading to many greater things.

Killjoy, years later, found words and decided to write some of them down and mail them to his only friend.

The opening line of the first one said, "Whitt, let me ask you..."

Wind knocked at distant windows on the second floor of the house, begging to be let in. Mike flipped the page over in case he'd missed something more, but there was nothing on the back. He let the note drop into his lap. "They're not dated. I thought this was the first letter."

"No."

"Is that how the first one started? 'Whitt, let me ask you...'?"

"Yes."

"Why isn't it here?"

Taking a sip of whiskey, Whitt let it wash around inside his mouth, finding the newly emptied spaces of his back teeth. The raw nerve pain made him hiss but nothing more. The single-malt scotch was too good, it didn't sear the way he wanted. "I destroyed it in a rage."

Mike nodded idly, knowing he probably would've done the same, at the time. "What did he ask?"

"If I would help him."

"Help him to do what?"

"He never got to that part."

Starting to see how difficult it might be to put real logic to any of this, the expanse and depth of absurd details that made up such a small part of the case, Mike asked, "Shouldn't the police have these? The originals? Aren't you committing some crime by withholding them?"

"No," Whitt said.

Mike turned again to glance at the empty wall, looking through time and space at the moderate proof that he'd once led a brighter life. Why did he need to stare in that direction to find his own memories? Whitt wondered.

The man's eyes glazed for an instant, then refocused as he gave Whitt the annoyed grimace. "His own handwriting. Such elegant script."

"Yes."

"What brashness. He isn't afraid."

"Apparently he doesn't need to be."

"Do you think any of it is true? These things he says about his childhood?"

"There's no way to tell yet. But probably not. It's part of his construct."

"Did they do a search on all the potential facts? The murdered mother and sister? Killer father?"

"They got thousands of hits going back twenty years, with no way to narrow it down."

Another rattle of noise, this time from the front of the house. The mailman had finally gotten to Mike's door, petrified at what might be going on inside. Whitt thought it might be fun to run out there and spook the guy, ask him for help in closing the car trunk, watch him get into his little mail mobile and veer crazily over nearby lawns.

He finished the glass off and thought maybe the whiskey was beginning to affect him. He hadn't even been casually buzzed since Sarah was born.

"What did the task force psychiatrist say?" Mike asked.

"Which one?"

"There was more than one?"

"Yes."

Another level to the case—the all-consuming canvass of story—that his father-in-law hadn't been fully aware of. Mike's chin came up and his eyes narrowed. There it was, some realization that there was more to this thing than he'd known. Than he'd ever wanted to know.

Look at me, old man, Whitt thought. It's a burden to have all this speculation, theory, opinion, conjecture, supposition, and assumption surrounding blood and pain, but no answers.

Picnic basket. His wife had actually had a picnic basket, didn't anybody understand what that meant? How perfect in beauty and truth and dream his life had once been?

"How many were there?"

"Eleven, including the profilers, behaviorists, and a couple of specialists they conferred with in London and Vienna."

"Did they come to any conclusions?"

"They all pretty much decided that he was male, Caucasian, in his early to midthirties, probably unmarried, incapable of forming a stable relationship, possibly abused as a child."

"In other words, even with all this documentation, this . . . vomit, they still have no idea what he's all about."

"No."

"Do you?"

"Probably not."

"There's more blood in your mouth, Eddie."

"How about if you just forget the blood in my mouth for now, eh?"

Mike looked at the next letter, his features taking on the stern cast of a man wanting to use his powerful hands for all the terrible things they were trained to do. But handling the paper so delicately, like an archaic document left behind by ancestors, possessing the origins of his people.

For further commentary on the roles humans play in modern European society—and by extension the Americas, though only in a tolerably acceptable capacity—please consult Schlegelmann in Paradozia E Significum Harlequenin. *I think we can all remember how the achingly shy professor carried on conversations with his own wife and mother by passing memos under his bedroom door. We would all feel so much more at home in our respective countries of the soul if only we could change our aspects, dimensions, intelligence, molars, blood types, and sexes at will, until at last we understood the similarities among them, and how these differences should be so utterly meaningless, based on such deceptive merits of identity.*

But would the resulting increased awareness help us in our cognizance of self and empathy of dissimilarity? Would you prefer an aboveboard and resolute belief system that values a combination of efficiency, proliferation, and longevity? Remember that Schlegelmann was shot through his bedroom keyhole by his wife, who had been driven mad by the fact that she could no longer turn over the mattress and believed he was often stretching out her favorite Merino riding dresses.

Whitt liked this one. *Increased awareness help us in our cognizance of self and empathy of dissimilarity.* Killjoy might be interesting to pal around with, in his off-hours when he wasn't killing kids.

Mike shut his eyes, took a five count, and then opened them again. Two huge, throbbing veins turned black on his forehead. "And what of these philosophers and professors . . . ?"

"They don't exist. More of his construct."

"This preoccupation with teeth is interesting. Dental pain is real torture. He might have had serious problems with his teeth or jaw. TMJ. Or it might be more symbolic of age. Baby teeth. False teeth."

"Taken at face value, the allusion as used in his notes, there's just not enough of a well-defined reference point for us to judge."

"And the Southern jargon coupled with the faux European sophistication?"

"Again, despite the content, there's nothing to give us a credible connection."

"Is that what the FBI profiler said?" Mike asked.

"One of them. The specialist in Vienna agreed. More

importantly, it's what I say. The other psychiatrists feel Killjoy probably speaks with a lisp or has a harelip, so he's socially and sexually inept and resentful. He can't comment directly on his deformity and so uses teeth as a way to objectify his embarrassing trait."

"You'd rather keep an open mind on the matter."

"Yes."

"Is he a biter?"

"No."

Trying to think like an investigator, getting into it, working the material from a variety of subjective viewpoints. In a few hours Mike would suffer some guilt over this, Whitt knew. It was the first swell of emotion that hit you as soon as you started seeing Killjoy as a human being.

Another heaving of wind rattled the den window in its frame. The day continued growing colder, the room becoming chill. Whitt folded his arms and tucked his hands into his pits to keep them warm. He wished he could laser the thermostat, make the monkey go and turn on the heat.

"You can't catch him, Eddie. No one can," Mike said, indifferently but with the resolution found in surrender. "I didn't expect you to pursue this . . . investigation to such an extent. To become so involved. I only meant—"

"I know. I've always known that. You expected me to bounce around for a while and feel like I'd accomplished something, then find another reason to go on with my day. Come back to work for you, take up where I left off. I appreciate your efforts to protect me."

"It's been five years since you started chasing him."

"If it's the money, then—"

"Of course it's not the goddamn money!" He grabbed the bottle of scotch and poured himself another glass. Man, what kind of relationship would they have if the whiskey wasn't around? Mike's trembling hand sent the liquor splashing over Killjoy's letters. He stared down in fear and some kind of anticipation, expecting a hidden message to reveal itself. This wasn't advertising, where you pounded the other guy with cost-effective product campaigns. This wasn't a young man's crusade where they pointed you at the enemy and patted you on the top of your buzz-cut head.

Whitt thought, There it is.

I'll never be afraid of this man again. He's no longer the father figure he was an hour ago. I've replaced him. I'm harder than he is. What I've carried for five years he can't handle for more than a few minutes. I can bear more weight on the structure of my soul.

Of course, Mike noticed it too, this loss of domination. He flipped through more of the letters, unable to read every sentence, just skimming. Catching a phrase here and there that stood out, seemed rational on its own, until combined with the others. A surge of sadness swept through Whitt's chest.

The old man drew back a bit, hiding in the corner of his chair. Because to get in so close just confused you.

"So what the hell does all this mean? Merino riding dresses? *Significum Harlequenin*?"

"It's metaphor."

"Denoting what?"

"Misery," Whitt said.

"That's ridiculous."

"No, it's crazy, which he is."

"How many children did he . . . ?" Mike sought a euphemism for murder that didn't sound too much like what the Marines would use in the field. Liquidate. Terminate. Dispatch. Execute. But he couldn't find one.

"Twenty-one that we know of, in a two-year period, beginning with Sarah."

"All the same?"

"All asphyxiated with pillows, if that's what you mean. He's not . . . cruel."

"But he talks of children's bleeding wounds."

"Yes."

Mike started to say something but had the good sense to stop himself. When he found Whitt's eyes again he said, "And all of them with his mark?"

"Yes. A frownie face drawn on each pillowcase in magic marker."

"Denoting them as sad children."

"Apparently."

"Before or after death?"

"I don't know," Whitt said.

"And then a period of inactivity for over two years?"

"Unless he was active elsewhere, or in other ways."

"And then this...this change of heart? He started giving stolen newborns to the families of the kids he originally murdered?"

"Yes."

"How many so far?"

"Six that we know of. Several of the families moved shortly after Killjoy's...new activity began. They may have taken the changeling children with them."

"Changeling children, my God."

"The feds don't want to look too closely for fear of treading on the parents' civil liberties. Killjoy says he's taken them from abusive homes. So far, that appears to be true in at least three of the cases."

"And again, you were the first."

"Yes, but there's no pattern after that. He's not bestowing changeling kids in the same order that he killed the children."

"So why you, Eddie? Why Sarah?"

"I don't know."

"And how many of the kids have been returned to their rightful parents?"

"Only one. The one he gave to me."

Transitive properties of our conscious mores. Remember Grossburg's Theory of Ambivalence, wherein he took two babies and using the intestinal mesh from a cadaver, conjoined them at the twelfth vertebra. If you're unfamiliar with the experiment, let me guide you to his masterwork—

* * *

"And this latest communication? What's it a metaphor of?"

"Repentance," Whitt said.

"Impossible."

Both of Mike's hands were shaky now, the exasperation so apparent. And he hadn't even caught the really good part of the letter, about the ballerina and the guy with orange sneakers with his prick cut off. "You think he's . . . trying to make up for the butchery he's committed? That he's seeking forgiveness?"

"Yes."

"But why, Eddie? Why now? Serial child murderers, by definition, are compulsive. They do not stop killing. They're incapable of diverting or diminishing their obsessions."

"Not unless there's been some kind of radical change in his life."

"Such as?" Mike asked, vanquished and dwindling, so small in his chair that Whitt could hardly even see him now.

Testament of Ya'al.

"Love," Whitt said. "I think he's fallen in love."

FIVE

Fifteen miles outside of Garden Falls the rain came down in a torrent, sluicing across the highway. Whitt held the wheel steady and snapped the windshield wipers to high. He was the only one on the road.

Before they married, he and Karen had discussed moving up here to Westchester, seventy-five minutes out of the city, but they thought it was still too close to the urban blight. Neither of them knew exactly what urban blight consisted of, but seventy-five minutes didn't seem far enough away from it, whatever it might be.

Besides, they both liked the beaches along Long Island's south bay, where they could live far enough out on the east end that they would escape the over-developed areas and the real estate squeeze. Close enough to visit Mike on the north shore, but far enough that Whitt didn't have to deal with his father-in-law and boss every day after work. He put in his days on magazine ads and then commercials, first writing them and then directing them, and eventually earned the respect that everybody at the office originally only pretended to give him because he'd married the boss's daughter.

Whitt didn't even mind the two-hour commute into Manhattan on the train, since he often did his best copywriting work on his laptop, surrounded by passengers. He didn't know why, but there it was.

Maybe the crammed conditions, the other riders crushed against him, hissing down his neck, gave him ideas for what kind of mouthwashes they could use, shampoos, clothes, what cars they'd want to be driving if they could afford to spend all that time in gridlock, waiting for their stalled lives to start up again.

The closer you looked the more you realized there was nothing upstate to draw your attention, to inspire or arouse you. Small green hills and back roads leading to deteriorating factory towns or clusters of dismal farming villages. When you were on the highway doing a double nickel, you breathed in the fresh air and spotted the old, corner gas station and thought, How quaint and charming, I could raise a kid here.

But when you got close enough to see the rot and feel the isolation, you just couldn't imagine forcing your child to endure such a dismal atmosphere. Gray faces with colorless eyes, dust settled on their foreheads. Dull axes on the floor beneath their drooping hands. Flesh dried and skinned back away from bone and teeth, dead in their chairs in the center of their junk storerooms and bait shops infested with night crawlers.

An abrupt beeping made Whitt tighten his grip on the steering wheel. The car hydroplaned for an instant and floated on the wet highway, veering toward the guardrail. He tapped the brake until the tires caught and he was in control again.

His cell phone so rarely rang nowadays that it took him a few seconds to recognize the sound. His first thought was always that Killjoy had planted a small bomb on him, something to snag his attention, maybe make him bleed without killing him, and that the sound was a countdown. He wasn't really afraid. It took about ten beeps before he realized, shit, the cell phone.

He answered. Brunkowski grunted Whitt's name around the cigar that wasn't there in the corner of his mouth. The connection was so clear that it sounded like he was in the backseat. "The blind one, Franklin Prott, he got away."

"How?"

"He's not blind. Or not completely anyway. He was being escorted to lockup, pulled the handicapped card, and nearly strangled a rookie."

"Stupid to leave a rookie with him."

"Yeah, we could all learn so much from you about every fucking thing. Anyway, he's on the loose. We don't know how many other cult members might be around, so he's probably got some contacts he can turn to for help."

"He didn't appear to believe the bizarre mysticism his mother force-fed him. She was responsible but might never have been personally involved with the murders. He was her hand. I think he was only in it for the killing. He's probably happy the old broad is being put away. Now he can go it alone."

"If that's true, then we've really got troubles. We don't know how large or extensive this organization may be. It sounds like he's considered some kind of prince among them, an authority figure. They might go to extremes to help hide him."

"How're the other Protts doing?"

"The old lady is fine. She loves to go on for hours about soulwinds and who the fuck knows what all else. She's already got another little group of whackos rallying around her in the lockup. We keep her separated from the other cult members we arrested. Most of them we still haven't ID'ed yet, and they're not talking. Seems like they're vagrants, ex–mental patients who've gone off their meds. The other kid, the brain-damaged one, he's lost without his mommy. He wants to know where his jars are."

"He talks?"

"Yeah."

"He never said a word while I was in that house."

"He's obsessed with what time it is, and which direction the windows of every room face, and like that.

Cosmic relationships, and the guy can't tie his shoes or wipe his own nose. He'll never see a day in prison."

Which meant they'd ship him off to an institution upstate, perhaps even Garden Falls. Whitt could drive up here and visit with Karen for an hour, then take the elevator down to see Merwin, talk about Mucus-Thorn-In-Brain, and play the government-head-smack game with him.

"Do you have an ID on the guy with orange sneakers?"

"No, not yet."

"He's the key."

"Why do you say that?" Brunkowski asked.

"Killjoy mentioned him specifically. That means he either knew the guy or saw him go into the house and get iced. If he knew him beforehand, then we've got a direct link between the victim and Killjoy."

"You're making too much of it. Killjoy is a watcher, he studies the families he hits. He cases the homes far in advance. He must've seen the guy go into the Prott house for tea and never come out again. But put that aside for now. Back to Franklin . . . he's going to hold you responsible for this shake-up. You didn't give them your real name, did you?"

"She asked to see my ID. I had to show her."

"And you don't carry a fake license around?"

"I never thought I'd have to worry about *two* maniacs coming after me."

"You're not very good at this, are you?" Brunk said. "Playing cop?"

"The police allow a blind lunatic to escape and you want to toss insults?"

Whitt pressed the OFF button and severed the connection. He eased up toward the next exit ramp, where one small sign mostly hidden by weeds alerted you to the fact that you were headed the right way toward the State Psychiatric Facility.

The first time he'd visited Karen here he'd expected to see electrified fences topped with razor wire and gun-toting security guards all over the grounds. Or at the very least lots of burly orderlies in white, carrying truncheons, cans of Mace. Grinning and waiting to catch some lunatic climbing down knotted sheets.

But the skinny guy reading a supermarket tabloid in the booth at the gate just lifted the semaphore arm and waved him on. No second glance, no crow's-feet at the edges of his eyes. Here it was five years later and the same skinny fucker was reading the latest issue of the same magazine, and he still had no stress wrinkles.

At the front desk of the main building Whitt gave his name, got his visitor's pass. A tiny Asian nurse with reams of black hair spilling from beneath her little hat told him to please take a seat and wait for Ted, who would be down shortly to escort him to Karen's room.

Whitt sat and watched the rain wash down and

throb against the windows, thinking about how much longer he could put up with this. When Killjoy was dead, would Karen return to herself and come back to him? Could he stand the humiliation of always having an orderly lead him through the grim hallways to his own wife?

It felt too easy to lose control of yourself in a mental hospital because you wouldn't have very far to go to find a bed.

Unlike many of the other patients, Karen's family had a lot of bread. She had her own apartment in the north wing of the facility, about twice the size of the place that Whitt rented and her father paid for. The staff took her out to museums, plays, the ballet, musicals, shopping, and even escorted her on vacations. Over the five years she'd been in the Falls, Karen had traveled to the Virgin Islands, the Grand Canyon, Rio, Morocco, and the Swiss Alps. Wherever she went she always made sure to send Whitt a postcard describing the weather and one or two other trivial details.

The ill children of wealthy parents knew how to live right, even if they were chaperoned by male nurses everywhere they went.

Ted, whose job was being Karen's custodial guardian, popped out from around the corner wearing lots of citrus colors: bright yellow pants, an orange-and-green shirt. A walkie-talkie mumbled on his belt. Ted liked to stand out and probably had half a dozen discrimination lawsuits in the works at any given time in any given place. It was cheaper for the facility to let the dress code slide with this one.

Ted was still pretty new to the Falls. He'd shown up about six months ago with a melodious voice that demanded attention from everyone in a fifty-yard radius. He had a bottled tan, absurdly white teeth, wispy, blow-dried hair, and a soft chin that was always freshly shaved. A hint of mascara and a touch of foundation.

He sort of sashayed when he walked, as if he was forever prepared to break into a song-and-dance routine. He remained pleasant and even amiable when the situation called for it, but there was always a smug sense of superiority about him.

Whitt hated Ted's guts and knew Ted felt the same way about him.

Somehow, they had become jealous rivals over Karen, protective of her in their own fashions but equally ineffectual. Whitt understood Ted's feelings, but not the entirety of his own.

"Hello, Mr. Whitt."

"Hello, Ted."

"She's in good spirits today."

The implication being, don't bring her down and ruin her any more than you already have. Ted of the white teeth and seventies porno hair was subtle but always made his point.

"That's good, thank you for telling me."

They walked together up the north wing corridors, past a dozen or so patients who ran the gamut from the shufflers and mutterers to the recovering alcoholics and acutely disheartened. It looked no different than any street in New York City, and reminded Whitt a lot of the morning rush to his former office.

"Very buoyant and animated," Ted continued. "Carefree, even. We went shopping down in the city over the weekend and she's still thrilled with all her new clothes and furniture for her apartment. Paintings, throw rugs, window treatments. It was time for a change."

All of it going on Mike's bill. They would've had to call him and confirm the orders, but Mike had said nothing about it to Whitt this morning.

"Glad you had a good time shopping with my wife, Ted. I look forward to seeing what kind of furniture and paintings and other things the two of you decided on. Especially the treatments. I love window treatments."

"She's delighted with them, and that's all that matters."

"Quite right."

Ted raised his fist and knocked a specific rappity-tap tune on Karen's door. At the end of it was a solid damning thump, and Whitt knew it represented him. Their own private code, these two. Whitt wondered if she'd tappity-rap-tap back from the other side, like kids playing a game across a shared bedroom wall.

"As I said, she's cheerful today, and I'd really appreciate it if you could help us—the doctors and staff—to keep her in as positive a mood as possible, Mr. Whitt. I know it's not your intention, but we've noticed that . . . well, after your visits, Mrs. Whitt seems . . ."

"Ted—"

". . . to be a bit despondent. Desolate, even forlorn. Perhaps it might be better if from now on you didn't discuss your daughter so frequently, but instead focused on beneficial and emotionally nourishing topics such as—"

They'd push you right to the fence and then through it, if you let them. "Ted, quit screwing around with me or I'm going to mangle those girlish looks of yours."

"Are you a fag basher now, Mr. Whitt?"

"If you're the fag in question, Ted, I just might become a basher in the next ten seconds. Now that you've escorted me to my wife's door and I know your magical little melody, get the fuck lost."

Ted's buoyant hair had a life of its own and roused itself when he got upset. The angel wings fluttered all over his head. "You're rude, crass, and not at all the proper influence that Mrs. Whitt needs in her life! You're vile! My comments are going into my report, Mr. Whitt!"

"I'd expect nothing less of you, Ted. Go on and dance with a cartoon bunny."

"What?"

Whitt slipped inside and slammed the door, then did a funky knockity-knock on it and ended with a backwards kick that rocked the doorframe. Give that prick a big finale for his report.

He turned, and there was Karen.

Since Sarah's death, the word "frail" always came to mind whenever he saw his wife. For a time, following the funeral, she'd become the image of her own mother just before the woman's death from breast cancer—weak, hunched, lifeless. He wold hold on to Karen and it was like trying to grab a section of air. No weight or force or voice.

A month after their five-year-old girl was buried, in a moment of extreme sorrow when he'd sobbed and babbled before his wife on his knees, saying words he could no longer remember, he'd clambered across the floor to her and hugged her tightly. She'd barely made a sound even as he felt one of her ribs snap beneath his hand.

In the emergency room he'd been stunned to learn that she'd dropped to under eighty pounds. They put her in a gown and he'd seen she was skeletal, with shadowed ridges and fierce angles to her contours. She hadn't eaten for weeks, and he'd been so nuts himself that he hadn't even noticed.

They jabbed IV tubes in her arms and up her nose and tried to pump life back into her. Mike hired a team of psychiatrists, who at least got her feeding herself again. They moved her to Garden Falls six weeks after Sarah's murder and she'd been here ever since.

The busted rib, though, got a lot of play. Ninety percent of murders were committed inside the family. The cops were already watching him, but now they were thinking, here's a guy who beats his wife, whose daughter was killed in a very bad way, who works in advertising. He's got a mean streak in him.

It wasn't until Killjoy iced the other children while Whitt was under surveillance that the cops realized he was only a victim. Just a guy with a crazy wife and a dead kid.

"Hello, Eddie," Karen said.

The backs of her hands had healed nicely, showing very little scarring from when she'd bite and scratch herself in agitation. They kept her nails short but it didn't stop the self-abuse that drove her on her worst days. Clawing, ripping at her own hands until she left bloody prints everywhere, acting like nothing was wrong even as you stared at the bone jutting from her skinned knuckles.

Some days he'd walk in and there'd be pieces of Karen smeared across her chin, bandages on her hand plucked open, matted with rust-colored blood.

He'd think, I have done a very poor job of protecting my family. I've failed at the only worthwhile duty a man ever has.

He looked around. He really did like the window treatments. She stepped forward and kissed him with some passion, but broke off quickly and drew away. "You taste like blood and good scotch. You've been talking with my father again, haven't you?"

Even in the bin she knew him better than anybody else. "Yes."

"You're too thin, you haven't been eating lately."

"Just eating better. I used to be fat."

"I liked you better that way. You used to feel like a man. Now you're like touching granite. Please take better care of yourself."

"I'll try."

She sat on the couch and gestured for him to take the chair opposite her. Just like her Dad, wanting him close but facing her. "I like the new furniture," Whitt said.

"I don't. Ted picked out most of it."

"If you didn't like it, why did you let him buy it?"

"Because someone needs to care."

She was right about that. These were the things that other people could afford to care about. Pictures on the wall. Stylish clothes. Throw rugs, end tables, serving sets.

"How's Sarah?" she asked.

The familiar despair would've filled him again, except it was always there anyway. "Sarah's dead."

"I know that," she said, because it was, after all, true. It wasn't *that* which took the precedence of heartbreak anymore. Sarah's murder had been pressed to the outer shore of her consciousness, where the memories floated in a cold, unmoving reservoir. "I mean, I know the first one is dead. But how's the new one?"

"There is no new one."

"Yes, the other one."

"There is no new Sarah."

"Yes, there is. You know what I'm talking about." Her features sharpened, the icy cast in her eyes refusing any argument. Her hand reached out across the coffee table. Soon it would grab his wrist. After that, she'd go for his throat.

The headshrinkers told him he had to be gentle but firm. Practicing it for him, showing him how he was supposed to do it. Even going so far as to mime particular actions, the way he should pat her shoulder, cuddle her, caress her back, turn her chin to look her in the eye.

Except he didn't have to turn her chin. She was always staring directly into his eyes, and it was him looking away.

The fuckin' psychiatrists were out of their trees if they thought a man could go through this all the time and not want to hurl himself under the 5:34 out of Penn Station.

He hopped out of the chair and Karen rose and hugged him then. Her arms tightened around him, and she lifted his shirt, pressed the flat of her hand against the middle of his back and he thought, Does she want me? He moved his lips to her throat and stifled a groan as her hand continued to roam.

They hadn't made love in the time she'd been in Garden Falls. The doctors, in their blatant, stark manner, had brought the issue up many times and urged Whitt to prompt her for sexual contact, thinking it would be a good sign if she responded. Admonished him, though, to practice safe sex. Who knew what her state of mind might be like if she got pregnant?

All these guidelines and rules and criteria working against what was supposed to be a natural show of love. Telling him to fuck his wife so she'd be sane again. Yeah, no pressure there, Doc. Never realizing how sick it made him feel, taking advantage of the woman who was Karen but was no longer the Karen he knew and had married.

Her hand drifted around his back some more until it settled on his gun holster. He'd forgotten to lock it in the glove compartment the way he'd always done before.

"What is that?" she asked. "I noticed the bulge when you walked in."

He didn't lie to her. He couldn't lie to her. That was the way you started your own construct, creating a world of pretense and fabrication. If he headed down Killjoy's path now, what would stop him from reaching its end?

"My .32," Whitt told her.

"What do you need a gun for?"

"In case I need to defend myself."

"Against whom? Me?"

When she spoke there was an airy, oblivious quality to her voice, like she was speaking to an audience she couldn't quite make out in the shadows. Her words weren't directed at him so much as they floated around him, near him.

"No, not you, Karen."

"Are you so certain?"

"Yes."

"Where's my daughter?"

"She's dead."

"No! The new one."

"There is no new one."

"I want my new girl. Where is she?"

This was where the truth would continue to drive his wife further from her own mind. As if the part had been written for him, he couldn't do anything except this one thing, allowing for the one answer he had.

He checked his watch. He'd been with his wife less than five minutes. "I gave her back."

"You did what?" Karen had that same knifing glare as her father.

"I gave her back to her real parents."

"No one gives back a child! No one!"

She was right.

Whitt, the father of Killjoy's first victim, was now, by this turn of circumstance, his accomplice. He'd stolen the changeling children back from the families who might love them. He'd broken the same hearts that Killjoy had broken.

"Where is the new one? Where's our second Sarah?"

"We don't have another daughter. That child wasn't ours. She already had parents."

"She was given to us!"

"By a killer. By the man who murdered Sarah."

"So what! Damn you, Eddie!" She clenched her fists and tightened every muscle in her body, struggling to subvert her own brand of frenzy, tamping it down into some dark corner. It wasn't enough. "God fucking damn you!"

She raised the back of her hand to her mouth ready to chew into herself. Whitt batted her arm aside, jammed his own fist between her teeth. She bit down with a groan of relief. His hands had hardened up since he'd begun his training, and though she broke the skin, she couldn't do much damage. Not like she could to herself.

His blood ringed her lips.

Finally, the tension drained from her, and in a slight daze, she managed to pull away. Karen glanced at him with tears in her eyes. She gave him a sad grin and he knew, This is as close as we'll ever be again. We'll never have more than this, what we have right now.

"Do you know where I was Friday night?" she asked.

"Yes," he told her, wondering what meds he might find here that would help him.

"I was in Sarah's dollhouse."

His breathing grew ragged. He thought, What's it called when you share somebody's hysterical vision? He should study up on shit like that, because he was becoming infected. "I know."

"I didn't see you there," she said.

"No, but I saw you, Karen."

And he had. Christ, he thought he really had.

He'd seen his wife inside their dead daughter's dollhouse, folding laundry. Sarah had been in her bedroom, playing a kid's game on the computer. She'd aged there, in a perfect world he hadn't made real for any of them. She was five years old when she'd died, and now he watched her blossoming into a young woman, losing at the game, but laughing anyway.

Whitt was starting to think maybe he needed a little therapy himself.

Now Ted walked into the apartment without even the benefit of his rapity-tap-bap. No doubt he'd been listening outside the door. He stormed over and let out a wicked squeal when he saw that Karen's lips were bloody. He clutched at the walkie-talkie and whimpered, and in thirty seconds two security guards were inside the room.

They escorted Whitt down the hallways to the front door of the main building and shoved him into the parking lot.

There it was, the completion of his pattern.

He got back into his car, drove out of the Falls and back onto the highway, headed for home.

Whitt had run through all the stations, and now had returned to the beginning.

Even if the fucker really was in love, it was time to get back to hunting Killjoy.

SIX

Whitt almost collided with Russell Gunderson and his two-year-old daughter Lorrie in a pastry shop on 54th and Seventh, the heart of the Manhattan tourist area.

He'd been sloppy, losing Gunderson in the crowd, so he'd slipped into the shop to get his bearings, and there was the man standing right in front of him, ordering a latte.

A brief rush of elation flooded Whitt's belly even as he realized how awkward the moment would be, how stupid he'd allowed himself to become. Still, the urge to say hello, to step up and make sure Lorrie was all right, was almost overpowering.

He turned away, made it out the door without being seen, and bolted around the corner. He should've moved off but wasn't quite capable of it yet, so he hung back partially shielded by parked cars, and watched Russell Gunderson walk out with a giant styrofoam cup of coffee, his daughter strapped to his chest in one of those papooselike rigs.

Whitt had spent one morning ten months ago being Lorrie's father.

He'd thought a great deal of her since then. On some days, almost as much as he thought of Sarah.

He remembered the initial wild sweep of joy he'd felt—far outweighing the surprise and confusion—when he discovered the baby in a picnic basket, left outside his apartment door nearly a year ago.

He imagined what he would've done if Karen hadn't been in the Falls. If she'd been at home, if there'd been a chance that the changeling child could've brought them both some peace in the aftermath of Sarah's death.

If they could've run with the child, would they have cut out and started over elsewhere? The way Pia and Edward Godard had. And Joe and Margaret Stokes.

He thought about it a lot.

Killjoy had left a letter in the picnic basket with the baby.

Let us consider the fortuitous meeting in the central plaza of Strumberg, spring 1819, and the fate that would bring together the quartet of sage engineers behind the formation of the Empire of Thought.

They were, in order of importance as dictated by the great historian Dr. Robert Pootattie (pronounced "Pootattie") of Syracuse University, in his seminal treatment on the subject, In the Order of Their Importance as Dictated by Me, the Great Historian Dr. Robert Pootattie: *Kellerman (pronounced "Kell-ehr-muhn"), T. (pronounced "Tee"), Rabbi Chaim Schlomo (pronounced "FuckayouJesus") and Fru Viberschwanzindorf (called "Fifi" by his cellmate Bubba Highbrinks, both incarcerated after the Marchand Alley peasant revolt of 1798).*

These four brilliant minds drew together to create an astounding movement of reason, logic, and sense. In less than eighteen months they'd drafted no less than six major documents in support of profound cultured and academic pursuits. Their organization had over forty thousand members across Europe and witnessed a growing movement in the Americas.

But soon after the second anniversary of the conception of the Empire of Thought, all four men suffered severe setbacks in their private lives. Kellerman's three underage mistresses became pregnant simultaneously after the orgiastic events following the Cheerleading Nationals, forcing him into such debt that pauper's prison loomed before him. T. lost both legs in a mysterious Scotch Taping accident. Rabbi Schlomo's matzoh ball soup canning factory was set ablaze by faulty matzoh. And Bubba Highbrinks, newly released from the Bastille, sought to renew his amorous relationship with Fifi.

And in their times of crises all four men turned away from reason and toward religion and the occult. Giving themselves up to forces greater than their own intellect.

One is not quite sure if one should laugh or cry in learning that all four men were struck down by the same carriage, driven by the same patrician, in different parts of the city on *the same day. The chances of such an act being purely random are astronomical, unless one sees the hand of God in all things.*

Three days later, after turning the child over to the police—but keeping the picnic basket for some reason, storing it in the back of his bedroom closet—Whitt found another note on his windshield. Written without preamble or the usual dreamlike, anachronistic constructs:

Why the hell did you give the child back, Whitt?
What kind of father are you?

"Eddie?"

Russell Gunderson stood at Whitt's side. His daughter Lorrie was humming and giggling to herself, holding a cruller, her face covered with cinnamon.

Shit, Brunkowski had been right. Whitt really wasn't very good at playing cop. Gunderson had not only spotted him but had walked right up and caught Whitt daydreaming about how to answer Killjoy's question. What kind of father was he? He had one dead child and had deserted another. What kind of a monster or fool did that make you?

"Hello, Russ."

"I thought it was you! I almost didn't recognize you. You've lost so much weight and you've really toned up!"

Russell Gunderson had an easy broad smile, a controlled strength within him that even the other pedestrians must've noticed, since they parted around him. No matter what clothes he wore they appeared casual and comfortable on him, perfectly fitted, of the finest material. Even now, wearing only jeans, a dark T-shirt with a sport coat, and a fancy pair of sneakers, he could still probably go into any interview and land the job.

Gunderson was one of the new breed of high-tech power stockbrokers who did most of their business online and via fax. He had an office with two laptops and three separate phone lines, and while his wife Anne put in long hours at her own boutique, Gunderson was a stay-at-home dad who spent a couple of hours on the computer in the morning and spent the rest of his day playing with his daughter, watching CNN and the Learning Channel.

So far, the Gundersons had been the only parents who'd filled out a report on their missing child, although Whitt hadn't known that when he'd called the police and arranged to return the baby. The other kids, probably abused for most of their young lives, came from families who didn't care enough even to look for them, or came by proxy from the likes of the Protts.

Whitt had kept a close eye on the Gunderson house over the past year.

The Protts were the worst case so far—not molesting or beating the kid, but since they'd planned on a human sacrifice and had bodies in the basement, you couldn't nominate them for family of the year.

So what did Gunderson do to his wife and baby?

Whitt had watched them for weeks at a time, parked up the road from the Gunderson home. He did the things that men with badges and licenses couldn't do— he peeked in windows, he hid under bushes in the backyard, keeping tabs. All he ever saw was a devoted husband and father, a man so much like Whitt had once been that Whitt would sometimes drop his face into the dirt and chew grass from Gunderson's back lawn, jealous and crazed. He wondered if Killjoy, in planning his kidnapping of the newborn Lorrie, had hidden in these same spots and done these same crazy things.

"You look fantastic!"

"I try to get into the gym more than I used to," Whitt said. "What brings you into the city?"

Gunderson took a sip of the enormous latte. "Anne wanted to do some window-shopping around Rockefeller Center, so Lorrie and I went to visit the new MOMA building."

It took Whitt a second to remember what MOMA stood for—the Museum of Modern Art. Nobody would ever believe he'd been raised in New York.

"Have you been there yet?"

"No," Whitt said, "not yet."

"You should make the time, the Pollocks are amazing. What you see in books doesn't do him justice. The texture of his work, the composition of it, using detritus from off the floor of his studio. Nails, cigarette butts, all worked into the paintings themselves. You have to get up close to appreciate it."

"I'll bear that in mind." Whitt had been an ad man for eight years. Getting up close to detritus was how he'd earned his living.

Lorrie, who'd been so close to becoming his daughter, hiccuped and giggled some more. She'd grown so much, becoming her own person. Her hair was scrunched up and squeezed into a modified ponytail, tied back with a black ribbon. She thumped her feet against Gunderson's ribs and the hollow thunk seemed to rattle through him and into Whitt's chest.

He lost control for a second and reached out, cupping Lorrie's chin in his hand, tickling her little mounds of baby fat. She gave Whitt a wide grin and guffawed. "Whoah ho! Ha!"

Realizing he might be sounding a touch too stuffy, Gunderson begged off the topic of modern art. "Well, it's not everybody's thing. How about you? What are you doing in the city this afternoon?"

"Had lunch with an old copywriter crony of mine. He's having trouble with his latest publicity package so we were talking over some possible revisions."

Lorrie stuck her tiny hand out and touched Whitt's

collar. He leaned in and made a face at her and she laughed and squirmed across her daddy's shoulder.

The only reason Gunderson still had his baby girl was because Whitt had given the kid back. *What kind of father are you?* He just didn't know anymore.

He thought he could probably get away with snatching her back. Step back, tuck in, and drop into a roll, aim the .32 from a crouching position and nail Gunderson between the eyes. Scoop the baby up and make a run for it. Drive to Garden Falls, lay waste to Ted, grab Karen, and be halfway to Miami by sunrise.

Sometimes it felt like the only answer left involved shooting a bunch of people in the head.

"It's really good seeing you. Have you got time to go sit and chat for a bit? Maybe in the park?" Gunderson asked. He took another pull on the coffee and tossed the cup in a nearby trash bin.

"No," Whitt said. "I'm afraid not. Thanks anyway." He shouldn't have touched her. Touching the changeling babies was when he was at his weakest.

"Oh, I'm sorry to hear it. Maybe some other time?"

"Sure, I'll take a rain check."

"Good running into you."

"You too, Russ."

Whitt held his hand out and Gunderson took it with force and insistence. He stepped in closer, eyes brimming with intensity. "Thanks, Eddie. Thank you for everything."

"Of course."

Gunderson faded back into the foot traffic on the sidewalk and Whitt watched the cinnamon-faced girl staring over her father's shoulder, directly at Whitt, still giggling.

Sarah's dollhouse sat in balsa wood and plastic perfection in the corner of Whitt's living room.

It had once been Karen's mother's. Chipped, broken, forgotten, restained, and repaired many times over the years. It was one of the very few items of Sarah's that Whitt had left. Like Killjoy's first letter, he had destroyed so much in his rages. Anything that caused him pain—and everything did. Thank the sweet Christ some of her belongings had been over at Mike's, or there might not be anything left to remember her by.

Somehow the dollhouse had escaped his rampages. Perhaps, even in his frenzy, he knew it was a sacred remnant that had to be protected.

Sarah and Karen would play with the dolls and the miniature furniture and furnishings for hours. They'd go through catalogues together, selecting just the right decor for the house. Tiny paintings for the walls. Centerpieces for the kitchen table. He'd get his credit card bill and they'd have spent six hundred dollars on the thing. Forty bucks for a dozen plastic eggs for the toy refrigerator, Jesus frickin' Christ.

He'd go on a tear around the place for about a half hour, and they'd both ignore him as they moved the family of dolls through their motions, having extended conversations on movies, celebrities, and favorite acts from the circus.

One afternoon his daughter clambered up his belly as he lay on the couch, nodding off, and she stuck the daddy doll up his nose, in his ear, walking the little plastic bastard across Whitt's forehead as it peered into his eyes.

"Hello there, Mr. Whitt," Sarah said, using a gruff daddy voice. "And how are you today?"

"I'm fine, thank you, Mr. Whitt."

"I would like to talk to you about your daughter."

"Certainly. What is it you'd like to discuss about her?"

"I think she needs a dog to take her to school."

"Is that right?"

"It is. A large dog that she can ride. Like a Great Dane."

"But, Mr. Whitt, a dog that big would eat too much. I don't think I could afford it."

"It could eat the nasty children at Sarah's school, Mr. Whitt."

"Are there many nasty children at Sarah's school, Mr. Whitt?"

"More than you would think, Mr. Whitt. They are loud and they often eat their lunches with their mouths open."

"Oh, that is nasty."

"You better believe it, Mr. Whitt."

would
over."

"Why must you m

"It's just a thing that I mu

"You may have nine days to mull,

"Oddly enough, Mr. Whitt, there are only
left before Sarah's birthday. Could this be a coinci-
dence?"

"You are not mulling hard enough, Mr. Whitt."

"I apologize, Mr. Whitt. I shall now get to mulling."

"Thank you, Daddy."

Now when he looked inside the dollhouse he saw
the three of them living there as they should be. Like
any other normal family, gathered around the television, at the dinner table, playing a card game in the living room. The mother preparing the girl's bedroom
upstairs while the father helped her with her homework. It looked like math. Simple equations. She struggled with long division, then later with algebra.

The man was fat and spent a lot of time on the
phone, usually cheerful and even a little boisterous,
but on occasion he'd growl and shout. His wife would
speak firmly to him about it, hands on his shoulders,
turning his heavy frame to face her when he wanted to
look away. Seemed like money troubles. Whitt could
tell by the thick atmosphere of the dollhouse, the way

...ugh again.

...was the life Whitt should've had, his wife and daughter with him.

He kneeled, staring through the windows, out at himself, and in at himself. The father in the dollhouse was looking out the window, watching Whitt.

Inside there, that other Eddie Whitt reached down and began dialing the tiny plastic rotary phone.

Whitt pulled out his cell and it rang.

The most difficult task he'd ever faced, besides letting the ambulance take Sarah's body away, was probably this. Answering a phone he knew wasn't actually ringing—that he thought *probably* wasn't ringing—just so he could talk with himself, a guy he didn't like much anyway.

But he did it.

You had to do these things if you wanted to catch Killjoy.

"Hello."

"You're much closer than you think, Mr. Whitt."

"I know he's nearby, Mr. Whitt," Whitt replied.

"Remember these words. Value. Transformation. Scarcity. Propitiation. Conversion. Connubial. Reformation. Incision."

"How will they help?"

"They probably won't, but you should remember them anyway."

"All right."

"Why did you give back the child, Mr. Whitt?"

"For Christ's sake, don't you give me that shit too."

"What else is on your mind?"

Some questions you couldn't put words to no matter how much you felt the need.

His other, smaller voice spoke one of them for him. "Did you want to ask me if you were insane?" A flat ugly chuckle resounded in his ear, a noise that Whitt had never made. "I was about to ask you the same thing."

They stared at each other through the small plastic window, until the father in the dollhouse hung up the phone, turned his back, sat in his recliner, and watched his daughter enter the room carrying lemonade on a tray. It was too sour. The daddy doll made a face. The girl laughed.

SEVEN

It wasn't yet nine in the morning when Brunkowski walked up the three flights of stairs to Whitt's apartment, stepped inside, and said, "You don't lock your door?"

Whitt was on the couch reading the latest clinical file on Karen, which was twenty-five pages long and essentially said there was no change in her condition. The doctors threw around the usual chestnut words like "paranoia," "delusional," "schizophrenia," and "aberrant behavior." They failed to mention how a paranoid schizophrenic behaving aberrantly could still manage to enjoy herself with her friends in Rio and the Virgin Islands.

Ted's report had lots of nasty things to say about Whitt, but at least he had said them in a subtle and somewhat astute fashion, which made Whitt feel a little better.

He shut the folder. "What do I have to be afraid of?"

Brunk thought about that for a second before shrugging. You didn't hide from the maniacs you were hoping to flush out in the first place. "Good point. Besides, it's a nice apartment complex. A charming neighborhood. Not far from your old house, right?"

"About a mile," Whitt said. "I wanted to stay close."

"Why?"

It took Whitt back. He'd never been asked before, never had to think about it. "I'm not sure."

"Can you see the Sound from here?"

"No."

"Not even on a nice day?"

"No."

"Too bad."

Brunk was taking his time getting to the point because he was uncomfortable showing up on Whitt's doorstep like this, spilling police info to a civilian right in his own living room. Whitt thought maybe he should offer Brunk breakfast, a glass of milk, but that didn't feel right either. He tossed the folder aside and waited.

"Listen," Brunkowski said. "Simon Robinson had a special delivery package dropped off on his office doorstep this morning. It was dressed in baby blues, wearing a little cotton hat and mittens."

"Another newborn."

"Maybe six weeks old. Robinson immediately turned around and brought the kid home. He and his wife Sandra—"

"Samantha."

"Yeah, that's right. The two of them were planning to stash the kid with her unmarried sister down in North Carolina for a while, until they could figure out a way to bring the baby into the fold. Raise it as their own without causing suspicion."

Whitt tightened his left fist against his leg, wishing the Robinsons had managed to pull it off. Jesus, was he working for the cops now, against his own kind?

What kind of parents would they be if they *didn't* try to make a run?

"What happened?"

"Robinson's secretary spotted the bassinet. He's an accountant in private practice, just the two of them in a tiny office over in Shoreville. She was walking across the parking lot when she saw him pick up the kid, get back in his car, and drive off pretending not to notice her. She wrestled with her conscience for about an hour, then phoned the local precinct. By the time a cruiser got over there, the Robinsons were ready to bolt, car running in the driveway, suitcases stowed. When the uniforms questioned them, the wife lost control and started screaming about how they couldn't steal her baby boy."

"Jesus."

"She attacked one of the cops and he had to cuff her."

"Their son, Paul, was Killjoy's fourteenth victim."

"Robinson broke almost immediately. He was crying his eyes out when he handed the kid over. The uniforms had to take the wife to Sojourner State Psych."

"Another job well done by our proud police," Whitt said, his pulse starting to snap in his throat.

Brunk tried to puff out his chest but couldn't quite pull it off. "Nobody wins in a case like this."

"Especially the babies."

Whitt imagined the scene. Robinson shocked but thrilled to find the baby on his step, like a scene out of some Victorian novel. *Ye take me childe inna yer lovin' heart, fresh and faire, lest she fall to doom in mournful November's dour aire.* About ten conflicting emotions filling his gut at once—fear, delight, excitement, remorse, shame. If Robinson had played it a little cooler, or moved a little faster, maybe he could've gotten away.

But pretending not to see his secretary, that was just dumb. He should've enlisted her help, brought her in on it, paid her off. But he must've been swayed more by his guilt than anything else, darting away like that, and she picked up on it. That's what had made up her mind for her.

Brunk took off his jacket. Beneath it, his shirtsleeves were rolled, and the tie, the same tie as the other day, remained loosely knotted and twisted the wrong way. That weird little tuft of hair stood on end, wafting left because Whitt was breathing harder than usual, the story getting to him. He wished he could've helped

Robinson. Whitt took a deep breath and the tuft drifted toward him.

"Did Killjoy contact you about the latest snatch?" Brunkowski asked.

"No."

"That surprise you?"

"Actually, yes."

"Maybe you're out of his loop now."

"He could be taking the next step. He not only wants to save the children from their abusive homes, he wants those families brought to justice."

"Then why didn't he send you a letter?"

"Maybe he has and I haven't found it yet." Whitt stood and walked to the window, gazed down at the neighboring yards, spotted a German shorthaired pointer just sitting there tied to a tree, staring back at him. "Or maybe he brought them to justice his own way."

"You think there's a dead family somewhere?"

"I don't know. He's been playing me all along, I don't think he'd stop now."

"Maybe he was hoping you'd clip the Protts. When you didn't, he decided to take a more active role."

Killjoy remaking Whitt in his own image? Expecting Whitt to purge his fever by icing somebody else instead of his daughter's killer? "A child murderer taking a more active role in killing abusive parents. That's his kind of logic, all right."

"I hate to say it, but in this case, looks like he was

right." Moving about the apartment now, Brunk peeked here and there, at things on the kitchen counter, up over on the bookshelves. Tact wasn't his strong suit as he nudged open drawers. "The kid had severe bruising of the chest and abdomen. Scarring of the rotator cuffs shows both arms had been pulled from the sockets at least a couple of times. If Killjoy took the fucker out who did that to a baby—well, maybe it takes one to sniff one out."

"So, all's forgiven?"

"I didn't say that."

"Sounds to me like you almost did," Whitt said, and couldn't keep the venom out of his voice.

The glass in the window frame moaned as if from a breeze, but there wasn't one. Whitt had grabbed hold of the sill, squeezed it so hard now that the molding was shifting inside the wall. His fingernails dug into the paint, maybe twenty coats thick over the ninety years the building had been around. Sinking back through the decades, his nails piercing deeper into time, fingertips beginning to bleed and leak into the foundation. Someday, all these small blood sacrifices were going to come back and give him power when he needed it most.

"You all right?"

"No. You a big believer in vigilante justice now, Sergeant?"

"If I wasn't, I would've locked you up a long time ago."

There it was again. The innuendo that Whitt was no different from Killjoy. It took Whitt a few seconds to release the sill, pull his fingers from the molding. He turned around. His face didn't change, but the force of his glare was enough to make Brunk take a step backward, that wedge of hair flapping all over the place.

"All right, I shouldn't have said that. At least not the way I did. What, you're getting sensitive on me now?"

"No," Whitt said. "What have you got on Grace Kinnick, the ballerina?"

"Still nothing. She's not listed as missing. Nobody in the dance or theater community knows her. And if her body is on the Prott property, we still haven't found her. You got any coffee?"

"No."

"How about a beer?"

"You're on duty, and it's 10:00 a.m."

"So?"

"So, no."

"Jesus, I got a brother who's a priest, and he isn't as uptight as you."

"And they say the Catholic Church needs to work on its image."

Down on the street, the dog started barking, the harsh sounds carrying across the neighborhood and merging with the noises of children playing up the block.

"There's something else," Brunkowski said, crossing his arms so the muscles corded, veins popping out along his thick wrists. It was as much a defensive position as an offensive one, Whitt now realized. "Mary Laramore. Her kid was number nine on Killjoy's original hit list."

"Yes, her son Tim." Whitt remembered a bland blond woman. Unmarried and a touch sad about it, but appreciative that somebody along the way had left her with child. A face heavily made up with eyeliner, shadow, rouge, lipstick—but still flat and ambivalent. Even when she spoke on the newscasts about finding her son's lifeless body on the bed beside her, a pillow pressed over his head, the sad face drawn on the pillowcase in black magic marker, her voice had a lethargy that Whitt completely understood and utterly despised. "Her boy was three years old. What about her?"

"Ever since Killjoy resurfaced we've been occasionally stopping in on the families still in the area, checking in with them. Five weeks ago she wasn't pregnant. Yesterday she looked about six months gone."

"She's faking it," Whitt said, knowing he shouldn't be saying it but unable to stop. "Hoping Killjoy will bring her a kid in the next few months. Then she won't have to make a run or hide the child anywhere. She's planning ahead."

"That, or you're not the only one getting letters that you're not handing over to the police."

The noises of the children were coming closer, down in front of the building now. Laughter, a dog barking. Sounded like they were playing with the pointer. A car roaring down the road slowed for a second, then picked up speed again. A girl screamed like she was being attacked. Whitt's shoulders tightened until he heard giggles again. You could go out of your mind just listening to an autumn day.

"You think he contacted her, told her he'd be bringing her a child soon?" Whitt asked.

"It's possible. When our guys questioned her she was very antsy, notified the chief and said they were harassing her. Brought in the local papers too. We need to back off for the time being."

"You're not even sure what you're backing off of."

"That's right. It's all supposition, and when I send out surveillance teams on supposition, my captain gives me the civil liberties speech. I hate that goddamn speech, it always ends with my job being on the line."

"This is the post–September 11 age. There are no civil liberties anymore."

"There are a few left, especially for white women who've had their three-year-old sons murdered."

"You could alert the feds again."

"Fuck the feebs."

An odd heaviness worked through Whitt's belly that he recognized as resentment. Thinking that Killjoy might have broken the chain with him and established a relationship with someone else, one of his other victims. Maybe this was some bizarre variation on Stockholm Syndrome. Sometimes you'd give your left arm to have just one normal thought or emotion the entire day. "I'll go talk to her."

"One more thing. Merwin Prott, the headcase, he's been asking for you."

"For me? Why?"

"Who the hell knows? But I think you should pay him a call. Maybe you'll be able to get information out of him that doesn't deal with cosmic knots, purifying light of phlegm gods, government assassins shooting his mother in the head, and shit like that. See if you can get an address where his brother might be hiding out."

"Is he still in county jail?"

"No, they moved him to Sojourner State."

Another psych facility, more prisonlike than Garden Falls, out on the Queens border. "You'll get me clearance?"

"Already done. He's under guard. Nobody wants him slipping away like his brother, even if he is found not to be culpable due to being mentally impaired."

Whitt wondered. Was there a chance Merwin, despite all the head trauma and scars, was only playing a role?

He had a hard time believing it, but he didn't like the fact that Merwin hadn't said a word the entire time Whitt had been in the Prott house, thunking his forehead in silence, but now was chatting to the cops and doctors, asking for Whitt.

He looked out the window again. The kids were gone and the brown pointer continued staring up at him until the front door of the house across the street opened. An elderly man in a hovercart came cruising down a ramp affixed to his patio. He untied the dog and held tightly to the leash, sailing along behind. The pointer barked happily and the old man made a similar sound. They crossed against the red light at the end of the block, nearly got sideswiped by an SUV, wheeled around the corner, and disappeared from sight.

EIGHT

An odd medicinal odor, some kind of high-grade cleanser, pervaded the place, reminding Whitt that he'd never been in a hospital for any reason other than a birth or death. They either cut the cord and handed you the kid, or you watched somebody you love fade farther and farther beyond your reach.

You learned the lesson of anguish early. Everyone did. Nobody ever got better, whether they were physically ill or only breaking down under emotional assaults in between vacations to the Yucatán. You put in your time for as long as you could, until there was no reason for the visits anymore. Then you buried what was yours, got drunk, and from time to time looked at old photos of the dead. Until it was your turn down the back alley of ashes.

Whitt sat before Merwin Prott at a white table in an exceedingly white little room at Sojourner Psych Center, on the D-Wing, where they stored the violent cases. Merwin had arranged his few belongings in bizarre patterns across the floor. Clothes, toilet paper, toothbrush, safety razor, and paper cups were laid out in meticulously wrought designs.

A cop and two attendants peered through the tiny reinforced window in the door, the three of them crowded there, nothing but eyes watching.

It made Whitt wonder what it must be like, having someone study your every move, jotting notes, trying out new medications and therapies. Could you ever find your balance inside a room like this?

Merwin continued to grin stupidly and pet his chest like he was soothing a beautiful woman. The surgical scars appeared fiery beneath the harsh brightness of the lights. What had somebody taken out of that skull? Or worse, put in?

And the hand, endlessly brushing, caressing a paramour so close it was a part of his own flesh.

From his gym bag, Whitt withdrew a sealed jar labeled "Hogarth" and placed it upside down on the table. He had a pocketful of rock salt and he sprinkled some on the jar. Merwin's eyes narrowed and darkened, the hand speeding along so fast that the friction had to be singeing his fingertips. He stood and rearranged the belongings, shifting their angles slightly.

Whitt withdrew five more jars: Pedantry. Airsiez. Colby. Terminus. Kinnick.

"Those were entrusted to me," Merwin said. "I am their caretaker."

They were the first words Whitt had heard him

speak, and he was surprised at the deep, mellifluous quality of Merwin's voice. Bringing it up from his diaphragm the way a trained tenor would.

Merwin didn't notice they weren't the original containers. Whitt had done a good job of reproducing what he'd smashed that day in the Prott house.

"Yes, I'm returning them to you."

"Thank you. Mucus-Thorn-In-Heart extends his gratitude and benediction."

"Sure," Whitt said.

According to Mrs. Prott, a new god was being born inside Merwin's heart. Perhaps he was trying to coax it out by rubbing his chest, to midwife it along.

"What about the other receptacles?" Merwin asked.

"I have them," Whitt told him. "All of them. Insensate. Testament of Ya'al. Ussel. Dr. Dispensations. O'Mundanity. And the rest."

"I need them. Please give them to me."

"What do you need them for?"

"Protection."

"From what?"

"From the Phlegm in Hair and the Orifice Eye. Oh, oh, the eyes of orifices forever staring from above, from the side, from beneath." Merwin pointed to the door, where the cop and orderlies gawked, like they wanted to climb through the small window. When you were in you couldn't get out, and when you were out you spent most of your time trying to clamber in. "Like them, there. There. There, you see?"

"Yes."

"Of course you do. They study the best way to shoot us in the head. They shot my mother between her eyes, the orifice eyes. We are nothing more than whore's bait without proper precautions and defenses. None of us are safe without the proper precautions. You are in danger, everyone is, but especially you. Don't you understand?"

"I do," Whitt said.

"The triumph of knee."

With his index finger, Whitt tapped the jars together and they rang a painful note. "The failure of urethra."

That got Merwin where he lived. "Yes! Yes!" He rocked in his seat, sniveling his lament, snapping forward and back. "Such grand failures, all-important, the unraveling of the webs and snarls and knots. What time is it?"

"It's late."

"Is it four?"

Whitt had purposefully not worn a watch because Brunkowski had mentioned Merwin was obsessed with time. "After."

"Oh, oh no. Where is my mother?"

"Didn't they tell you?"

"They tell me many different things. They give half-truths and mix them with lies."

"Yes, they do, but I won't. She's in the county jail."

"They're going to shoot her in the head again."

"She'll survive."

"Perhaps."

"She's strong."

"The most powerful of us all."

Whitt was having a hard time fighting off the feeling that he'd had this conversation many times before, or ones just like it, in Garden Falls with his own wife. Where he played along until he became enmeshed in the heady rituals, beliefs, and fabrications. Where did you go when they started talking like this, so sure of the worlds in which they lived? Much more certain than Whitt was in his own life.

He was susceptible to the force of another's fantasy pulling him closer and closer toward the big edge. He wasn't sane enough anymore not to lose a little ground.

"How is the god in your heart?" he asked.

Merwin patted his chest with a slower and somehow sadder motion. The way a child might try to comfort a dying animal on the side of the road. "Weakening."

"I'll do what I can to help."

"Thank you."

"But I need to know, Merwin...where is your brother? Where's Franklin?"

It was the question to ask. Merwin's body seized up so fast that the sound of his elbows and knees cracking erupted through the room like gunshots. His features collapsed in on themselves, head wobbling on his neck, jerking and twitching wildly, those shining scars growing more prominent.

Whitt held his palm up toward the door, hoping to keep the attendants outside a while longer.

After a minute Merwin calmed and relaxed in his chair. Sweat glistened on his face, writhing in the trenches and dents in his head. "I hate him so much."

"Why?"

"He is forever a slave of Mucus-Thorn-In-Brain. The god in skull. Bound. Chained to the rock."

"Aren't you?"

"No. Transformation is all in the Cosmic Knot. We value it above all else."

Remember these words. Value. Transformation.

Whitt tried to take it seriously, but not so seriously that he started clocking himself in the forehead. "Is that why you need to stab them thrice in the heart, with the point of the blade aiming north?"

"Yes."

"And then the throat must be cut so . . ."

". . . so its evil incantations will dribble to the floor instead of being raised to the cosmic masters. Then the genitals must be removed."

Whitt plied his memory to find the exact words. "Or the seed may infect another vessel and give birth in its dying throes."

"Yes."

That's how it was done, letting such grotesque gospels roll off the tongue with the flourish of conviction. Merwin smiled beatifically, because he was now with someone who understood not only what was done but what there was left to do. "There is virtue in the ceremony. This is what we value. My mother and I, and the rest who belong to our beliefs."

"But not your brother?" Whitt asked.

"He has been breaking from us for some time, but our arrest drove him from the quintessence of what we are, what we do. He was afraid when he should not be. He was angry when he should not be."

Whitt stared at Merwin Prott, that dulcet voice beginning to lull him now. The words filled with more sincerity than he ever could've guessed at, considering the state of that home, the mania of Mama, the bodies, the wee-wee nabbing.

"Where might Franklin go?"

"He aids forces to which I'm not privy. He has friends of which he does not speak. Perhaps one of them has taken him in."

"How do I find them?"

"If you want to find a man, you have to learn what he loves and what he hates, because you'll discover him there, moving from one to the other."

"What's he hate?" Whitt asked.

"Everything."

"Okay, so what's he love?"

"Music."

"What kind of music?"

"Music you cannot hear."

Whitt had to fight not to sigh. Maybe some of this shit would help later, but for now he had to let Franklin go. A blind guy on the run, let Brunkowski worry about it.

Whitt asked, "Who was the man with the orange sneakers buried in the basement of that house?"

That medicinal smell grew even stronger as Merwin leaned forward. Jesus, it was on his breath, in the toothpaste they used at the facility. Worse than the turpentine. Whitt could barely stay in his chair.

"Mr. Jameson," Merwin whispered, the stink inflating with each syllable.

"Who was Mr. Jameson?"

"He tried to drink the soulwind out of my mother."

"Tell me more. Why did he come there? Did he want to join your . . . persuasion?"

"He brought the ballerina."

"What?"

Sometimes you could be overtaken by the strength of your obsession. Whitt could see the ballerina on the stage, in *Swan Lake*, although he'd never seen *Swan Lake*, dancing on her tippy toes, doing these funky leaps through the air, *jeté, jeté*.

The other swans appear holding hands, people shouting *bravo, bravissimo*. She spots him in the audience, a gaze formed of love, and extends her hand.

You could only think, My Christ, every woman in my mind is either insane, unreal, or dead.

Whitt's mouth dried, as dusty as the Serbian desert, but he managed her name. "Grace Kinnick?"

"Yes. And the child we needed."

"She was the baby's mother."

"Yes. Will you still help us to retrieve it?"

"Of course."

The eyes in the window still staring in, wide and un-blinking.

"Thank you. Is it four?"

"No," Whitt said. "It's not four yet."

Merwin showed visible relief, the tension in his body dissipating. He exhaled heavily and let loose with a girlish giggle. "Oh, that's better, that's so much better then."

"Why did Jameson and Grace come to you with the baby?"

"To speak with my mother. So many people wanted to talk to her, at all hours, for an assortment of reasons. So she could heal their pain, so she could realign their spines. So she could evoke their love. Guard them from the doom arriving in varieties of form, in faces, in phlegm."

Whitt's stomach tumbled, thinking of people out there so miserable that they'd seek solace in a woman like Mama Prott. "But what did Grace Kinnick and Jameson want to talk to your mother about?"

"Phil."

Whitt was starting to get annoyed. Whether Merwin was being consciously resistant to the questions or not, it was having the same effect. Yanking every goddamn answer out inch by inch. Whitt had learned to dig up a wealth of patience these last few years, but even that had its limit.

His throat heated and a heavy flush worked upwards, through his entire head, until it felt like his teeth were on fire.

He took the jar labeled Kinnick and began to nudge it toward the edge of the table.

Pushing it slowly but hard enough that the salt granules on top began to fall off. Merwin's eyes popped wide open as if his lids had been cut off. He started bopping in his seat like an anxious child, going, "Eh eh eh!" He became so agitated that he stopped stroking his chest. His nostrils flared, the wet scars gleaming. The cop outside the door thumped hard, about to turn the key and bust in. Like they'd ever be fast enough to get the job done, whatever the job might be.

Here it is, Whitt thought, everybody's about to make his move.

"My mother called her a ballerina because when she came to the house, she wore no shoes. Merely thin pink slippers."

"So, she's not a dancer."

"Perhaps she was, but not truly a ballerina."

The jar sat at the edge of the table and Whitt kept his finger on it, tapping the "K" of Kinnick. "Your mother told me Grace came for the truth because she'd been tormented by her parents for driving her toward perfection in ballet."

"Mama gets mixed up sometimes. On account of her brain leaking out after she got shot in the head."

"Okay. Then why was Grace Kinnick after Phil? Who's Phil?"

"Her boyfriend. Jameson's son. You see? You understand?"

"No, tell me."

"Your aura is so black."

"Enough about my aura, just tell me."

"Phil. Phil who did not know how to pray but cried each night. Bad genetics. Afraid of his father, afraid of becoming his father. Phil wanted to paint the house. He didn't want to kneel at the altar with Grace, swollen with child. Bursting. He feared Jameson's wrath. He feared the warped DNA. His father's fury. Phil had failed. His responsibilities lay elsewhere. In painting the house. It was his thread in the knot."

There it was, the truth at the heart of the matter. Phil had run from his pregnant girlfriend, trying to escape his father, Jameson, who wore orange sneakers—and just who the fuck wears orange sneakers? Bad genetics meant what? Phil and Grace were cousins? Coming across the cult somehow, people who promised him love and attention and no commitments except maybe he could paint their hovel. He'd never gotten around to it.

"What happened to Phil?"

"Franklin."

So Phil was dead somewhere on the property too.

His girlfriend and his father—Grace Kinnick and Jameson—had come to find him and they'd been murdered as well. Anybody who went to that door got wiped out. Whitt figured if he'd shown up at that church meeting, he would've been tossed in a shallow grave too. For pocket change, for testicles, for babies.

"There's blood in your mouth," Merwin said.

Clutching the table, Whitt glared at Merwin Prott's sutured skull and thought how easy it would be to grab both sides of it and squeeze until all those deranged thoughts came spritzing out his ears. A couple of swabs with the mop and all that madness packed behind his eyes would be gone forever.

"It's leaking down your chin. You'll mark the floor and ruin my rites, the protocol of redemption."

Whitt wanted to make sure who he was dealing with here. He whispered, "Government, government, government." Merwin thumped his forehead three times and his eyes started to roll back.

Okay, then. Whitt shoved the jars toward him, one by one, taking his time, almost sad to give them up. These souls deserved better than to be back in Prott hands, even if they were fakes. You start believing and you start making things happen. He hoped the attendants would clean this place out fast.

"What about the others?" Merwin asked.

"I'll bring them to you soon."

"Thank you."

"Sure."

"When Mucus-Thorn-In-Heart is born, we will re-member your kindness."

"Good, I'm glad somebody will."

"I wonder, is it four yet?"

Whitt stood and walked to the door, but something was nagging at him, chewing at his nerves, and he couldn't let it go. "Merwin, why did you say that I was in danger? Me, especially?"

"Because you are transforming. In transition, con-tinuous, and contaminating. *De-purifying*. It's obvious, so clear."

"Sure."

"Your aura. My mother can help. Go speak to her. There is a corrupter whose hand is around your soul, constricting and twisting it into the void. Soon he'll own you entirely, and place you in his jar."

"He already has," Whitt said, and wiped the blood from his mouth with the back of his hand.

NINE

Outside Mary Laramore's house, parked on the street and staring up the road at a couple of kids throwing a football around, Whitt called Brunkowski and gave him all the information he'd prized from Merwin Prott.

Whitt's nerves buzzed so loudly, his pulse still clattering, that he had trouble hearing Brunk's responses. "What?"

"I said we already know all that."

"What? How?"

"We had the place wired. He gave up the right to an attorney. Gave us permission to tape him."

"That's not the same thing as bugging the room."

"Like you said, there aren't many civil liberties left."

"You didn't tell me the room was wired."

"No, I didn't."

Like that, the noise faded away and Whitt felt in control of himself again. "You're a real fuck, you know that?"

"Yeah. Anyway, we found out that construction worker Paul Jameson of Hoboken, New Jersey, reported his son Phil missing about three weeks ago. There's no sheet on Grace Kinnick, but I made a few calls. She's been living with the Jamesons for four or five years. She's Jameson's niece, daughter of his dead sister. He had no wife and no money but he took her in after her mother died. Grace and Phil were cousins. I suppose that's why he ran when she got pregnant."

"Mama Prott told me the baby was unpure, its blood tainted. Phil must've explained his whole story to her. Merwin said something about bad genetics, warped DNA."

"Guess that sort of thing worries them even in Hoboken."

"Have they found more bodies?"

"Yeah, but not them. Two elderly guys with their packages removed at the other house."

"Any luck finding Franklin?"

"Not yet."

"He's only a blind serial killer, nothing you should put at the top of your to-do list."

"Listen, you—"

Whitt hung up.

He shifted in the driver's seat and watched the kids up the block trying to have a football game with only five players. You could get nostalgic about anything. He'd hated football and never liked playing with the guys from the neighborhood, but there was that wistful tug at his heart. The same way people at their twentieth high school reunions could only talk about how much fun they'd had back in the day. The teachers they'd adored, the great friends they'd had. Completely forgetting how much they'd hated every damn day of it. You were incapable of facing the past without the cushion of sentimentality.

Whitt didn't want to face her.

Not another mother.

How awful had it been for her, finding the body of her child, the pillow over Timmy Laramore's face with the frownie face staring back at her? Alone with no husband, no one to scream with, nobody's arms to fall into the way he and Karen had fallen into each other's. He could hardly bear to think about it. Running in tiny circles, flapping your hands in the air, wailing on the chest of your dead child, hoping to awaken from the nightmare.

As he climbed out of his car, vertigo hit like a pipe wrench across the back of his neck. He nearly went down, but managed to hang on to the side mirror by his fingertips, staying on his feet as the world spun away from him. He'd been more keyed up than he'd thought. He couldn't remember the last time he'd eaten. He was getting even more stupid.

Cold sweat broke over his body, his face slick as if from tears, rivulets streaming down between his shoulder blades. His stomach bucked and he dry heaved a couple of times before he got his back braced against the car door and felt the rush of dizziness pass.

He knew that, one of these days, Killjoy would be waiting for him at his weakest moment, and finally step up.

Mary Laramore met Whitt on her front stoop wearing an ankle-length sundress. She seemed more blond and a little less bland than when he'd first met her. The touch of sadness was still there in her heavily made-up face. Somebody had taken the time to teach her the proper way to apply eyeliner, shadow, rouge, lipstick. Her expression was flat and ambivalent but actually kind of sexy now.

Obviously pregnant when you looked at her belly, but not when you watched her legs and back. Whitt had learned to spot the subtle gestures and signs of pregnancy, first when he'd watched Karen grow heavier over the months she carried Sarah, and later when he'd directed a couple of commercials about maternity wear.

Four pregnant women walking about a Mommy-To-Be store, discussing brand names and which were the best padded bras to soak up leakage: Two of the ladies actually pregnant, two with preggers padding. You could tell immediately who the fakes were, and though Whitt was willing to let it slide, Freddy had ordered that the actresses be replaced with two more pregnant women. Cinema verité, he wanted only the real.

At least he wasn't letting mommies-to-be loose in the Rockies.

So it was easy to see that Mary was faking it, crossing her arms now in a way no woman in her sixth month would. Laying her forearms across her belly, resting them on it. She ought to be pressing her hands to the middle of her aching back.

She narrowed her eyes and said, "You're Eddie Whitt."

"That's right."

He pulled the kind of face you were supposed to pull when you first notice a woman is carrying a child.

"Congratulations," he said.

"Thank you. Why are you here, Eddie?"

He couldn't shake the feeling this wasn't the way a private eye would be handling matters. He really was a poor investigator. Not as bad as the feebs and the cops, but pretty bad anyway. It was no surprise Killjoy was still on the loose.

Whitt should've had some kind of plan ready, some front, a lie, anything instead of just standing there staring at this fake pregnant woman, unsure of what the hell to say next. "I think you know I've been investigating the case."

"Yes, I know you have been. The only one who has been. Considering the FBI and the police haven't made the slightest headway in all these years." There were suddenly deep furrows piercing her features, folding that painted face all the wrong ways.

"But you know that Killjoy has resurfaced."

"Yes, I read about it. In the papers. I notice your photo in there, on occasion. You've been busy."

What a way to put it. Whitt waited to see if she'd follow up, ask about the bodies in the Prott house, the changeling children, anything at all. But she simply stood there, kind of wary, prepared for him to make some sort of play.

He thought about the discipline and single-mindedness it would take for a woman to stick a foam pillow under her dress every day and wait for a killer to come drop off a stolen baby. Not merely the temperance, but the faith she showed in Killjoy.

He'd spent his whole life taking care of everything that needed to be done, and he didn't think he'd ever inspired faith like that in somebody.

"May I have a glass of water?" he asked.

"What?"

"A glass of water."

"You want a drink of water?"

"Yes, please."

"You haven't told me why you're here yet. I'd like to know why, Eddie."

"Sure, I'll tell you in a minute, but my throat is parched."

She gave him the look his mother used to give him when she'd lost all tolerance for what she called his shenanigans. The eye roll replete with the chin cock, the fist on the hip, the wag of the head, the expulsion of air. But Mary Laramore turned and stepped into the kitchen, got a glass from the drainboard and turned on the tap.

Whitt moved through the house, noting there were no photos of her son Timmy anywhere.

He slipped into her bedroom, pulled her flowered bedspread back and saw two pillows in clean, yellow cases there. Smelled the rich scent of fruity fabric softener. He lifted one, held it in his hands. Look at this, he thought, look how crazy I'm being. They locked up the wrong one of us, Karen. He pressed his face to it and stayed that way until he heard her storm into the room. Mary held the glass by two fingers, a thin trail of spilled water dappling the carpet behind her. She stood there in silence as the foam pillow returned to its original shape, erasing the indent of his strange expression. He couldn't quite make it out as it faded. Had she been smiling? Scowling?

How soon before she smacked him in the head with a lamp and called the cops?

As her hand trembled, water splashed over the sides of the glass, onto her belly. "How dare you?"

In lieu of a plan, he decided to talk.

"You know what I used to do?" he said. "After the feds were through with it, checking for prints and hairs and fibers, I used to sleep with the pillow he killed my daughter with. That sound wrong to you?" He didn't wait for an answer. "Thing is, it was so precious to me, because that pillow was the last thing that had ever touched the face of my baby Sarah. It still had some portion of her on it, her smell...I mean, it really didn't, but I still believed it did, that it might." He didn't look at Mary Laramore, didn't look anywhere, really. "There was nothing else. In a fit I destroyed it all. The photos, the toys, the drawings stuck up on the fridge. Even her clothes, can you believe it? Nobody knows what sick is until they see a parent destroying his kid's finger paintings. Crayon drawings of her and Mommy and Daddy all together out on the lawn, a dog in every picture even though we didn't have a dog. She wanted one but I had to mull." His voice faded for an instant and he thought he'd gone too far, but he continued. No, it probably wasn't nearly far enough. "Tearing up my baby's jumpers, her little booties. My wife Karen was already...growing ill by that time, and this weird thing with the pillow, my obsession with it, only made her state of mind worse. But I couldn't see it, I was already in the deep end myself. The two of us wrestling through the night to hold this pillow to our chests. Sometimes when we made love—we still did that for a few months afterwards—it was only so we could get the other to give up the pillow. After she left for the Falls—after I sent her, after they took her—I didn't have either of them anymore, just me and the pillow, the object used to smother the life out of my baby. The murder weapon, you know, and I used it to help me sleep. I'd have the strangest dreams. Some nights I'd imagine I was very small, lost among mammoths, scurrying across the feet of raging giants. It felt as if everything in my head, everything that came to me in that specific darkness, had been filtered through the ... the device, you see? It was like sleeping on a stick of dynamite. A machine gun. A machete. A vial of nerve gas, a land mine. A flamethrower. An inoperable tumor. Any type of killing machine, and I couldn't let it go. Couldn't even put it out of my own bed. I had to keep it as close to me as possible, all night long, in the dark, because it was the only way I knew how to hold on to my Sarah."

At the end of it he was out of breath, sweat dripping in his eyes.

Mary had shaken all the water from the glass and her fake belly was soaked.

She opened and closed her mouth twice before she managed to whisper, "How did you let it go?"

"I'm not sure," he admitted. "But there were days when I sobbed into it and held it and couldn't get out of the bed. The dreams had me pinned down. But eventually I knew I had to get up and out of the house."

"Why?"

"Because I have to catch him," Whitt said. "I have to kill him."

Mary threw herself forward, faster than any pregnant woman could, and grabbed hold of his jacket.

"Oh God no, please don't. Not yet! Don't stop him yet!"

"Mary—"

"You had your chance. Now it's my turn! Don't you see?"

"Mary—"

Whitt lifted her dress and she drew back a step, and then another, and another, until she was pressed up against the far wall like he might seduce her. She hated him for it but she wanted it too, of course. The burden of it finally released from her.

She closed her eyes, threw back her head, and lifted her chin so he could press his lips to her throat. He felt the girdle there and yanked down on it until the pillow jumped into his hands. The frownie face stared at him.

He tossed it on the bed and pulled her to him. She shivered so violently that she nearly rattled out of his hands.

"Don't throw it away," she said.

"I won't. He's not a hero, Mary. No matter what he does next, he's not a hero."

"I—"

"Remember what he did to you."

"I do, but—"

"What he did to you and your son Tim."

Whitt had always thought, If any of these people are like me, they might've done the same thing, and destroyed everything of their children.

From his jacket pocket he withdrew a sheet of paper. It was a copy of the original article about Timothy Laramore, a close-up of the kid smiling. Not quite four years old, his moppish hair flying every which way. Whitt held the picture up to her, and when she refused to take it he put it in her hands and repeated, "Remember what he did to your son Tim. Think of your boy."

That painted face cracked, inch by inch, from her eyes to the corners of her mouth, the heavy pancake foundation and thick wads of rouge flaking away. Shadow beginning to run as the tears she'd been holding back for Christ knows how long finally burst from her eyes, her mouth red with something other than lipstick. Mary's tongue swung back and forth like a pendulum as she tilted her head back and let loose with a dying animal's cry of loneliness and desolation.

He held her tightly but she broke away. She flopped onto the bed and convulsed in her grief, turned her face to the murderer's pillowcase and screamed into it, *"That savage, fiendish son of a bitch killed my baby! He suffocated my baby boy!"*

"Don't take anything he offers, Mary."

"He killed my Timmy, oh Jesus!"

"Reject him and his gift. Don't forgive him."

He let her weep for more than an hour, sitting beside her while she kissed the boy's face until the newspaper ink ran. She slept for a time and he kept patting her back and rubbing her shoulders, doing the simple, ineffectual things he'd tried to do with Karen in the beginning. When Mary Laramore awoke, she stared at Whitt like she didn't recognize him.

"Has he written you?" he asked.

"Yes," she said.

"Let me see the letter."

There was a full minute of hesitation as Mary fought back the need, the appalling awful desire, to keep Killjoy to herself. Whitt understood it perfectly. Then she rolled over and drew the note from the nightstand, folded and refolded a hundred times already. When Whitt saw the distinctive script, his heart began to batter his ribs, maybe trying to soar.

You are not alone in this precious housing of your skull. We live here together within the bone, the sweet spot, the temporal mandibular joints, these ridges of your brow, within the cranial cavity, inside every molar. Neurochemicals slither to the cadence of your compunction, atomic structures break down beyond the laws of physics, in contrast with Krantzein theory, Wesserrami ideology, Glocustertian principles, Xoxovinquinski equations. You know this because you speak in silence, and the silence itself continues to talk back.

There is no darkness. When you close your eyes there are visions, torments, lightning storms of disgrace and outrage, the face of a man who did not love you enough to stay. We are consumed by that which reaches down from around the frontal lobe, the hand within the head.

It still perplexes scholars today that Xoxovinquinski's most famous equation, which was started on his deathbed and finished on the floor by his hunchback hydrocephalic son, Leonard, remains a constant even in this improbable age:

I h8 {evreel}/ b4 + b(Wair) = 1(MO) ded [mE like b()()beeZ 2)

Clearly proving that it had been Leonard all along with the foresight, inferential logic, and mathematical genius to re-shape the very graphs used in fundamental black hole–white star postulates. Even after he was made president of Oxford, sat on the board of the London Guild of Intelligentsia, and spent so much time positing the curvature of space-time in his applesauce, in his porridge, in his mashed peas, attempting not merely to track black hole activity but also re-create it within his own brainpan—for purposes unknown to those of us with IQs only slightly higher than the average ladies'-night-out bowling score (106)—Leonard never frowned on the common man and continued to be kind to kittens.

Whitt, did you feel a pang of jealousy when you saw this letter?

Don't fret.

You're still the only real friend I have.

Are you ready for another girl?

"What the hell does it mean?" she asked, the tears still heavy in her throat.

"It doesn't mean anything, Mary."

"It must. There must be a reason."

"The reason is he's having fun. He's always been having fun, even in his misery."

"Is that why he calls himself Killjoy?"

"He didn't name himself. I named him."

Mary had newsprint dried to her cheek. "What? How?"

"That's what they tell me anyway. When the police first interviewed me, after he'd murdered Sarah, I said he'd killed my joy. The reporters leaped on it."

"No wonder he thinks you have a . . . a . . . connection. You gave him his name. Like a father would."

The explanation, given to him like that, hit Whitt so hard that he almost fell over. Mary's face dropped and she reached for him, and Whitt pressed his back to the wall trying to shake off the nausea, the immediate disgrace he felt.

Him being Killjoy's father. My Christ, what a thing to say.

She said, "I'm sorry, I didn't mean that to come out the way it did."

"That's all right."

"You're ill, you need a doctor."

"I'll be okay in a minute."

"You're the only one who can do it, Eddie."

"What?"

"The only one who's willing to do what has to be done. No one else is strong enough. I wasn't. None of the other parents are. The police, the FBI . . . all those psychiatrists, the manhunters . . . none of us. Only you."

He thought, I'm the only one who gave the kid back. What kind of father does that make me?

"How are you going to kill him?" Mary asked.

"I've got a gun."

"No, that's not good enough. Not a gun. Use a knife. Stick it in him! And you twist it and *twist it and twist it!*"

Whitt thought about shoving the blade in, scraping bone, and then twisting it. Listening to Killjoy scream. Maybe that was the way to go, after all.

TEN

A smear of black motion coming up fast behind him reflected in the driver's window as Whitt stepped to his car. He dodged to the right, a painful grin branding his face.

Thinking, Finally, I'm about to meet him. He couldn't take it anymore and had to come out from the gloom.

Let's see him draw a frownie face on me.

As Whitt turned, something heavy brushed past his ear. A sweep of air brushing back his curls while he continued to spin around, the way his sensei had taught him, sweeping his left arm over to strike with the elbow.

He took in several things at once as the moment expanded to encompass first himself, then his immediate surroundings, his car, then up the lawn to the house:

Bill McConnelly, whose son had been murdered, whose wife could no longer come to full term, who had lost a new child because of a busybody neighbor, now brandishing an old school Louisville Slugger. Solid wood, none of this aluminum or graphite shit, the damn thing would've caved in Whitt's head if it had connected. And McConnelly would never have survived Whitt's blow if he followed through with it. Whitt feeling the superb frenzy humming through his muscles, McConnelly looking like he hadn't eaten or slept in three months, the point of his chin raised just right, as if daring Whitt to strike him. Split that jaw so perfectly that the bone fragments burst upwards into the guy's brain. And behind him, there, creeping across the lawn, a calico missing the top of one ear, its tail flicking with great intensity. At her front window, Mary Laramore peering out from the curtains, the hate still there and the newfound strength as well. Her lips puffed out as she mouthed, "Oh."

It was going to hurt.

Whitt couldn't stop his rage or the strike, but he altered course, shifting slightly to bring the brunt of his attack away from McConnelly and to the bat. His elbow struck the middle of the Slugger, where it was thickest, missing McConnelly's fingers by inches. The crack echoed up the block.

A brilliant, crystalline pain tore through Whitt's arm, but he swallowed it down, the way he'd kept silent the last time he'd seen Bill McConnelly—a year ago, when McConnelly had wildly and repeatedly punched him in the stomach.

McConnelly screamed as the bat splintered. Most of

it hit the side of Whitt's car, but one thick spear tore through the air, rising for an instant, before swooping down toward the calico. Mary Laramore's scream vibrated the window, but the cat simply eased aside and ran for the weeds.

"You son of a bitch," McConnelly said.

"With my back turned." Whitt's arm was numb, and he checked to make sure it wasn't broken.

"I'll smash your face in too."

Since his brief interview with McConnelly eight or nine months ago, when he'd mentioned the possibility of Killjoy's delivering them a child in the middle of the night, the man had gone skeletal. He'd once been fat, like Whitt. With a face sculpted from flint, all sharp angles and points, his eyes going so far back into his head that they seemed to have been jabbed inside with an ice pick.

He stood there with his fists up, hollowed out, gutted. He threw two weak punches that Whitt avoided. The lingering fury wanted Whitt to do something more, any goddamn thing. With his hands, the gun, even his feet. Quit taking shit off every bastard with a grudge of some kind.

He groaned, trying to hold the fever back. He hissed, "Stop it, McConnelly."

The man was trying to work his way up to speaking. His lips quivering as if speech was only a faint memory, the tip of his tongue jutting, white and dry. "It's your fault. My son is gone."

"Your son is dead."

"My other son. My new child."

"You don't have a new child."

"We did!"

Almost the exact words that Karen had said to him up at the Falls. *I know the first one is dead. But how's the new one?*

"I had nothing to do with that."

"That bitch across the street from us knew all about our case because of you. Because you keep it alive. Always in the papers and on television! Always spouting off, on the hunt! Because you wouldn't let it go, my boy is gone!"

Everyone willing to forgive Killjoy except Whitt.

Was it true, was he the prick here? Or had Killjoy driven them all so far out of their heads that he'd created his own little fan club, a kind of love cult? A religion devoted to a bitter god with a soft pillow.

The Brotherhood of Sleep.

The Holy Order of Asphyxiated Babies.

McConnelly picked up the busted bat, hardly more than a stick, and made a few tentative swipes at Whitt with it.

All this time Whitt had been training himself to be a stone killer, and he couldn't feel anything more than a great swell of compassion for Bill McConnelly, even while the guy bared his teeth.

"You don't want to do this, Bill. This isn't going to help."

"And what will?"

"I don't know."

"What will? Killing him?"

"No, that won't bring your child back. Nothing's going to do that. You've got to learn to live with it."

"Don't you get it?" McConnelly shrieked. "Don't you understand anything? I can't! I've been trying and I can't do it!"

He drew the stake back over his head, preparing to plunge it down into Whitt's heart. And Whitt thought—I can't hit this guy again, I can't, I've got to move out of the way, but for some reason I can't seem to do that either—and McConnelly brought the stake down with all the thrust of his heartbreak behind it, pulling it in close as if to hug the Slugger to him like the kid he'd lost, until it jutted from his own spurting chest.

ELEVEN

Mike Bowman stood in the doorway, hands behind his back, waiting. Dressed in a black suit, narrow black tie, black shoes so polished that they caught the kitchen light and flashed it all over the room.

It was the first time he'd ever been to Whitt's apartment, although he paid the rent on it. He craned his head, spotted Whitt at the window like a soldier at watch, and said, "I saw the news last night. How is he?"

Whitt didn't turn to face his father-in-law. "He punctured a lung, nicked his aorta, but they think he'll live."

"Thanks to you, Eddie."

"Hardly."

"Don't trivialize what happened. You saved a man's life yesterday."

Whitt stared off in the direction of the house he'd lived in with Karen and Sarah, less than a mile away but as remote as the other side of the world. Rain throbbed against the glass and he brought his hand up to the pane. He looked over his shoulder and said, "Come inside, Mike."

At that last instant, watching McConnelly with the stake quivering between his ribs, the blood bursting from the guy's mouth, Whitt had felt shame overpowering the astonishment, alarm, and everything else. The real reason he'd saved Bill McConnelly's life, laying his hands over the wound to stanch the flow of blood, was because he didn't think he could carry another straw of guilt.

McConnelly had taken a header on Mary Laramore's front lawn, spritzing across the grass before knocking the stake loose. The sucking wound so loud and obscene, whistling to Whitt. That sound, another sound he'd never forget.

The blood kept erupting over Whitt's hands and he'd been forced to plug the hole with his finger. Jamming it into the man's chest, damn near into his broken heart.

How was McConnelly going to live with *that* on top of all his other distress? The idea that the man he held responsible for the loss of his new child had actually had his finger inside him, stirring up his sorrow. Bill McConnelly hadn't even passed out through it all, just sat there with his eyes full of shock and resignation, staring at Whitt and saying, "Leave it go. Leave it go."

Mike stepped inside.

Whitt turned. At the moment, all he could think

about was how Mike would've been the one who found Whitt behind the wheel in the garage, eating the pipe, if he'd gone through with it that day. Amazing how you could carry humiliation around for the things you never even did.

"How's your arm?"

"The EMTs gave me some painkillers. All I needed was some sleep. It's okay now."

"That's good," Mike said. "I'm going to the cemetery today. I'd like you to come with me."

"No," Whitt told him.

"Please."

"No, I'm sorry."

"I insist, Eddie."

"You can't."

Mike's face, going hard-core Marine again, as the man shifted his weight up into his shoulders, dropping his chin tight against his chest, like he would charge forward and bull his way through. To where? Where did the man think he was going to go?

Whitt almost looked forward to it, thinking about what the fight would be like. So much of his mind consumed lately with the idea of shattering bones, breaking cartilage, kicking at kneecaps, blasting someone in the brain, his fever broiling his everyday thoughts. It had to stop, but probably not yet.

First thing he thought he'd do was scuff those shoes. Mike still thinking that the strength of his will was enough to make the rest of the world bend to him.

That slight flaring curl of steel-gray hair had been brought low today by rain. The windows chattered just loud enough to keep you distracted, keep you turning back to see if somebody was there. Mike's eyes never shifted but he was taking everything in—the state of the apartment, a little more run-down than usual. The dollhouse, the torn-open packages of miniatures on the floor. The half-eaten ham sandwich. Whitt had been getting sloppy, another bad sign.

The brutal power inside the man pulsed, growing and diminishing from one second to the next. He prowled forward, toed the empty plastic packages, turned and put a hand on Karen's psychiatric files stacked a foot high on the coffee table.

Clearly Mike wanted to sit, do his little mano a mano gig over whiskey and stare into Whitt's eyes, but the place wasn't set up that way. Anywhere he sat he'd be off to an angle, unable to glare directly into Whitt's face. No liquor on hand, no photos on any shelves in this room or the next.

"You've never been to Sarah's grave."

"I was there when they buried my girl, Mike. How about if we don't get into this now, eh?"

Whitt lit a cigarette, wondering if Mike would feel in charge enough to ask him to put it out. Apparently not. Mike just watched him smoke. It was another tiny victory in his own home, but he made sure he blew the smoke away from the man.

This wasn't about Sarah or the cemetery at all.

"It's the letters," Whitt finally said.

"Yes."

"You can't get them out of your head. I told you it was a bad idea for you to read them."

"He's laughing at the world. He's having fun."

"In a manner of speaking, yes."

"Why do you qualify it?"

"Nobody goes crazy happily. Pain brought him to this." Whitt went on, further than he meant to go, but unable to stop himself, knowing what would come. "To his first incarnation, and now to this new one."

"You talk about him as if he's a holy figure."

"No, Mike, I don't talk about him like that at all."

"I think you do."

Certain trials force you toward a clarity you do not want. The precision of pain reshapes and remolds you like the hand of the father once did. Whitt knew everyone close to him would judge him as he continued his course—find him lacking in heart, spirit, intelligence, nerve, but fixated and full of mania, just like . . .

Before he realized he was moving, Whitt was already on Mike. Holding the man by his tie, yanking him nose to nose. Good, this was all right, let the guy look him dead in the eye now, the way he liked. See what he could see so deeply in there, what judgments he could pass, decisions he could make.

Whitt waited, wondering which move the old man

would make—jump left, use one of those Marine tactics, judo chop to the sternum, then go in for the clench, the long, drawn-out lovey hug? He shivered thinking about where the next instant would take him.

But Mike Bowman did nothing.

He'd dealt with his share of men on the edge in the military, on both sides. The troops failing to rally, the enemy priming for a suicide mission. He simply looked at Whitt, waiting for him to let go of the tie.

The shine of those shoes worked into Whitt's eyes until he saw spots and the borders of his vision became purple and blue. He was holding his breath. Another mistake his sensei used to point out.

"I'm sorry, Mike."

"It's all right. I understand what a trial this has been for you."

Whitt let go, moved back to the window, opened it, and let the drizzle spatter against his face. It was all right to become distracted for a little while. A moment's slippage was acceptable. If you kept the string of the bow too tight, the arrow couldn't fly. Buddha had said that. He didn't know how the hell he knew that Buddha had said it, but there it was anyway. Maybe he was wrong.

Mike was suddenly behind him. One hand out as if to pat Whitt's back, but frozen there. "I feel...very feeble. Ineffectual."

"You're not," Whitt said.

"And something more. Perhaps it's paranoia."

"It's natural. This is something we never get to the end of, never solve. The enemy has no face."

"I've dealt with faceless enemies before."

"In the jungles? The deserts? Wherever the hell you've been?"

"Yes."

"They had faces. They were on the other side. They wore different uniforms, raised different flags, isn't that so?"

Mike said nothing.

"Even if you didn't know why you were fighting, at least you knew the color of the other guy's skin. This isn't the same."

The pieces snapping together for his father-in-law, the man at last seeing an exit from the impotence. "Yes, you're right. This is different because it could be anyone. It's possible he's walked past me a hundred times and I wouldn't know it."

"It's not your fault. That's enough to make any normal man of vengeance feel apprehensive."

He mouthed the phrase quietly, tonguing it for a minute. "A normal man of vengeance. I've never heard it put that way before."

Whitt was still a little loopy. The painkillers were good stuff. He should at least finish the sandwich too. "Regardless, it's the truth. Or so I see it anyway."

Mike's hands could strangle a man, pluck out an

eyeball. Crush a larynx, flail a chest. Angle along a daughter's cheek, carry a granddaughter from the bassinet to the crib. Those hands would never get close to Killjoy.

Whitt glanced down at his own fists, covered in red with another father's blood just this morning, knowing only one thing, comprehending a single certainty.

These.

"Don't be guilty, Mike. You're humanizing him, trying to feel what he feels in order to discover why he does what he does. But those aren't your natural thoughts. You have to stop now and let me do what I've decided to do."

"All right. But I'd still like you to come with me to the cemetery."

"No," Whitt said.

"You should see her."

"She's not there for me to see."

"It's a matter of acceptance."

"If you say so."

"I've seen more death than you ever will, son."

"Sure. But not your own kid."

"No, not that. But these rituals have meaning. Services. Prayers. Graves."

"They mean nothing to me."

"It's the first step toward peace."

"I don't believe that."

"It's for your own sake."

"I can't do that. I'm sorry."

With an impatient sigh now, chin raised again. "You're never going to heal this way."

"That's the fuckin' point, old man."

Whitt almost missed the familiar fear he'd felt in his father-in-law's presence. He missed what the man had represented to him, the authority figure. Whitt had paid a hell of a price to be harder than an ex-Marine, and suddenly his head got light, the vertigo coming on strong.

Repentance. *Testament of Ya'al*. Value. Transformation. *Significum Harlequenin*. Incision. The words continued to amass without real meaning, but taking shape nonetheless, in Whitt's mind and probably in Killjoy's too.

Mike started for the door. All he had to do was pay for his daughter's tickets to Vancouver, Ted's shopping sprees, read the reports, visit once in a while, and he was doing his fatherly duty. Taking care of Daddy's girl. He didn't have to go any further than that, the lucky prick.

Still, he couldn't leave in silence. He wasn't going to take all of Whitt's crap without giving at least a little back.

"Eddie, I have to ask you something."

Of course he did.

The man would never be able to stanch the questions he shouldn't give voice to. That he should not give form to, that should never be answered. He was incapable of forgoing, of allowing, of refraining. The man couldn't keep his goddamn mouth shut.

"Are you playing with Sarah's dolls?" Mike said.

"No," Whitt told him, and finally cracked a grin. "They're sorta playing with me."

TWELVE

Whitt was getting slow again. McConnelly never should've gotten as much of a jump on him as the guy had. If it had been Killjoy, Whitt would be dead now. He needed to get back into training. He needed to get to Freddy's cabin.

So here he was back on the set. Grips and best boys hid in sharp corners, sneaking sips of beer and Dewars & Coke out of poorly concealed bottles in bags, making triple time because it was after six. A few other folks milling about, makeup girls staring into mirrors, two actors in face paint, wigs, wearing fringe jackets asleep in their chairs. Some quick math showed that about thirty grand was sliding into the sewer.

Shouts resounded down the corridor to Freddy Fruggman's office. Freddy paced in there, flinging himself around in a dance of anger, vibrations making the ceiling tiles groan.

Whitt walked in. Freddy slammed the phone down, but it was a wireless and he never pushed the button to disconnect. A small, tinny voice continued to dribble from it. Something about discrimination, casinos, firewater. Freddy leaned over and looked into the face of the cell phone and shrieked, "Fuckin' Nazis!" He slapped it off the desk and Whitt caught it in his left hand with a casual grace, hit the disconnect button.

"Who?" Whitt asked.

"Those Indians!"

"Indian Nazis?"

"Yeah, Nazi Native Americans, they're mad about my latest ad campaign and commercial. I've got their tribal lawyers breaking my ass wherever I go. They've got protestors outside my apartment building, for Christ's sake."

"What happened? Something to do with the hovercart?"

"No, no, this is the other commercial we were working on. Started airing last night. The alternative medicine man one."

"I must've missed this," Whitt said. He'd finished his ham sandwich and caught a nap but the painkillers kept him feeling like he was in a place without much gravity or many boundaries. "What happened?"

Freddy made a flustered noise like he couldn't believe what was going on, the trials he was being put through. "To sell herbal supplements. We dressed a guy up in a wig, put him in a teepee with a buffalo head on a stick. Herbal remedies for hemorrhoids, some colon cleanser, aids for regularity, bladder control, that sort of thing, and now the Indians are rioting. They got a fleet of attorneys. None of this jumping off the rez crap, these guys are serious. It's worse than when they were protesting Columbus Day."

"You couldn't find an herbal supplement that didn't have to do with piss or shit?"

"It's herbs, man, that's all herbs help out with. They grease your guts, unless you want to smoke them."

Whitt wasn't so sure about that but let it slide. "Which tribe?"

"Who the hell knows? One of the ones out West."

"That'd be about all of them."

"Yeah, but the tribal lawyers all went to Harvard and Yale. Explain that one to me."

"What do you plan on doing?" Whitt tried to put a note of sympathy in his voice and failed pretty badly.

"They want some free commercials made to promote their casinos. They're mad about the stereotype, want to show them in three-piece suits, gold watches, short haircuts, welcome to Apacheland, home of the ten-million-dollar slot machine jackpot."

"Apacheland?"

"That kind of thing. I got to pay for it myself, but it shouldn't be too bad. Might even be fun, so long as they comp my stay at the casino." Freddy threw his bulk down in his chair and swung himself around for a minute. He shut his eyes and relaxed, all of the tension slipping out of him at once. Man, what a gift, to be able to do that. Just let the anxiety escape. "Besides, it doesn't much matter, the execs are happy with the alternative medicine man campaign anyhow. It's already a major hit for the herbal company."

"Did you ever get the quads the monkeys?"

Freddy said, "No, they settled for dogs. Canine companions. They do tricks, help around the house too, but you don't laser things, you just tell them, 'Hey, go bring me the phone,' and they go get it." Freddy stopped whirling in his chair, leaned over his desk, and peered deeply into Whitt's face, that little head jutting forward. "The hell are you asking about the monkeys for?"

"I was thinking of getting a few."

"A few? What do you need a few trained monkeys for? Something wrong with you you're not telling me? You got spinal meningitis or something?"

"Not exactly."

"What's 'not exactly'?"

Whitt couldn't stop thinking about it. Drawing Killjoy into a trap and, when the guy appeared, instead of Whitt drawing his .32 and putting one between his eyes, he'd yank out the laser, zap the kitchen cutlery with it, and watch as twenty monkeys grabbed cleavers and steak knives and got to work.

"Stop that," Freddy said.

"What?"

"What you were doing."

"What was I doing?" Whitt asked.

"Laughing in a way you shouldn't."

"Oh."

"You okay? You don't look okay."

He was pretty sure he wasn't okay, but that wasn't the issue here. "I need to borrow your cabin for a couple of days."

"Sure. Go up there and relax. Meditate. It'll be good for you. Go break that pattern I mentioned."

"It's already broken, but I didn't do it. Mike did. He showed up at my place. It was the first time he'd ever been there. I wonder how that will change things."

"Change things how?"

"With Killjoy."

"You get another letter?" Freddy shook his tiny head, erasing the question. "Forget I said that, I don't want to know. Listen, going to the cabin is a smart idea. I've got some Caruso CDs, you'll like them. Take some time out for yourself. You need to rest. You look like shit."

"I must mull."

"What?"

"Mulling is what I must do."

Freddy Fruggman, of all people, showing an expression of concern. The guy who let the quads go in the Rockies, lending a hand. "Eddie, listen—"

"Caruso, eh? That might be fun. That might be just what I'm after."

"You're not going to listen to any fucking CDs, are you?"

"I don't think so, Freddy."

"Eddie, why are you doing this?"

Whitt spoke clearly, doing his best to keep any emotion from his voice, getting to that place where Freddy wouldn't be distracted, so the two of them could talk honestly. "I need to get faster. Stronger."

"There's not an ounce of fat on you!"

"It's for Sarah. Remember how hard you cried the day we buried her?"

"Yes, of course—"

"It's never gotten any easier since that day, Freddy, never. You looked like you were going to jump down into the grave with her, but I did it. You understand? I'm there. I have to be there with my girl or I can never catch her killer."

"You're talking crazy."

"How else can I talk?"

"Eddie, you can't catch him. No matter what you do, what you give up, how much you train, you won't ever find him. He's air. He's the monster in the dark."

"Everybody telling me I can't catch him. If I was the sensitive type, I might be offended by that."

"You are the sensitive type."

"Yeah."

"He's going to finish this thing with the babies and then go away. He'll be done. He won't be able to hurt you anymore."

"Another one," Whitt said, letting out the laugh that wasn't a laugh. "You're another one who's willing to forget about him."

That riled Freddy enough to get him glowering.

"Don't you say that. I'll never forget what he did, but you have to learn to live with it. Eventually. Otherwise, you'll wind up like Karen. That's why she's in there, don't you know that? Because she can't accept what's happened. She'll never accept it and she'll never get out. You want that to be how the story ends? You and Karen shacking up in the Falls together? Playing house behind a barbed wire fence?"

"No," Whitt said. "I don't think so. Besides, Ted's a pretty crappy decorator."

"Who the fuck is Ted!"

"That doesn't matter."

Shutting his eyes, relaxing the muscles in his little face, Freddy let the tension roll out of him once again. Whitt felt it drift by him like a ripple on a pond. But Freddy couldn't quite get it all this time. His shoulders still hunched with the stress.

"Be careful with your gun," Freddy said. "There's hunters up there this time of year. It's duck season."

"It's not duck season."

"It is, I just got a letter about it."

"You pick up your mail from the box every four months. It's long past duck season."

"Well, if it ain't ducks, then it's deer, and if it's not that, it's moose or buffalo."

"You can't hunt buffalo, Freddy."

"Up there they do!"

"There's no buffalo in New York."

"Up there they hunt everything! They're savages, you know that!"

Maybe they were. Maybe everybody was when you got down to it.

"Eddie," Freddy said with an awkward, sad expression, "if you can catch him, I wish you'd hurry up."

"Whatever happens, it'll happen soon."

"How can you tell?"

How could you explain it?

He said, "The hell you listening to Caruso for?"

And Freddy, still flushed with his frustrations, replied, "The great sad clown? Why else? He calms me."

THIRTEEN

The cabin sat out on the edge of thirty-five acres of woodland up in the Catskills, about twenty minutes west of Woodstock. Whitt had to pass the exit for Garden Falls to get there, feeling the almost sexual lure of the hospital as he drove by the ramp, sensing his wife. Hearing Ted knocking his rappity-tap tune on Karen's door, the two of them planning ingenious schemes together in the safety of corridors choked with psychotics. Whitt wondered when it would be his turn to relax and go mad. Visit the Virgin Islands.

Easing down on the accelerator, the thrum of speed working through his body, it reminded him of when he'd pick Karen up for a date and tear down Sunrise Highway out to Montauk Point. Cruising with his girl snuggled against him, bracing herself on his arm, as he kicked it to eighty and they hit the desolate pine barrens. Darkness pulsing across the road, no other car in sight.

He'd wheel through the Hamptons and Karen

would fiddle with the radio, pick an oldies station so they could ride to the crooners, the chilly salt air breezing through the vents. She'd work him up by placing a hand on his knee, going no farther than that. Just a touch in the right place. For the first time in his life he could see an inch beyond the present and feel his future becoming real around him.

His girl, his job with her old man's company, the wedding on the horizon. The world ahead heavy with promise. She'd whisper to him, *"My love, my lover, my man."* Words that at first sounded like a foreign language because he'd never heard them said that way before, to him, in this way.

Racing through the small wealthy towns that peppered the east end, charming in the way that only incorporated villages thick with millionaires can be quaint. His long-standing dreams of wealth still important but not nearly as much as they'd once been. He and his girl as they fled along the coastal streets past shadowy mansions branching across the moon, wavering in the roiling surf. That hand on his thigh, fingers tapping to the fifties tunes, vowing abandon, until Karen slid forward and the seat fabric groaned, and she pressed her face into the crook of his neck and licked. He nearly went off the road.

That's how it had been.

Whitt floored the accelerator and sped by the pickups and Freightliners, barely allowing himself the luxury of imagining what it would be like to just keep going. Shuck the game, the responsibilities he'd taken on, the others that had been laid in his lap by remorse. You could do that. Some people could do that. They went on. They hobbled on, brokenhearted and maimed, maybe crazy too, but they went out. They went to Lake Tahoe and bought new clothes and went to work in the morning. Some of them.

Eventually he came to the exit leading up into the mountain range and he pretended like he had a choice to pass it by. He held the steering wheel locked in his hands, forcing himself to keep to the course. Until at the last moment he swung hard and angled up the ramp. He weaved his way through a series of turnoffs and began to thread up dirt roads leading into the front hills, maneuvering toward the cabin.

It was the kind of place every urbanite wished for, even if he didn't realize it. Even if he hated the stink of pollen and the silence that ran counter to city life. There was always an area of your mind that wanted to live apart from the crowd, in a land you didn't know anymore.

The four-room cabin was built on a couple of feet of cinder blocks, and when Whitt got out of the car he heard things running and scuttling under there. Another time, that would've spooked him. Dealing with a serial child murderer had its advantages—you learned to let a lot of the smaller frights slide.

Whitt opened his trunk and brought in his luggage and a few days' worth of supplies. He had to go out to the shed, fill the generator, and get it going. He had to fool with the circuit breakers before the lights would come on. Once the electricity was working he had to turn on the pump to get the water running.

The place was fairly clean, even if Freddy hadn't been up here since duck season. He lent the cabin out to a lot of his friends and the last ones had done a pretty good job of tidying up after themselves. Whitt checked around and found a stack of fashion and entertainment magazines from two months back.

Freddy's stereo system was small and expensive, set up on a poorly made shelving unit. CDs lay on a coffee table made from a lacquered tree trunk almost four feet wide. Whitt put one in and hit Play and sure enough, Caruso started filling the cabin with Italian anguish. He shut it off.

Whitt had set up the back room as a gym almost a year ago. He spent more time at the cabin than Freddy ever did. He'd cleared a couple acres of land, chopping down trees, grinding stumps, and moving rocks. In the gym he worked out the tightness in his muscles and practiced the moves he knew, waiting for the moment they'd finally come in handy.

A heavy bag, speed bag, weights, and hefty mats on the floor where he could do his tumbles. It wasn't the way to go about it. He should be in a ring sparring or back at the dojo training with a sensei.

But Whitt wasn't that kind of student. Three years ago, he'd been kicked out of three dojos within six months. He didn't have the capacity to find the reflective quality in martial arts, the betterment of self. He didn't want to learn how to find inner peace, or even how to fight. Just how to stop Killjoy, quickly and effectively.

Besides basic blocking, kicking, and punching, Whitt only knew about a dozen really solid moves. But they were enough for him to handle about 90 percent of the trouble he was likely to get into. For the next 9 percent he carried the .32.

He didn't want to think about the last 1 percent.

Whitt carried rocks in the morning.

Through the middle of Freddy's property ran a river that had overflowed twenty years ago and drowned thirty-seven people down in the valley. The floodwaters had smashed through the woodlands and washed all the rocks to the ridge, leaving five acres completely infertile, covered in nothing but rubble and shattered logs. All this gorgeous forest around you and then, breaking over the rise, you're suddenly standing on the moon.

It was a good way to get a hernia, throw out your back, pull a hamstring, crack your vertebrae. Any of another dozen stupid injuries, but Whitt liked the harsh, redundant nature of it. There was a sanctity to the repetition, the sheer mindlessness involved. You just picked up a rock from over there and carried it twenty-five feet to over here, dumped it, and went back for another. And you did it again. And again.

With no concern for life or death.

Justice or law.

Wife or daughter.

Just stone and sweat. Whitt and Killjoy.

The act never fully cleared his mind, but it came as close as anything else had these past five years. By the end of each morning he was so worn that he crashed for two hours without dreaming. His hands were blistered but strong.

After the nap, he'd loosen up and hit the mats for a couple hours, repeating the few moves he knew, the martial arts he'd picked up from his senseis. Leg sweeps, strike zones, kill areas, seeing men around him as he moved.

One guy, appearing and reappearing, faster than the others and nearly on him before he turned. Sometimes it was Mike, sometimes himself.

Killjoy had no face, so it was impossible to spot him in the room, coming up from behind. The one you're after is the one you can't see, even when you're pretending. Whitt put on Caruso and tried to picture the killer, detail him enough so the enigma wore away. Doing his best to dissipate the awful myth.

Now when he forced himself to see Killjoy slipping into the cabin, he saw a guy with a pillowcase over his head, the frownie face drawn in magic marker easing closer.

No weapon except for black-gloved hands, small and almost feminine. No strangler's fists, almost dainty fingers. Perhaps as short and thin as a child himself, the frown forever unchanging. The hands gentle, even loving.

The foolish, wasted motions you went through hoping for your one chance.

After the martial arts, Whitt would get to work on the bags. Twenty minutes pounding the shit out of the heavy bag, another twenty spent on the speed bag.

He'd shower and relax for a while, flipping through the magazines. Freddy had a well-stocked wine cellar, and Whitt would uncork a bottle, pour himself a glass, and sip it. Pretending to be interested in the fashion articles, the movie reviews. It was an important factor, playing at being normal.

Finally, with an hour or so of light left, he'd draw his .32 and go outside.

A month after Sarah's murder, he spent a week working with three shooting instructors learning what he had to about handguns. It only took about two days to learn the basics. Everything after that was just further honing and practice.

The last time he'd been to the cabin he'd set up bottles on the posts of a wooden fence. The way you see it done in every Western movie where the hero starts off as a greenhorn from back East but eventually learns to outdraw the guy in the black hat.

At first, Whitt felt ridiculous shooting at the hundreds of beer cans and bottles Freddy had left stacked in their original cases out back of the cabin. But the more he did it, the less foolish it seemed. He'd brought thirty boxes of ammo and kept them in the trunk.

Who knew, if he ever got rear-ended just right, sitting at a stop sign and some little old lady who couldn't see over her dashboard clunked into him, doing fifteen miles an hour on a side street, it'd be like Normandy beach.

So now in the evenings he set up the bottles and shot them down. Hearing spaghetti Western sound tracks loud in his head every time he drew the .32, straightened his arm, and pulled the trigger. Never firing all six shots, always leaving one in the gun so he wouldn't ever be caught totally defenseless.

Afterwards, in the night, he'd play music.

All in all, the boxed set of Caruso CDs was actually very good. Whitt had never enjoyed opera before. But in the dark, listening to Enrico kick out "Vesti La Giubba" from *I Pagliacci*, that tenor voice full of passion, stretching the violent octaves, robust and full of sincerity, it soothed him.

The primitive acoustic-recording technology still came through with sharp fidelity, warm tonal quality filling the entire cabin, working across Whitt's sensibilities. Somehow getting down into his aching muscles. He kept replaying "Celeste Aida" for the broken high note, enjoying it because it showed the man wasn't perfect. The jarring error making the music that much more beautiful.

By the end of the week he felt sharper than before, but there was something still missing. He practiced shooting the bottles and cans again. He sighted on one after the other until he realized what was missing, what he needed.

He found a linen closet with extra blankets and bedding. He grabbed five pillowcases and grinned like a baboon, knowing he was doing it but not caring much. He moved deeper inside to meet his own fever.

He dug around in the kitchen until he found a magic marker and spent an exceedingly long time drawing the frownie faces, doing his best to add the particularly refined *élan* that showed in Killjoy's art and penmanship.

He carried the proper-sized stones back from the dead patch of land and up the path to the back fence. It was difficult as hell lifting the stones high enough to stick them on the posts, but he managed it. Then he draped the pillowcases over the head-shaped rocks.

How insane a thing was this? How much closer to the edge was he now from an hour ago?

Or was it a natural reaction to what had happened, and what still lay ahead? What would Karen's doctors say now? You could push yourself to the edge just worrying about it, so there wasn't much point. Killjoy had given Whitt a lot of leeway in life.

So Whitt practiced his diving rolls and fired at the

frownie faces, each of his first five shots hitting damn near perfectly between the eyes. He reloaded and fired again, reloaded once more but the ricochets off the stones had set the pillowcases on fire. Eventually the rails caught and then the entire fence ignited. Whitt stood back and watched the writhing flames, and somehow it was like watching the waves at Montauk Point coming in.

He wanted to see Lorrie, the daughter that had almost been his. The one he'd given back. The act that had damned him in his crazy wife's eyes.

He packed up his belongings and loaded the car.

When he got in he noticed a piece of paper on the windshield.

"Huh," Whitt said.

It was another note from Killjoy.

Whitt didn't allow the frustration to touch him.

The idea that the maniac had been here in the driveway while Whitt was out back pretending to shoot him. You couldn't let ironies like that deflect your intentions, not when you were already halfway out of your head. It was the kind of thing you rolled with when you'd just spent a couple days carrying rocks and listening to opera.

We are in need of equals. Without them we are too distinct. Harmony cannot exist without brotherhood, and within that enveloping fraternity must be, as always, a moderate sense of sibling rivalry.

I, like all of us, am fascinated with saints. The martyrs who stood on the rock, at the cliff edge. Broken upon the wheel, the rack, the cross.

Most notable among them is, of course, Saint Bugelfaust: apostle; evangelist; martyr; mystic; scientist; confessor.

Born in Uffizi in 1332 to a noble military family, Bugelfaust was studying at Padua when he was attracted to the Order of Snooty Preachers, then less than ten years old. He was ordained in Germany and taught there before going on to the University of Sicily, where he became a master of olives and sheep in 1358 and subsequently held one of the Mount Etna chairs of theology. Among his early students were Stroonzie Defranco, Popgun Fromaggi, and Thomas the Unhappy Castrato.

Despite his zeal and austerity, Bugelfaust was exiled from Rome as a result of nationalist repression and upheaval. As a penitent he wandered Europe, entering the monastery on the island of Iona in 1367. Soon afterwards he was elected abbot after winning the championship medal at the Self-Flagellation Olympics. His great written works at that time include In the Bathhouses of the Holy Land, *an account containing information about the Holy Land based on a pilgrimage made by a Frankish bishop posing as a towelboy. He is best known, however, for his* Life of a Street Trolling Pimpdaddy, *a biography of the missionary and philanthropist who converted the ancient Picts and founded the Iona monastery and local brothel.*

Bugelfaust had, on his journeys, shown an intense interest in natural phenomena, especially breast-feeding and break dancing, and he seized on Aristotle's scientific writings. He occasionally contradicted them on the evidence of his own careful observations, usually through binoculars from across the street of Madame Leilani's House of the Dancing Pants. It is believed that his fetish for glazed donuts and sweaty fat women began at this time.

As a theologian, Bugelfaust was outstanding among the medieval philosophers but perhaps no more innovative than his pupil Thomas the Unhappy Castrato, who proved to be a legendary metaphysician of the time. In his eight-volume manifesto Summa Theologiae No-Dicka *(circa 1380), Thomas attempted to reconcile Aristotelianism and Christian teachings under the auspices of Bugelfaust's principles of Jelly Rolls and Lardy Jugs.*

Bugelfaust's attempts at monastic reform led to his imprisonment in 1380 and 1382; it was in prison that he began to compose some of his finest poetry. The themes of his verse concentrated on the reconciliation of human beings with divinity through a series of mystical steps that begin with silverware in the rectal orifice and continued with renunciation of distractions of the daily world, such as donkey riding. These unique poetical achievements combine both the rational and the irrational, the desires for mysticism mated with the philosophical precepts established by Sheepherder Billy Jo.

Bugelfaust's greatest verse, all of which have been translated into English, include the moving poems "He Ain't

Heavy, He's My Buddha," "Miss Dolly's Comin' Down the Mountain for the Mornin' Milkin'," and "Lama de Amor Lama Spiriti Fideli" (Living Flame of Lamas Puts a Burnin' in My S-s-s-soul). In his best-known lyric, "Shut Yo Mout' Be-Yotch 'Fore I Whip Dat Ass Agin," he described the spirit's progress in finally attaining union with the Heavenly choirs.

Upon his release from prison, Bugelfaust continued his zealous promotion of the interests and prestige of the Roman church. He instructed Saint Paul III to intervene in the case of the Altar of Invasive Dildomia, in which an influential group of pagan senators attempted to block the removal of ancient life-sized statues depicting the Orgy of Apollo from the senate house. St. Paul failed in his mission and the loathsome statues were indeed transported to private chambers, along with eighty pounds of guava jelly.

In September 1394, after forty days of fasting, Bugelfaust prayed upon Mount Alverno when he felt his libido physically leave his body. Terror mingled with joy as stigmata abruptly appeared on his body. He was carried back to Cologne, where he spent his remaining years chasing nuns around the Maypole, even in November. He died of impacted hemorrhoids in the summer of 1399, and on his deathbed he was heard to cry up to Heaven and say, "Oh solo mio, mia assa hurta" which translates to, "My Lord God, I convey my soul into your merciful hands."

Although Bugelfaust's name was "accidentally" left off the general table in the sixty-first volume of the colossal Acta Sanctorum of the Bollandists, *which notes nearly 20,000*

saints, he is still mentioned nineteen times in the highest ec-
clesiastical authority of the Martyrologium Romanum.
Regardless of the Rogomils' and Waledanses' objections to
the glorification of Bugelfaust, he was venerated and eventu-
ally canonized in 1694 during a witch-burning/bra-burning
gathering in Hexenhaus, Germany.

Summarily, it is said that Satan appeared at Bugelfaust's
burial and saluted the passing of his greatest enemy before
vanishing in a plume of brimstone.

We are in need of equals.

Without them we are too distinct.

You roll well.

Whitt crumpled the note and tossed it in his backseat. He drove down the mountain, watching the coil-
ing smoke of Freddy's burning cabin rise over the hills
as he hit the highway.

PART II

HARLEQUENIN

FOURTEEN

On his belly in the freshly cut grass, Whitt lay in the Gundersons' backyard and peered through the TV room window.

Russell and Anne Gunderson sat with Lorrie, watching a kid's animated movie. Surfing dinosaurs, some kind of sea race going on, a caveman on the beach making sand castles. Enraptured, Lorrie lay on a cushion between her parents, ignoring the adults as they occasionally spoke to one another and laughed along. Passing popcorn back and forth, giving Lorrie her juice bottle.

When the movie ended, the girl made excited motions until they played the DVD extras—two more animated shorts featuring the same characters, the caveman back on the beach building a raft out of boulders. She hardly ever laughed, hypnotized by the screen.

It reminded him of the last movie he'd taken Karen and Sarah to see. Silly f/x as some teenagers found a troll and brought it back during their parents' anniversary party. Lots of bright colors, the troll a neon green that could fry your retina. Each of the three kids wearing an outfit in a distinct hue: blue, orange, red.

Wait, the critter's name, it was Crowfield Crenshaw. With a tag line he repeated maybe a hundred times during the flick. Showing his green teeth, running across the floor causing mayhem, tripping the waiters so the cake came down on the mother's lap, squeaking with his green lips, *"Let's try that again!"*

The names of the other parents and their dead children flitted in and out of his mind.

Pia and Edward Godard, their daughter Jamie. Joe and Margaret Stokes, their son Albert. Mary Laramore, her son Timmy. McConnelly. How he'd gotten to know McConnelly.

Somehow Whitt had failed them all, and they him. He shouldn't have to be the only one putting this dopey crusade before everything else. They could've been jumping in instead of wandering around wearing fake bellies and plunging sticks into their own hearts. The rotten unhelpful pricks.

"Jesus," Whitt whispered.

He clawed at the grass, leaving gouges in the manicured lawn. His temples burning, the soothing anger having slid up on him like that.

So, Whitt had to get down to it: What was Gunderson doing to his baby that had caused Killjoy to take her?

Even now, seeing Lorrie prompted a surge of elation through Whitt's chest. She watched the caveman's raft sink and started to gyrate excitedly, clapping. Then the credits began to roll, and when the screen went black she kicked up a fuss and started crying. Whitt checked his watch. It was after eight. Late, time to get her to bed.

But Anne Gunderson shrugged her shoulders, seemed to be telling her daughter that they'd only watch TV for a little while longer, and replayed one of the caveman shorts. The woman was tired, had probably put in a lot of overtime at the boutique she owned. She nodded in and out while the cartoon started again.

Russell cleared the coffee table and carried the dirty dishes and glasses into the kitchen. Whitt shifted and crawled closer. He watched Gunderson as he wrapped leftovers and placed them neatly in the fridge. Anne roused herself and followed him into the kitchen. There, the two of them held each other, propped against the counter, kissing briefly and often as they spoke.

Whitt wondered, Holy Christ, are they going to do it? Are they really going to do it?

And sure as hell, they did—they washed the dishes together. She soaped and rinsed, and he dried with a checkered towel.

Whitt shook his head. He buried his face in the dirt, trying to bear up beneath the assault of memory. So many contradictions and conflicts over something as simple as this. Looking at the little girl again he felt love, and foreboding, and frenzy. Holding that together within him was the guilt that he could care so much for a child that had been his for only one day, that he could think of her now instead of his own daughter.

Never stop thinking of Sarah.

Never give an inch to Killjoy.

Sarah had been blue beneath the pillow. Whitt started to chew the grass, liking the taste of the dirt and grit on his tongue. Christ on the cross, he couldn't wait to shoot Killjoy in the head, just so he could go and check himself into the Falls, hug his wife to him, and lie in bed waiting for a shot of lithium.

He spit out mud, the chill wind slithering across his throat. He watched the rest of the cartoon as if he was a part of the family. He'd once possessed those qualities of Russell Gunderson. The easy smile, the carefully bridled strength, the ability to be casual and cultivated at once, even now, reseating himself on the couch with his girls, watching a cartoon he'd just watched a few minutes ago.

Why the hell did you give the child back, Whitt?
What kind of father are you?

Whitt chewed the questions side by side. What had Gunderson done? Besides hit the fuckin' MOMA, chatting up the Pollocks? How did he make it onto Killjoy's radar?

Whitt twisted in the grass, thinking, Or what had the wife inflicted on the kid?

Anne putting in all those hours, dealing with customers, retailers, the rush-hour traffic, gridlock, the shitty fall weather. How short a fuse did she have?

He pressed his cheek to the grass again, remembering back when he'd owned his own house and used to enjoy doing yard work. Cutting the lawn, trimming hedges. After a day at the office he'd come home and sweep. He grooved on it. Somehow the act relaxed him, the sound of the bristles touching down on the cement, the clearing off of pollen and dead leaves. After forming little piles he'd return with the dustpan and toss the mound into the garbage can in the shed.

Mike would come over and sit on the patio, wearing his suit and tie even in eighty-degree heat on a Saturday afternoon. With his legs crossed like he was in a business meeting. The guy would try to find nice things to say, like, "Your gutters are quite clean, Eddie. Do you do them yourself or do you have a boy come by?" As if he had a Filipino kid stored in the shed with the mower and the garbage can. Mike would look around some more and pull faces like his shoes were swimming in shit. Karen would be near the edge of the grass and Sarah would run around the lawn acting like she was being chased by a Great Dane.

Karen would sit and Whitt would get up and get the broom.

He knew it had something to do with his own father,

who'd always been out back sweeping a yard no bigger than twenty by twenty, half of it eaten up by a cement patio with a little green plastic roof that banged in high wind. But the man would get down on his hands and knees to clean grit out of the expansion lines, the crannies and cracks and crevices.

In every photo Whitt ever saw of his father the guy was washing the car or standing up on the roof putting on new shingles. Bare-chested, a cigarette hanging out of the corner of his mouth, looking slicker than grease.

All of that compressed into the simple motion of sweeping. Sometimes Whitt would be out there in the dark with the back light on, cleaning up a few stray leaves, while Karen stood in the back door holding Sarah, watching him, trying not to laugh.

C'mon, really, when you got down to it, you've always been at least half off your rocker.

And now—

In the grass, like a sniper in one of Mike Bowman's unknown wars.

He'd been watching them on and off for almost ten months now, peering in windows, hiding like a thief in the darkness, hinged on his day as Lorrie's dad. That swipe of joy he'd felt, strong enough to brush aside all bewilderment, when he'd opened the door to find the baby in the picnic basket, with the note.

* * *

The Empire of Thought.

One is not quite sure if one should laugh or cry in learning that all four men were struck down by the same carriage, driven by the same patrician, in different parts of the city on the same day. The chances of such an act being purely random are astronomical, unless one sees the hand of God in all things.

Once again Whitt was overpowered by the feeling that Killjoy had done this same thing, lying here in this exact spot, watching, waiting to steal the kid. Lusting for Anne Gunderson, wishing pain on her—on all mothers. On all fathers as well, wanting to make Russ howl so loudly it would shake the entire picturesque neighborhood. Killjoy loving and hating the family at the same time, wanting to be with them but fearing them, and fearing himself if he was to somehow become one of them.

Better to eradicate, to work your will on others. Disrupt the happiness. Hear the screams, the moaning. See the terror. Sure. So much power in his hands, and all he had to do was hold a pillow in place for less than a minute.

But he hadn't killed Lorrie, he'd stolen her, given her to Whitt. Implying Whitt was the better parent.

But why?

Lorrie was still entranced with the caveman raft film as it ended once again. This time Gunderson picked her up and she didn't argue, simply yawned as he pressed his cheek to her forehead. Her hair scrunched up and brushed into that funky ponytail, tied with a black ribbon, the same as when Whitt had last seen her.

Is that why Killjoy had chosen the family?

To make Whitt do these things, think in this way, eat the dirt?

To get him ready to go barreling through the glass, grab the kid, and run into the night?

Killjoy was the father, the daddy now. Twisting little boy Whitt into any shape he wanted. Maybe that was the root of it all.

Whitt himself was the real changeling child, and he didn't see the hand of God in much.

But the hand of Killjoy, the corrupter, that was everywhere.

FIFTEEN

Whitt woke inside the dollhouse and looked out the bedroom window to see his apartment endlessly huge and malevolent around him.

He saw himself out there right now, on the phone with Freddy's voice mail, saying, "I just got your message. I'm sorry, I didn't think it was windy enough for the flames to carry. I'll pay for the cabin. Well, Mike will pay for it, if I can talk him into it. Anyway, it was just four rooms, and the wine, and the Caruso CDs. You were right. I liked them, they really were calming."

Whitt lay on the miniature plastic bed that had cost $27.50 and picked up the phone on the nightstand but couldn't get a dial tone. The pounding of his own colossal footsteps pacing across the kitchen floor drove into his throbbing head, all this tiny dollhouse furniture bouncing with each step.

You wanted to shout to yourself, Stop moving, just go sit in the fucking corner. Go try putting the rage at ease until it's time to take action, until you implement the plan.

He turned over and buried his face in the pillow. He wondered how long he could hold himself here. As his vision began to blacken, he realized, This, this is what my baby last felt in the world. This softness sealing across her nose and mouth, this comfortable darkness.

He got up and walked downstairs. He sat in the corner in a leather chair in front of the fireplace. Squeezing himself down smaller and smaller, becoming the rock in the wind.

When he looked up again Karen was sitting across from him, on the couch, sipping tea from a china cup that had cost him $12.50. He very clearly remembered the intense shock he'd felt when she'd mentioned how much she'd paid for the miniature. The price so staggeringly high, and him thinking it was such a waste since you really couldn't play with the damn thing anyway. What was the point if Sarah couldn't actually have fun with it?

But then he'd spent the day watching the two of them moving the dolls through the house. Seeing how imaginative and sharp his daughter was in the way she expressed herself. Karen moving the mommy doll through the kitchen, asking, "Shall we bake some cookies?"

And Sarah saying, "Oh think of the mess, how can we be bothered?"

"You're so right, so right!"

"Let us put on Vivaldi and dance a waltz!"

"Oh yes, oh yes!"

So Karen, shooting a glance over her shoulder at Whitt, shrugged her shoulders because she didn't know how a Vivaldi concerto might go, or how Sarah, at only five, would know such a thing, and began to hum something not even remotely classical.

Sarah rose to take his hand. "Daddy, let us dance."

"I don't know how to waltz."

"I'll teach you."

"Okay."

And with his wife humming like that, he danced with his daughter, doing a version of a waltz, more like the Watusi really, the two of them shaking their hips, and he'd thought, Where did this kid come from? This can't be mine, nothing this beautiful and amazing could possibly have come from me.

Now, inside the dollhouse, Karen sipped tea from that cup. "If it's a dream, it's a rather pleasant one. I love you, Eddie, and I'm always so glad to see you. I'm sorry it's such a burden for you. Everything. Me. This."

He could think of nothing to say to his love. He used to call her from the office several times a day, just to speak a sentence, a word. To hear her voice, it seemed the most important triumph of his entire life. He'd read her French poetry in bed for hours until his voice was almost gone and she screamed, "For the love of Christ, speak in English will you!"

Whitt stood and moved to her but felt an almost

painful urge not to touch her. As if that would damage the home.

"Eddie?"

"Yes?"

"Come here."

"No, Karen, not yet."

"You don't have to be afraid."

"Yes, I do."

"You're safe here."

"I don't feel very safe."

The other Whitt, the one out there, still free to an extent, hung up the phone and tossed it on the coffee table, on top of the latest clinical report on Karen's condition. He wondered if you stacked them side by side, which file would be thicker, his or his wife's.

He walked into the kitchen and reached for the phone on the wall. He worked the rotary dial. It was fully articulated. You got what you paid for with these miniature decorations.

Out in the apartment, Whitt's cell phone rang. He drew it off the table, taking Karen's file with it. Thirty pages hit the floor and scattered against his legs. He saw Ted's name all over the place, explaining how much they'd spent on their last shopping trip to Saks.

Whitt said, "Hello?"

"Hello," Whitt said. "You're never going to catch him at this rate."

"So, you're just another naysayer."

"You've never said 'naysayer' in your life. How'd it feel?"

"Kinda fucked, actually."

"Thought so."

"Go farther."

"What? How?"

"Don't ask me, Mr. Whitt. I'm doing everything I can. I've got my own problems."

"Worse than mine, Mr. Whitt?"

"At the moment, I'm of the opinion that I do."

"Then you're pretty fucked yourself."

"You have no idea."

"How do I get to where he is?"

"You're asking me?"

"Yes."

"Well, you find out what he loves and what he hates. You find out how he found you."

"Then what?"

"You know what."

Whitt paused.

The meeting of yourself is the meeting of a stranger.

The man you're becoming has much less in common with the man you were.

Whitt stared at himself across the room.

"You hunger for his hate, Mr. Whitt."

"What the hell's that mean?"

"I'm not sure, but it's the truth. Your truth, at least. Right now. Mine too."

"You're an idiot, Mr. Whitt."

"Perhaps so. But then, why did you call me?"

"I didn't. You called me."

Whitt hung up and looked over at the dollhouse to see himself in there, trapped and a touch terrified, growing even smaller, the rock in the storm. While Karen brought the $12.50 miniature china cup to her tiny lips, calmly sipping her tea.

SIXTEEN

He walked into Brunkowski's office and Brunk was already in his hard-boiled mode, leaning back with his feet propped against the desk. His suit rumpled enough to make it look like he'd been smacking some dealer in the head with a telephone book. He didn't ask Whitt what he was doing there, just started talking as if he'd phoned and told Whitt to get his ass down to the precinct immediately.

"We still haven't found the ballerina," Brunk said. "And I know she's not a ballerina, but that's what's stuck around the office."

"How about Franklin Prott?" Whitt asked.

"No sign of him."

"They must have another house. The cult."

"We figure it that way, but nobody's talking. None of the other members in custody, and not the Protts. The mother has about twenty new members from Gen Pop. You should see her. They treat her like a queen."

"Her line of shit gives the hopeless something to believe in."

"Something really stupid."

"Yeah, but she says it with such conviction the others fall in line."

Whitt could just imagine Mama Prott, the High Priestess of the Cosmic Knot, speaking with hysterical excitement, overjoyed to find an audience of captives. Handing out all her charts and graphs, the pages overflowing with nonsensical references to reproductive organs that had to get the chop. How many cigarettes did they charge in the joint for Whore's Bait and Failure of Urethra?

Brunk shifted his feet around on his blotter. "Until somebody wakes up out of that deviant dream and sticks a shiv in her ass."

"There are no records to trace her real estate holdings?"

"On the books, she doesn't own a damn thing under her own name. Not the house she was in, not the other church house, none of her skeevy belongings, nothing. Everything she's got, all of it is supposedly donations."

"There's another house," Whitt said, "and Franklin's there."

"Probably."

Killjoy might know where the cult's other house was. He'd watched them for much longer than Whitt had. He'd seen them murder and dispose of Jameson's body. Maybe other bodies. He'd know where Franklin would be holed up.

"Coroner know how long Jameson was dead?"

"Almost a week before you dug him up."

"Killjoy was watching long in advance."

"You think your friend might know where Franklin is?"

Whitt had to take three deep breaths before he could speak in a normal tone of voice. Brunk knew the button. "Call him my friend again and you won't be getting a Christmas card from me this year."

"You really are getting sensitive," Brunk said.

"Yeah."

Brunk frowned, trying to look tough from that position, with his feet up. It wasn't happening. The expression made all the creases of his face buckle in.

Whitt ignored him. His thoughts tumbled, and he could feel the faint tinges of fever settling over him. All this time that Killjoy had been sending letters, and Whitt had never thought to send one back.

"I want to talk to Mama Prott."

"That's not going to be so easy," Brunkowski said.

"You can make it happen."

"Possibly, but what is she going to give you that the headcase son couldn't?"

"I'm not sure."

"But you want to risk it."

"What's the risk?"

"Maybe Mama doesn't hate her blind son the way

her other kid does. What if she gets word to him to come pay you a visit?"

"That's what you're hoping for, isn't it? I may be a shitty investigator, but I'm still pretty good bait, right?"

Brunkowski dropped his feet to the ground, did a slow lean forward, peered into Whitt's face. He stood and Whitt sat back and waited for it, for Brunk to hit his favorite pose. Like waiting for Crowfield Crenshaw to squeak with his green troll lips, *"Let's try that again!"* Brunk rested his fists on the desk, forearms corded, the rolled sleeves so tight they creaked against the press of his muscles.

Whitt wondered if now was the time when they'd get into the brawl they both wanted. But then again, he thought that every time he was nose to nose with this guy.

"Don't feel bad about it," Whitt said. "You don't have many options left."

"Don't be such a goddamn know-it-all. Anyway, I listened to the Merwin tape. I know he told you to talk to his mother. That why you want to do it? Because Merwin Prott said the old lady could help you?"

"Maybe."

"They're playing you."

"So? What, you care all of a sudden? You're playing me too. Can you get me in to see her or not?"

"If she allows it."

"She will."

"'Cause your aura's black?"

"Yeah."

That made Brunk take a step back, the tuft of hair flopping the other way. He knew he had to find a new tough guy attitude now, the current one wasn't working as well as it should. He decided to go for the old fists on his hips stance, which didn't do much to inspire anxiety. Whitt's mother used to angle into the same posture all the time, whenever he was late for dinner or didn't wash his hands when he came in. She knew how to do it right, to really put the fear of the Big G into you. Brunkowski finally just sat on the corner of his desk. "What makes you so sure?"

"She liked me."

"Yeah, well, don't forget . . . that old lady happens to like plenty of people. Just check out her basement."

"I already have."

Whitt figured they were done here and spun out of the chair toward the door. Brunk got to his feet again, the heels of his shoes clopping hard on the tiled floor. "Listen, there's something else. The commissioner created a new task force to nab Killjoy."

"Another one, eh?" Whitt had to force himself not to grin even though the last thing he felt like doing was smiling.

Weird, wasn't it, trying not to do the thing you would never do anyway.

This would be the third task unit in five years, not counting the feds or the seventy-five-year-old Viennese psychiatrist they'd consulted with. "How much man-power do they have on it this time?"

"Just one, working out of this precinct."

"They call one cop working alone 'a task force'?"

"Yeah, and it's womanpower this time."

Whitt stiffened and moved so fast toward Brunkowski, finally doing what they'd both been aching for, that Brunk actually shifted his eyes to his empty gun in its holster.

Whitt hissed, "They're sending a woman after Killjoy?"

"A policewoman. Back off a step."

"She got kids?"

"You heard what I said."

"Just answer me, eh?"

Snorting, Brunk actually eased away, his hair doing nutty things on top of his head because Whitt was almost panting. "Two."

"Oh Jesus Christ."

"Killjoy never went after any of the other cops or feebs searching for him. And one of them was a woman, as I recall."

"Yeah, the Vienna specialist, who was seventy-five."

"Oh yeah. I met her once but could barely understand a word she said, with that accent."

"You people shouldn't be doing this."

"Thought you were more liberal in your thinking than that."

"You know why I'm saying it."

"The thing is, you really think you're in charge," Brunk told him. "You got to stop acting that way."

You had to take whatever you could in stride. These monkey wrenches that kept getting tossed around, you dodged them when you could and the rest you tried not to take in the teeth. Whitt sighed. This was just more wasted efforts from the cops, like they didn't have anything better to do with their time. He speculated about what kind of trouble the woman had been in, whose toes she'd stomped on, that they'd put her on the case alone.

He backed down to salve Brunk's ego. "What made them suddenly decide to go with a new task force? She do something to rub the chief the wrong way?"

"Something like that. She was an NYC cop for a while before moving up into the feebs in DC. She's an opinionated lady, thought they'd fouled up the way they handled a few cases, including Killjoy. All the profilers tripping each other up, nobody making any progress. The kind of person who goes through cases she's not assigned to, you know? They routed her out of DC and back to Manhattan, and from there she was rerouted here to Nassau County, told to take a swipe at it herself."

"Nobody's so opinionated that they'd turn a case like this over just to humiliate her."

"Well, there's more to it."

"Undoubtedly."

"She was having an affair down there with one of

her ranking agents. He was married to another fed. When the wife found out, a shitstorm hit and everybody in the office got their pant cuffs spattered. This one, she pulled up stakes and came home. Her boss, the ex-boyfriend, is giving her the case as a way of shoving her face farther in the mud."

"Unless she solves it."

"You think that'll happen?"

"No," Whitt said, "he's mine." Knowing how stupid it sounded, but it was the truth.

"So you keep saying."

"But maybe she can help me," Whitt said.

Brunk's lips curled every which way. "Christ, you got nerve."

"The word you're looking for is 'verve.' I've got verve. Zest. Flair."

"And I can smell it from over here."

Whitt wondered how many regulations Brunkowski had broken so far just by talking to Whitt the way he did. Giving him so much inside info, treating a civilian like a PI, a bad one at that, but one who was expendable and could be put to good use.

"She's going over all the Prott information as well."

"Why?" Whitt asked, genuinely curious. "The chief thinks the cases are connected?"

"They are, in a fashion. Depending on how deep the connections lie, this all may lead back to Killjoy. But it's not the chief so much as the feds."

Whitt could feel the thickening atmosphere in the

silence between them, and he understood what it indicated. "She's investigating me too."

"Yeah. Of course."

"So . . . you asking about 'my friend' . . . was that your inelegant way of hinting that the feebs think I'm in cahoots with the man who murdered my daughter?"

"More or less. Showing up at the Protts' to find the body didn't go far in alleviating suspicion, and refusing to turn over Killjoy's letters didn't win you any supporters either. You're always there in the wrong place at the wrong time."

"If I *am* Killjoy or working with him, then you've announced your intentions. Sometimes you're a pretty piss poor investigator too, Brunk."

"Maybe I'm doing a double fake out."

"Yeah, that must be it." Whitt could barely ease the words from his mouth, his back teeth champed. He stuffed his hands in his pockets as the heat crawled across his body, sweat threading across his scalp. So now they were going to try to pin murders on him because he refused to go back to a life he didn't have anymore. "I don't give a shit so long as she doesn't get in my way."

"Listen—you've got to stop believing you're a cop. This isn't your job. You know you're not. Don't trip up the real investigators."

"So is she a police officer now or a fed or what?" Whitt asked.

"Still a fed, I think. Well, actually, I'm really not sure. Maybe she quit the feebs. I don't talk to her much."

"Just wag your chin at her and go 'hey you'?"

"Something like that. She's only been here two days."

"She here now?"

"Yeah."

"Okay. Introduce me."

SEVENTEEN

Sometimes when you ask, you actually get.

Tie trailing over his shoulder, Brunk marched Whitt to the back of the station house, past the crowd. Fellow officers, a couple of drunk car thieves arguing over who'd forgotten to fill the tank before the high-speed pursuit, a snickering guy with a neck wound, and a prostitute complaining to her lawyer that she'd given head to the cop who arrested her and he'd still arrested her. The lawyer said, "Next time, you don't do it in the back of the cruiser behind the cage."

"That's what he wanted!"

"It's too easy for him to finish, zip up, and just shut the car door on you so he gets the bust too."

"I know now."

"You gotta get his pants all the way off, in the front seat."

"I know now!"

Whitt followed Brunk to the back of the room, over to a desk where a woman sat.

Brunk's introduction was about as diplomatic as a ref telling two heavyweights to come out and shake hands, have a good clean match. He nodded at Whitt and said, "This is Whitt," and then aimed his chin in the direction of the woman and said, "Diana Carver. Figured you might want to talk to him." Without another word Brunk snaked his way back to his office and shut the door.

Diana Carver stood, held her hand out, and said, "Hello." Whitt took it, and they openly inspected each other without being embarrassed about doing so.

He didn't know what she was seeing or what judgments she'd make. But he stood there looking at a lady in her early thirties, with a heart-shaped face and short, black curling bangs that feathered into points off her forehead.

Her features had all kinds of that girl-next-door cuteness. The even white teeth, the warm smile. The dimples that weren't really dimples but just the way the lines around her mouth folded in. A small nick of a scar near her eye and another at the corner of her mouth. From split skin, he realized. She'd taken a couple of hard shots in her time. Who was the brute? A perp or her ex-husband? Or the ex-boyfriend who was her ranking officer in the feebs?

She stood nearly as tall as Whitt. About five-nine in serious heels, but she had this way of rearing up so that she seemed a little bigger than him, and it felt like she was looking down. They were already getting into it, the subtle dynamics of domination, force of personality. All the quirks beginning to bleed to the surface.

Even with the smile, her eyes were extremely dark and kind of angry.

She must've seen something about him that she really didn't like and it made her grimace, a faint checkerboard of wrinkles appearing over her brow. Could she read the mark of Killjoy upon his soul? There was something about her Whitt found vaguely unsettling, and more than that, he thought she was damn sexy.

This is not good, he thought. This is, in fact, a very bad thing. I shouldn't be thinking like this—

But he had trouble taking his eyes off her. She wore a sleeveless gray blouse and tight black jeans that showed off every contour, just the way they should be doing. She'd missed a loop on the belt around her waist. The belt was scuffed in that spot because it was where she usually kept her gun clipped.

They were still softly clenching each other's hands. No wedding ring for her. He continued to wear his, at first out of respect for Karen, and later for reasons he was unclear about. He suddenly was aware of it in a way he hadn't been for a couple of years.

Her fingers were strong, nails clipped down to nothing with no polish on them. His calluses brushed hers and there was an electric tingle in the scar tissue. The middle two knuckles on her right hand were distended. She'd busted her fist at least a couple of times.

"So," she said, "you're the famous Eddie Whitt."

He didn't know how to answer so he said nothing. It was happening to him more and more, not knowing how to answer and then standing there like a fuckin' mute. It became apparent she wasn't going to say anything more unless Whitt coughed up something. So he went, "Yeah."

"There's quite a lot of paperwork on you."

"There's a lot of paperwork on everybody, you just happen to have all of mine in one place. Hope it doesn't give you eyestrain."

"I'll manage."

"I think you will."

He tried to take his hand back and she held on, shifted, and used her weight in an attempt to tug him forward. Jesus, she was a little powerhouse. Was she gonna do some judo now? Flip him over her hip in front of everybody?

His three senseis would die of shame. Whitt yanked her to him instead, thinking this was the kind of scene where she falls into his arms, they laugh, then go running through huckleberry fields. But she didn't like the hold and angled her knee in front to catch him in the goodies if need be. Everybody after the goodies. Goddamn, you couldn't even shake hands with somebody nowadays without them trying to snip your package off.

"What is it with you, lady?" he asked.

"You're carrying."

He didn't catch it at first. Carrying? What, diseases?

Then he realized she'd spotted the slight bulge of the .32 beneath his jacket. "You do have good eyesight."

"Are you going to give us trouble here today, Mr. Whitt?"

"Only if the two drunk thieves try to take my car. Otherwise, I'm the soul of restraint." He wanted to add "Agent Carver" or "Officer Carver" or even "Miss Carver" but didn't know which term applied.

"Somehow I doubt that," she said, still with the death grip on his hand, the knee directed toward his crotch.

"I have a license to carry. Would you like to see it?"

"Yes," Diana Carver said, with a faux grin like she was trying to calm a mental patient during a hostage situation. The smile reached her eyes though, and the little scars faded in laugh lines. It was extremely appealing and his belly twitched. What the hell was happening here?

"Return my hand to me long enough to get it out," he told her. "We can resume shaking in a minute."

The false grin didn't falter, but the heat in her gaze grew a notch, like she was hoping he'd start something so she could pull his arm out of the socket. She released him and he got his license out. As she checked it over, her eyes kept flashing up to see if he was making any moves.

"This is because you often carried huge deposits for your advertising company?" she asked.

"That's right."

"But you no longer work in advertising."

"Go take a gander at my father-in-law's books and you'll see I'm still listed as an employee."

"That's in case the IRS checks, not if the police do."

"If you want me to turn my gun over to you, I will."

"Why?"

"I have another at home."

He didn't, but it sounded hard and made his point. She'd been hoping to see where he'd fold and buckle, what his weak points might be. If he had something to do with Killjoy beyond the obvious. In a way, he appreciated her tactics. They proved she was willing to go under or over the wire if need be, using whatever means she had to get to the truth.

There was an empty box on the floor beside her chair, which had probably held a few personal items she'd brought with her from DC to Manhattan to here. Only one photo on the desk, showing two children laughing on a couch tangled together in a hug, a boy and a girl, maybe three and four. He wondered if they were with her here on the Island, or if she'd gotten the boot so quick she left them in DC with her mother or her ex.

He thought about what guts it would take to buck her bosses and stick her nose in cases where it didn't belong. That meant she thought her married boyfriend would catch her back, but the guy had cut her loose instead. Why? To save his marriage or his career?

Returning the license, she said, "Why are you here, Mr. Whitt? Exactly what is it that you and Sergeant Brunkowski have been discussing?"

"The Protts," he told her.

"I see. You appear to have a very . . . odd relationship with that family."

"It wasn't my intention to have any relationship with them. It just sorta happened."

"Is that so?"

"Yes, it is so."

It didn't take long before you were fed up with the minutiae of the combative personality dance and just wanted to skip to the next level, whatever it might be. Let her take a run at him later, if she wanted, but first he had things he had to find out.

"Can you show me where and how Franklin Prott escaped?" he asked.

"Yes."

"Thank you." She led him down a corridor past a couple of offices, toward the entrance to the cells on the second floor of the precinct. He kept checking her face, watching the little feathered bangs bop and weave across her forehead as she moved, the two tiny scars looking very deep or practically vanishing depending on the light.

She showed him a window and said, "Here. Prott was being escorted by a single police officer, back from the interrogation room to lock up. He apparently overcame the officer and jumped from here."

" 'Apparently'?"

"The officer in question doesn't remember much about the incident."

"Brunkowski said he was a rookie."

"He's been on the force for three years," she said. "A good cop."

"You checked his record too?"

"Yes." She was sensitive to the tone, and didn't like the implication that an officer who'd made one mistake shouldn't be exonerated. "Prott faked being blind and overcame him, throttled him into unconsciousness."

"I've met Franklin Prott. He's not faking. He is blind."

"That's impossible," she said. "Look at the jump he'd have to make without being able to see what he was doing or where he was going."

They stared out the window at the parking lot below, the heavy street traffic just outside. Across the road was an area of brush that led off to a Little League field. They couldn't see farther than that from here, but Whitt knew there was nothing but factories and car garages beyond. A blind man could never have made it on his own.

"He must've had help," Whitt said. "One of the other cult members?"

"Just waiting around the police station until Prott decided to jump through a window?"

"He probably would've gotten mowed down trying to cross the street on his own."

"You're the one insisting he's actually blind."

"I'm not insisting, I'm just saying. It's the truth. The guy can't see."

Diana Carver nodded the way people nod when they think you're lying—only capable of lying—even to yourself. It made her breasts jiggle and he felt a tug in his guts, wondering how it was possible that he was attracted to her. He hadn't felt anything like this for a woman since Karen had gone into the Falls.

"I'd like to set up an interview and talk to you at length, Mr. Whitt."

"I'm available now."

"No, I'm busy this afternoon, and I'm still in the middle of reviewing the case."

"Cases. Killjoy and the Protts are separate matters, despite their intersecting over the ballerina's baby."

"You mean Miss Kinnick."

"Yes, that's exactly who I mean. Grace Kinnick."

"And yet, the perpetrator intentionally brought you into the situation."

"You may as well start calling him Killjoy now."

"A name you gave the perpetrator."

"In a manner of speaking, yes," Whitt admitted.

"I see," she said. With that heavy milieu of a wagging

finger in his face. "Are you currently in therapy, Mr. Whitt?"

"What?"

Maybe she noticed he was watching her jiggle because she crossed her arms over her chest. "I believe you heard my question."

"Yes, I did. The 'what' was merely an expletive designed to show my affront at the question."

"You still haven't answered it."

"No, I haven't. No, I'm not currently in therapy. Isn't that in your files?"

"I wanted to make sure they were up-to-date."

Now Whitt had to put up with someone else who was going to give him the stink eye every time she ran into him.

"If you'd like me to fact check your records for you, I'm always at your service."

"I sense a great hostility in you, Mr. Whitt."

"And yet I remain the life of any party. Incongruous, isn't it?"

"That's one way of putting it," she said, the counterfeit smile back in place, and those fierce dark eyes burning into and through him.

EIGHTEEN

Freddy Fruggman's number flashed on the Caller ID but there was no message, so Whitt called him back, ready to face seven kinds of hell for the fire. Freddy answered with a growl and immediately covered the receiver while he shouted at people all around the office.

Maybe the alternative medicine man Indians were on the warpath, shooting burning arrows at the set. Whitt distinctly heard one woman shouting about putting in a call to her union representative. Freddy said, "You do that, Little Miss Sunshine, and all they'll do is double your dues. Trust me, I used to play croquet with those guys. You know how much representation you're going to get from a union rep who fuckin' plays croquet?" More angry chatter and a high-pitched groan of outrage and acquiescence. Freddy said, "And stop using that new antihistamine, Gloria, it's making you cranky."

Whitt figured it was a good point to cut in, and said, "Hello?"

"Who is this?" Angry that somebody was saying hello to him.

"Hey, Freddy."

"What? What's this?" Whitt heard creaking as Freddy shifted in his chair, settling deep so he could really give it his all, get into Whitt's face from twenty minutes away. "No, no, listen, 'Hey, Freddy' is not the opening I expect from you."

"No?"

"No, see, I'm waiting for something like 'I'm sorry about the fire I started and then left to ravage your property!'"

"I already said that on your voice mail."

"So that's it? You apologize to a machine so you don't have to say it to me?"

Whitt turned his face away from his cell phone and let a hiss free between his teeth, feeling strangely put upon although Freddy was in the right. You don't burn down a man's cabin and not feel regret about it. But somehow, Whitt just didn't. "You're absolutely right, I'm sorry about what happened."

"You burned down my fucking cabin is what happened!"

"Right, and I apologize."

"My cabin, man!"

"Yeah, but really, it was just four rooms."

"That was my getaway, my little piece of heaven! The girls loved it there too!"

"Which girls?"

"Any girls!" Freddy yowled, really and truly yowling, doing this weird tremolo thing with his voice the way guys do in horror movies after they've fallen into a bucket of radiation and start mutating into giant katydids, crawfish, Chihuahuas.

"Any girls?"

"The girls who liked a little piece of heaven, man! Fresh mountain air is better than raw oysters. The chicks loved the place. And my wine! You know how much that wine cost me?"

"How much?"

"Who the fuck knows! But the girls loved it."

"If they were so turned on, why are they bringing *Vogue* up there?" Whitt asked, realizing afterwards that this probably wasn't the way to go with the conversation.

"What's this? What's this you're saying?"

"Nothing."

"What was that? What's that?"

"Really, Freddy, it wasn't much of a cabin."

"Look at this, the backtalk I get—"

"I'll get Mike to rebuild it."

"I don't want your father-in-law's money, or yours either! It was an accident, I understand that. But at least you could show some remorse."

"I am. I do. I'm sorry."

"You sound like you're saying 'fuck you, Freddy' when you say that."

"And you call me sensitive."

"You are sensitive."

"Yeah, but everybody is. I didn't mean to wreck your love life."

"You didn't. I have no love life, but I get laid a lot for a fat guy. The girls liked it there, but they like my apartment and the view of Central Park even better. They don't bring *Vogue* over to Fifth Avenue. That's Seventh Avenue shit." Speaking softly, maybe with his hand cupped beside the receiver. "This Gloria, she does this little act where she comes out with a baton that's got two fuses on the ends she can light. She dances around the room naked and deep throats the thing, then spits flames."

Whitt smiled, his first real smile in days, maybe weeks. "Sounds erotic."

"It's not really, but it's still interesting to watch."

"So she would've set the cabin on fire eventually anyway."

"Probably."

"What's going on over there with all your yelling?" Whitt asked. "Trouble with the tribal lawyers again?"

"No, that deal is settled. They comped me and a three-man crew last weekend at one of their casinos. We spent an afternoon doing a promo shoot. Which reminds me, I'm not gonna be around at the end of the month. Gonna go back and do a couple of commercials for them, and I'll pay for it with what I win at their craps tables."

Whitt said, "Freddy, you don't know how to play craps."

"Gloria does, and I'm taking her."

"Who is Gloria anyway?"

"One of the makeup girls. But she better get some new goddamn allergy pills or I swear I'll leave her here. Talk about mood swings."

"Because of antihistamines?"

"Worse than menopause, let me tell you."

"So what's the trouble now?"

Whitt could hear the air going by Freddy's phone as Freddy spun himself in his chair, around and around. Footsteps plodded into the office and abruptly scampered away. Somebody who knew not to disturb Freddy when he was spinning. "I'm thinking of quitting the biz."

"Ah."

"You don't believe me, nobody believes me, but I think I'm going to do it. This last setup, it's for a new brand of TV dinner, right? So I have this guy, works hard at the office, comes home to his TV dinner, watches a movie, drinks his beer, goes to bed alone but he's content, right? No they tell me, no, he should have the family around. The whole family, they should all be having TV dinners together, the Mom calling her kids in from the backyard, you know, 'Come in, Billy and Sophie, come get the dinner your Mommy slaved all of four and a half minutes over.' Then they all sit down together at the kitchen table eating their TV dinners, smiling at each other. What the fuck kind of family is this, they unwrap the cellophane off their dinners together, microwave them in turn, four and a half minutes each one, but somehow they eat them at the same goddamn time? Then they go out for ice cream. Where's the realism in any of that?"

"Freddy, you just did a commercial for colon cleanser showing a guy in a teepee with a buffalo head on a stick."

"That was hyperreality, but it was real, man!"

Freddy paused, drawing out the silence. Whitt knew Freddy was screwing up his courage to broach a new subject.

Hang up, Whitt thought, he should hang up, hang up right now, but he couldn't force himself to do it. Seconds ticking off like lemmings hitting the water.

Freddy Fruggman, on the phone, probably with the same uncomfortably sorrowful expression as the last time they were face-to-face, he took a breath, started to speak, stopped, and tried again. "Eddie, I saw the rocks. I saw that you moved all those rocks. Fucking hundreds of them. And the bottles and cans. You know how many? Five years' worth of bottles and cans I had stacked out there, and you shot nearly all of them to pieces."

"Some of them I did last time I was there, when I put in the gym."

"You did something like twenty last time. This time, maybe a thousand. How much ammo did you have?"

"'Thirty boxes."

"How much you got left?"

"Not much. What're you really asking?"

Freddy could get down to it when he had to. "Are you ready yet?"

So could Whitt. "Yeah, I am."

Gloria stepped into the office again, still sniffling—either from crying or maybe it was why she needed the antihistamines—and said something about turning in her resignation. Freddy consoled her with baby talk for a minute, the heavy hand patting her ass loudly, whap-whap-whap-whap, until she giggled.

Then, back into the phone, "So you really liked the Caruso?"

NINETEEN

There she was, Mama Prott, already waving to him, her turkey neck going fucking wild.

Whitt thought he would have to talk to her through a plastic partition, maybe on the phone, but they brought him right into a visitor's room that was mobbed with people. Kids running around, mothers handing over chocolate cake and cookies, guys making out with their girlfriends.

There were two female and two male guards, all four standing against the far wall like they were waiting for the firing squad. Eyes darting but none of them moving their chins.

Mrs. Prott was seated on a small, four-tiered set of bleachers, in the center of a pinwheel of empty-faced women. Brunkowski hadn't been kidding. Mama Prott really had gathered quite the entourage in jail.

Everything around him screamed hazard, threat, stupidity, menace. So of course he walked right in. Maybe thirty prisoners, fifty visitors. How easy would it be for one of these ladies to grab a kid and yank him under the bleachers, hold him hostage with a nail file? Cut his throat just for good measure, for no reason at all, except she had nothing more to lose behind bars. He wanted to shout at the parents, tell them to take their children out of here, run for it, except that these ladies in gray, most of them were the kids' mothers.

Mama Prott gestured for him to come over. The women surrounding her stared angrily at Whitt's approach. He was surprised to see how the minicult spanned the breadth of racial barriers: two skinny, slack-jawed white chicks, a couple of older black women, and one heavyset Latino lady who looked a little crazy and was actually baring her teeth.

All of them wearing the same blue smock as Mrs. Prott, even though it looked like prisoners were allowed some leniency in their wardrobe. Others wore jeans, the prison-blue blouses unbuttoned, sleeves rolled up or cut off.

The similarity of their wardrobes gave Mrs. Prott's group an even greater cult feel. No wonder she appeared so happy, waving to Whitt with those fingers fluttering. She was plugged into a highly receptive audience.

When he got within a few feet of her he caught that familiar smell. It wafted into his face on the air currents made by the kids running around like crazy. The stink of turpentine from the herbal tea she'd served him in the house that day. Who knew, maybe it was the same colon-cleansing stuff Freddy was doing commercials for.

On the floor around her was a tapered white line of sand. No, it was a ring of salt, one of those magic circles she'd mentioned.

How the hell did somebody smuggle this much salt out of the prison kitchen? Where was the profit in it with which to bribe the guards?

Those four against the wall acting like they didn't see anything when there was a two-inch-thick ring of salt sprinkled all around the bleachers. What'd she tell them? Get me a ten-pound bag of salt and some of that alternative medicine man herbal remedy for hemorrhoids and your soulwind will be safe with me for eternity?

Whitt walked to her, knowing it was going to get bad before the end. Mrs. Prott, High Priestess of the Cosmic Knot, was already speaking with the near-hysterical excitement he'd come to expect, shouting, "Don't scuff the markings! No! Here, sit, sit with us!"

The women around her all held sheets of paper in their laps. Whitt could make out star charts, Teutonic characters, numbers doing all kinds of strange things. It seemed that each woman had copied the basic style of Mrs. Prott's nonsense and then run with it, creating more and more bizarre representations, seals, and ciphers. The white chicks had the best handwriting and artistic ability, really doing delicate work. One of the black ladies had her pages turned in his direction. Among all the ancient mystical alphabets of the millennia stood out GET YOUR OWN CRACK, MY MAN IS DEAD.

"Your aura is even darker than the last time we spoke," Mama Prott said, arms slightly open as if she wanted to hug him to her.

"Is it?"

"You know it is. You take pride in the fact, Mr. Whitt."

"Do I?"

"You know you do."

That stopped him because he didn't think he took much pride in anything about himself lately. He wasn't sure that a black aura seen by the murdering leader of a goofy-ass cult was the kind of thing that would build his ego. But who knew, maybe it did. You rolled with whatever they handed you.

He decided to respond with, "Okay."

"You speak from the heart of the knot. I can see that much. You've a great gift. One of travel. You move from place to place inside yourself, outside yourself."

Somehow this was leading up to her wanting to shear through his *vas deferens*. He grinned at the other women, wondering if he could maybe bring them to his side. Say to them, Heya, cross the salt and come over here where we don't chop off other people's sexiest extremities.

The ladies were leaning in a touch, still staring but not saying a word. None of them acted as if they'd even heard a word of the conversation. Showing no human interest. Nobody nodding, shaking her head, licking her lips. It had to be a pretty tough trick. He wondered if the other cult members, the ones who'd been arrested with the Protts, were remaining silent too, wherever they might be.

Mama Prott tapped at the spot between her eyes where her brains had leaked out. She stroked the area the way her son had petted his chest. "Thank you for returning Merwin's jars to him."

"How did you know I did that?"

"He called me. Oh, don't look surprised, of course we're allowed to talk. He is my son, and a character witness in my trial."

Whitt said, "He is the caretaker, isn't he? Of the vessels."

"Yes. And those he watches over thank you as well. Hogarth. Pedantry. Colby."

"Terminus. Insensate. Ussel. Dr. Dispensations."

"They speak of you highly."

If a few jars were going to speak of you, it was nice to know they spoke highly.

"I'm glad," he said, thinking, Why am I here again? How is she supposed to help me catch Killjoy? Why do I do these things?

She showed off her brown, crooked teeth. "You lie at the center of it."

"Of what?"

"The snarled fabric of our lives."

"Ah."

Now the other women all began moving as one, shuffling the papers in their laps, nodding wildly, as if Mama Prott had given them a prearranged signal. Like she says "snarled fabric" and they all start wagging their heads like their neck muscles have been cut.

"In the knot," she said.

"A knot that spins and spins like a wheel across the great ecclesiastical galaxy," he said, quoting her.

"Well, no, not exactly this, but similar, in the microcosm."

"Ah."

"You continue to transform."

"Sure."

"You understand value."

"Sure."

"Of conversion."

"Reformation," he said.

"Yes. Metamorphosis."

You weren't supposed to converse with a lunatic. It only gave credence to her construct.

But he couldn't help himself. Why was he here if not to converse with her? Get her talking. He said, "We all do it, every day."

"No, not everyone. But you are in transition. Continuous and profane."

"Contaminating. *De-purifying*," he said, repeating Merwin's words. Now that he heard them from his own mouth, he felt slightly insulted. Look at what the loonies are saying about me now, how goddamn nasty.

"The hand of the corrupter is squeezing your soul out of existence."

"My soul is squeezing back," Whitt said, believing it. Killjoy had been fucking with him for years now, but it was because Whitt had somehow gotten inside Killjoy's life, inside his head. If only he could figure out how. Where it was they were tied together.

She smiled, tilted her head into a pose that a very young girl might think was sexy. "You see, there it is, your ego. Your vanity. Believing yourself capable of great feats against great evil."

"I'll give it a whirl anyway, when the time comes."

"But it's already arrived, many times over, throughout eternity."

"Sure. Where's Franklin, Mrs. Prott?"

"I'm not the one to ask."

The turpentine stink was starting to get him a little high, like standing for too long in a room being painted with the windows shut. "What?"

She let out another delighted squeal that suddenly broke off. "Yes, yes, you're getting even stronger now. More adept, even more sensitive in your search. Astonishing, your aura is brilliant, illuminating."

"I thought it was black."

"It is. A black star. It's genuinely beautiful. Do you see, girls?"

The women all groggily nodding as one, looking at him and not seeing him, perhaps not seeing anything at all.

Children laughed and whisked past behind him, Whitt turning to see them and seeing nothing, the kids already threading through their parents' legs, Mama Prott's turpentine odor mixing with the smell of freshly made bread, cookies, corn muffins. Whitt realized the guards still hadn't moved an inch, not a millimeter, like plastic statues of modern art symbolizing something about blind justice or consumerism. The kind of shit you see in the MOMA apparently, alongside the Pollocks. The stuff you stare at and go, I don't get it, I just don't know what the hell I'm supposed to be seeing here.

"You're learning how to use your other attributes," she told him.

"What? Which?"

"To put this dominion into words, to name the thing, is to weaken it."

"Where's Franklin, Mrs. Prott?"

That insanely sweet dark smile on her face, such an expression of self-satisfaction. "I could tell you, but it's not for me to do so."

"Not for you?" Whitt glanced around at her minions, thinking maybe one of them would give it up, if that's the way this new religion worked. Another voice of God hidden among them, somebody who'd spit up some answers. "Then who?"

"You already know that."

How active had Killjoy been in that house? Had he sat with the Protts, discussed the Failure of Urethra with them the way Whitt had?

"If I could talk to Killjoy, I wouldn't need you or Franklin at all."

"You don't need us anyway, don't you see?"

"Something led him to your house."

"Something led him to your house. To all our homes."

Whitt was starting to understand a little piece of it. "Did you see him, Mrs. Prott?" That smile on her face was mirrored by the other women, everybody so safe behind their little wall of salt. "Did you speak to him?"

Invisible children rushed by again, brushing up against Whitt's legs, one of them tugging at his sleeve. But whenever he looked there was nothing but a fleeting shadow, the kid already moving across the room. Wasn't there some kind of time limit for visitors? What the hell was going on in this romper room? It was so ridiculous he almost let out a laugh, thinking about playing hide-'n'-seek with Sarah, and how she'd always run into the bedroom closet and giggle behind the clothes as he counted to twenty. Karen in the kitchen yelling for them not to stretch out her cashmere. Both of them yelling back that they wouldn't. Whitt standing there outside the magic circle of protection, turning, and turning again.

"He spoke to me," Mrs. Prott said, infected gums on display. "About you."

TWENTY

It went back to teeth. Killjoy with his mouth open, always needing to talk. To make contact even with the families he'd already destroyed. Tongue forever wagging, lecturing from afar. He could chew his lips for hours but he'd never be able to keep silent for long, not that murderous prick.

"You didn't tell me that last time," Whitt said, pulling a grin. His charm was exceptionally limited.

"I thought you would already know the face and caprices of your enemy. After all, that's why I enlisted your help."

She was right. She really had been asking him for help in getting the ballerina's baby back after Killjoy had stolen the kid. Whitt hadn't been playing the Protts as much as they'd been playing him.

You weren't supposed to converse with lunatics. It only gave credence to their constructs. He was going to keep thinking that until maybe he shut the hell up.

But here he was, giving it his all. No wonder there

were so many nutcases around. Probably because there were so many guys like Whitt who kept talking to them.

"What did he look like?" he asked.

"I didn't see him. He entered the house while we slept and sat on the end of my bed in shadows. He asked me not to turn on the light and I didn't, out of respect, and fear, I suppose. He is a powerful force."

"You never called your sons to come help you?"

"No, I was too afraid. I both hated and admired him in that instant, sensing his place in the tapestry. The baby was in his arms. I heard it snoring."

"What did he sound like?"

"His voice was electronically disguised."

"What?"

"He had one of those microphone mechanisms that throat cancer victims hold against their necks."

Whitt thought about that, about how—

—how bush-league that was for Killjoy. Effective, maybe, but so amateurish. It must eat away at him, having to do something that second-rate. He was more of a dilettante than a force, when you got down to it.

So Whitt saw the scene. Killjoy walking into that house, feeling...what...? Anger that the cult would dare sacrifice a child? Understanding the need to sacrifice a newborn, because he'd done it himself. Conflicted, but not pissed off enough to direct his hate toward them, not daring to try his hand against Franklin Prott. Leaving all of that for Whitt, later on.

Knowing that Whitt not only could handle it, but that he would. Thinking, *My partner will be in after me to clean up this refuse.* Still fearing Whitt enough to make sure that his face was never seen, his voice went unheard. Under those circumstances, that must've steamed his ass.

"What did he say?" Whitt asked.

"Are you prepared?"

"He said 'Are you prepared?'"

"No, I ask you, are you prepared?"

"For what?"

"The answer."

"Oh. Sure."

"He said that he loves you."

Whitt's stomach spasmed, like someone was shoving a knife in, twisting and twisting. "Terrific."

"You are his only friend."

"Yeah," Whitt said, "yeah, yeah, fuckin' yeah. I know."

"He called you his favorite father. His first father."

Here they were just going around in circles, not breaking much new ground anymore. Was Killjoy as tired of it all as Whitt was becoming? Couldn't they move it along, confront each other once and for all? Both of them in the middle of main street, pulling guns, see who draws first.

"Anything else?" he asked.

"He said you would come to need him. As he needs you."

"'That just isn't going to happen."

"It already has."

Sometimes you wanted to see if somebody else had the same soft spots you did. Whitt asked, "You admired and hated him in that moment, when he sat on your bed. Couldn't you have stopped him? Isn't he *other*? Didn't he need to be struck down in the purifying light of Mucus-Thorn-in-Brain before he tried to steal your breath?"

Telling it while she fluttered her hand at him, like he was absurd, so silly. "No. He only kills children."

The new cult members were moving now, just a bit, maybe an inch to the side for each of them, as the impact of Mama Prott's words stirred them from their stupor. The women held their hands up, the way a bride does when she waits for the ring, fluttering their fingers to mimic Mrs. Prott. All of them sort of waving at Whitt now. Foolish man, strange boy, so silly. Nodding with snapped necks.

Kids brushed past behind him, but he didn't turn this time, maybe at last catching on.

"You're surrounded by dead children," Mama Prott said.

"You're not being particularly helpful to me, lady."

"The circle allows me to see them."

"Don't look too closely, my black star aura will blind you."

"You brought the children with you."

"That's enough now, eh?"

But it must be true. He felt it again, his past and future brushing up against his legs, small hands grabbing hold, but nothing there, nothing ever there.

Next she was going to tell him he had blood in his mouth. He refused to turn anymore, and the old lady picked up on it. "As I told you, there are many casualties sprawled across both sides of the veil."

"You told me, all right."

That thick gray neck wobbling, alive in some unholy manner. You slash her throat and who the hell knows what's in there that's going to come out after you. She showed her teeth and said, "There will be more sacrifices."

"Sure. Where's Franklin, Mrs. Prott?"

"You know what must happen now," she told him, giving away nothing.

"Where's Franklin, Mrs. Prott?"

The kids, if there were kids here, stopped moving.

They stepped up beside him, standing nearby, waiting. The tension inside and outside of him equalized. A few seconds passed where he felt like he was floating, his head higher than the rest of his body, just out of reach. They were at the edge, one of them ready to push the other one off.

Mama Prott raised her hand out to him, a loving and gentle gesture, and for an instant he wanted to take it, maybe rest his face against her the way he would his own mother. He stepped over the circle and she said, "You have to die, you realize. So you can be reborn into light and sanctity, even more mighty than you are now."

He had time enough to say, "Ah shit."

The Latino lady, nearly 220 pounds of solid muscle, swooped off the bleachers and lunged at Whitt. She held a screwdriver sharpened into a dagger. He'd been staring at her a minute ago and had seen nothing but the crazy pages in her lap, so how could he miss a knife in her hand?

He barely managed to get his arms up in time to grip her by the wrists, before they fell over backwards. They hit the floor hard. She tried to knee him in the groin, seething and bursting with a sudden, immense hate.

He hadn't been expecting it at all. His own incompetence scared him worse than anything.

"Holy crap, lady!"

"God wants you dead," she said in a heavy accent, her muscles solid as stone. "Jesus, he say you got the devil in you!"

"No I don't!"

Whitt arched his back, trying to look behind him, hoping the fucking guards would get moving soon but he couldn't see them anywhere. A few people shouted, but nobody screamed, no alarms went off.

"Mary dee Virgin say you evil!"

"Stop, will you!"

"That's why I bring the drugs up in my pudenda. For dee church!"

Look at this. He's got to wrestle some Catholic Colombian mule for his life while Mama just sat there and smiled at him. This gal must've been ramped up on her own supply because he was gaining no ground with her. He could've head-butted her in the nose and maybe killed her, but she reminded him too much of his tenth-grade religion class teacher, Sister Roberta Ignatius.

"You da bad man!"

"I am not! Roberta stop!"

"Who Roberta?"

Maybe Whitt screwed around too much because he didn't want to waste his energy on anybody except Killjoy. That seemed psychologically plausible. It was foolish, all his training, carrying rocks, the mats and speed bag, and him down here struggling like a son of a bitch, worrying about what kind of penance he might get for slugging a mule who looked like a nun.

He shifted his weight, got the mule leaning to the left while he pulled right, then drew her toward him and snapped the edge of his hand against her wrist. The shiv skittered across the floor. Whitt chopped the woman in the shoulder, got his knee into her belly, and lashed out. She went flying ass backwards and dropped at Mrs. Prott's feet.

"You'll have to be stronger than that for my Franklin," Mama Prott said.

He grinned and blood dripped from his mouth. It splashed against the scuffs in her magic circle, maybe

healing it, completing it again. A horn sounded and immediately guards were all over him, corralling Mrs. Prott and the other cultists. Visitors shrank back to the far walls, children shrieking everywhere.

When he got back to his car, Diana Carver was parked beside him. She stood leaning against the passenger door. "So did Mama help you out?"

"She tried to have one of her new followers stick a shiv in my ear," he said.

"Maybe she doesn't like you as well as you thought."

Hearing his words come back at him like that proved that Brunkowski talked to Diana Carver a little more than he'd admitted at the station.

"In that lady's head, killing a person is doing them a favor," Whitt told her. "It sets souls free, lets them go back to the big cosmic web of the universe. She's crazy about me."

"She's certainly crazy anyway."

"Yeah."

"Did you get anything out of her?"

"You want me to do all your work for you?"

"No, but I would like you to start being more cooperative."

Whitt stared at her, hoping to hide the fact that he was checking out her rack again. The sweet rush of lust filled him, and the guilt hit him nearly as quick. "Whatever I say is already tainted. It has to be if you're going to continue investigating me. You've got to keep your options open."

"You let me worry about that. I'd like to talk to you."

"At length? Ready for our formal interview?"

"Yes," she said.

"Does that mean you've finished reviewing the case?"

"Yes," she said.

"Great. Let's get a burger." He grinned again. It didn't work any better on her than on a visitors' room full of cult loonies. "I know this place on the other side of town. Terrific onion rings. My treat."

TWENTY-ONE

Diana Carver slid opposite him into the booth and tried hard not to look like a woman who didn't even want to touch the silverware in this place.

Whitt was petty enough to enjoy her discomfort. Anything to even the playing field, however he could do it. He made an effort to avoid looking into her face, but wasn't doing very well. Every time he glanced at her he was left a little breathless. She knew it and was using it.

It wasn't too much to expect her to take the lead, her being the cop. But she remained silent, tossed her hair a bit. The feathered bangs rippled before draping back into sharp points ringing her face.

"You've had trouble here," she said.

He sat up straighter. "Wow, that's pretty good."

"You've got that self-satisfied look on your face that guys get after they've kicked somebody's ass. So what happened?"

Diana Carver really had been doing her homework.

Who knew how long she'd been on his tail, the famous Eddie Whitt. He cocked his head and looked at her again, seeing her in a new light. Always seeing this lady in some kind of new light, there was that much to her.

There was a lot of bustle and noise, and the smell of burned meat. Whitt occasionally ate here when coming back from the Falls, feeling empty and hungry and not wanting to head back to his apartment just yet.

"Made a scene once," he said. "A father was screaming at his son. Little boy maybe seven, eight years old, cranky from a long ride down from New England, wouldn't eat his hamburger. The father started lecturing, got the kid crying, feeling guilty."

"And you whupped him bad," she said with a half-grin that told him she knew the truth already.

He felt stupid but committed to finishing the story. "No, I just got in his face a little. His wife got scared, flopped over on the table hyperventilating. Somebody called the cops. Local press got wind of it, media picked up on it."

"Bet they painted a rosy picture of you."

He figured she'd already memorized the headlines. "It was easy for them because there was so much built into it. Crazy guy who lost his daughter beats up an 'abusive' father"—he made the quotes in the air with his fingers and she mimicked him—"after visiting his wife up in a mental hospital. Tied in with Killjoy, made me look like a protector of children, got the ball rolling all over again."

"The story that never dies."

"Not yet," he said, knowing it would be dead soon enough, one way or another.

"And are you?" she asked.

"Am I what? Crazy?"

"The jury's still out on that," she said. She came this close to putting a mocking tone in her voice, but backed off just in time. "Are you a protector of children?"

"I don't like seeing men screaming at their kids, if that's what you mean."

"It's not."

Diana Carver looking at him, him looking back. How much else did she know? And how much did she want to know?

"You're staring at my scars," she said.

"Yeah."

"You like them?"

Whitt figured this was another power tactic, a way to take control of the situation. Call attention to the fact that he was checking her out, but stop him cold when he wanted to know more. It was going to be fun, hanging out with Diana Carver.

"Sure," he told her. "I bet a lot of guys do."

"Takes the edge off my looks."

"Adds to them. Not only sexy, but makes you seem tough too."

"Because I am."

"Yeah, well, I believe it. How'd you get them?"

She angled her chin away. In this light the nicks appeared much deeper than before. Maybe she did it on purpose, depending on the situation and what she wanted out of whoever she was dealing with. She turned back and the scars were nearly gone. "I'd rather not say."

"Okay."

Like any cop, she was trained to change the subject fast, get a suspect off his guard. "You've been watching Russell Gunderson."

Whitt had been waiting for it since she'd shown her face. "Yeah."

"Late night stake-outs in his backyard. But you're not a peeper. You're just keeping your eye on them."

"Sure," he said. He had to do something with the rage and fever, but not even Brunk knew about this weakness. He imagined Diana Carver sitting in her car with a set of high-powered infrared binoculars trained on Whitt, as he lay in Gunderson's yard chewing grass and going out of his head. Careful about the way he worded it, Whitt continued. "I still feel a connection to Lorrie."

"I would guess you might, seeing as how she was left on your doorstep."

"Were you watching him or me?"

"You," she said.

The waitress appeared like an assistant in a magic

trick, nowhere in sight and then suddenly there. Exceptionally proud of her name badge, thrusting the thing nearly into his nose. BONNIE. BONNIE. BONNIE, so you'd never forget it. Then Whitt realized she was shoving her ample tits at him. Trying to nab a better tip, or just doing it because she could.

He ordered a cheeseburger, onion rings, and a beer. The tension in his gut had eased up a touch, but left him hollow.

Diana Carver said, "The same."

She did that rearing up thing again, getting taller than him from her seat so she could stare down. Maybe he was slumping. He wondered why it was so important to her. Did it come from working with the feebs? Or because of her ex?

Even with the smile, her eyes remained dark and angry. She'd slept badly last night. She'd been sleeping badly for a while.

There it was again, something about her Whitt found unsettling. Like she could see maybe ninety seconds into the future and the weight of the knowledge was killing her. But she wouldn't share with you whatever it was she saw lying ahead.

"Tell me about yourself," Whitt said.

She folded her strong hands in front of her on the table. "Mr. Whitt, despite the circumstances and current surroundings, I'll conduct the interview, if you don't mind."

"But I do."

"Excuse me?"

It was easy putting him on edge, a little harder to do it to her.

He liked this part of it. How the feds and cops came at him like a suspect and then were shocked when he didn't fall in line. "Ms. Carver, I can choose to assist the efforts of the police in this matter or I can choose not to. That's my right. What you don't fully comprehend is that I've played this game for five years. I've answered about ten thousand questions from my living room to lockup, from here to Quantico. I've been befriended, threatened, cajoled, coaxed, flattered, implored, bullied, and harassed. All because the man who murdered my daughter sends me letters."

"Don't you find it strange?" she asked.

"Of course I do, but it's not my fault."

"You should let the law enforcement agencies handle it."

"How about if we don't push that point, eh? Brunk said the whole reason you're here is because you're an opinionated lady who knows the feebs fouled up the way they handled this case in the first place. All the profilers coming to different conclusions, nobody making any progress. Interbureau collaboration notwithstanding. You're the kind of person who goes through cases she's not assigned to. From DC to Manhattan and rerouted out to Nassau County. They told you to take a swipe at it yourself."

"My, you do have the ear of the department, don't

you. You're not a police officer or a private detective. You're not even a bounty hunter. You have no license."

"I know. Weird, isn't it?" he admitted. "That he'd afford me such inner circle courtesy?"

"Yes, it is."

"Still, why don't you follow his lead and do the same?"

"I am." She snapped on the vapid smile again, not trusting him an inch.

Bonnie brought the food out and gunned her titties at Whitt as she slapped the plates down. She took her time placing the bottle of beer in front of him, trying to do something sexy with it. He grinned and she said, "Let me know if you need anything..."

"Will do."

"Enjoy."

He watched her wriggle off, really shaking it across the floor. Some truckers on the other end of the room whistled.

Diana Carver unfolded her napkin but made no move toward the food. "You want to go crack a few collarbones now?"

"And ruin this delicious meal?"

"Don't feel so flattered by Bonnie."

"I'm not."

"She turns tricks in the parking lot."

"You've been here before, Ms. Carver. You've been asking around. You've been following me up to Garden Falls."

She let it pass since it was an obvious statement. He thought about her up at the hospital, talking to Ted, and Whitt's stomach tightened. He took a deep breath and Diana Carver said, "She figures we're unhappily married and hopes you'll come back sometime so she can make better cash off you."

Whitt sighed. "I thought maybe she wanted to go to a movie."

"I'd like to know what Mrs. Prott had to say to you."

"Okay."

"Did she give you a line on Franklin?"

"No. It sounds like he's broken from the pack. His brother doesn't like him much either anymore. If they knew where he was, they'd give him up. If for no other reason than to have me take a run at him."

"Why would they want that?"

"They're hoping I'll join their little group, start burying guys with funny-colored sneakers on and no dicks. Save the cosmos that way."

She nodded at that, once, a small but sharp up-and-down action with her chin. What they called an economy of motion. No wasted energy.

"And how about information on Killjoy? Did she know anything more about him than she first let on?"

"She's scared of him," Whitt said.

"For her life?"

"I don't think so. More for her soul. She thinks he has great power in the cosmic cycle of life and rebirth and all kinds of other mystical shit. Her belief system

takes pieces of just about every religion out there and
screws them up even worse. She may be a lunatic, but
she knows enough to realize Killjoy is a whole other
kind of crazy."

"I wonder if that's true."

Whitt said nothing.

"You still attest that Franklin Prott is blind?" Diana
Carver asked.

"Did you expect me to change my mind?"

"I thought you might come to an understanding
that you were wrong," she said.

"I come to that understanding a lot, but not when a
blind guy is looking at me with dead eyes that don't
work."

"It doesn't make any sense."

"You won't last long on this case if you look for
much logic, Ms. Carver. You get in the center of it and
throw a stick, you'll hit about twenty-seven maniacs. I
just had a run-in with a woman who thinks Mama
Prott is the Virgin Mary. They should keep Mama in
solitary. They're going to have a lot of problems pretty
soon." He swigged his beer. "You're not going to find
your normal rationale here."

"I wasn't looking for normal, exactly. Just a line
on how a supposed blind man might escape from a
second-story window of a crowded police station."

She studied him while he continued eating, enjoying
the food. Like he was an obstacle to overcome, a piece
of machinery that had broken down and needed to be

handled carefully so it would last long enough to get into the shop. Maybe he only liked her so much because she hardly noticed him there sitting right in front of her. Looking at him the same way Karen did.

"You have a boy and a girl," he said.

"I'm not going to talk to you about my personal life."

"It's not like I'm asking you on a date."

"I refuse to discuss—"

"Okay. I've got the check."

"What? You've got the check?"

"Yeah. See ya."

She reached to grip his wrist, and he let her take it. She hit him with that heated gaze and said, "We're not finished here yet."

"Sure we are. Mind if I take your onion rings home?"

"Mr. Whitt—"

"You don't know what you're missing."

"You can be charged with—"

"Obstruction. Yeah, I know."

"Don't take it so lightly. I'll make it stick."

"Oh, bullshit, lady. I'm the fuckin' king of obstruction with you people. You'd think the wheels of justice had come to a complete halt thanks to me and all the goddamn obstructing I do.

"Did you kick his ass?" Whitt asked.

"Whose?"

"Your married boyfriend in the feebs. The one who

demoted you. Did you smack the crap out of him for that?"

"I was *not* demoted."

"Whatever you call it. Rerouted. Kicked to the curbside."

She tried to sit even taller but she was already at her max. So she just tightened her lips, probably thinking about taking a poke at him, or maybe wanting to kick the hell out of Brunkowski for talking.

"That's—"

"Yeah, none of my business. Except it shows me how involved you're willing to get in this case. Bucking your bosses, putting it all on the line. But I still don't know why."

"You don't have to know." She slapped her palm down on the table. Like saying, this is solid, this is real, what you're seeing now is every truth in the world. "All that should be important to you, Mr. Whitt, is that I intend to solve this case and bring Killjoy to justice."

"Is that right?"

"Yes."

The flames in her dark eyes wavered for an instant, dimming and brightening as she tried to come to a decision about what to say next. How open she should be. How much she should lay out in front of him. Taking a chance and going for it.

"What's your connection to Killjoy?"

He'd misjudged her. It wasn't just that she didn't trust him. She was coming down on the side that he was either Killjoy or in league with him. Whitt was pretty sure if he made any fast moves, Diana Carver would put one in his forehead and sleep just fine afterwards.

He stared hard at her, the black star within burning. "He killed my daughter."

"I mean why is he obsessed with you?"

"I have no idea."

"The answer rests with you."

"I know that," Whitt said.

"You're certain it's no one from your past?"

"I'm not certain of that at all. The FBI and NYPD investigated me from my birth certificate on up the chain. If it is somebody from my corner of the world, nobody was able to make the connection, including me."

"But still, it's there. You're there. In his head."

Whitt, the opening scene of Killjoy's construct. "Yeah."

"Is he in yours?"

"Sure, he's gotta be. That's the way I'm going to catch him."

She didn't want to hear that. Everybody acting like it wasn't his place. "You are very close to having me arrest you."

"No, I'm not," he said. "Why were you so interested in this case, Ms. Carver? Brunk said you thought the feebs messed up several other investigations as well. What about this one grabbed your attention?"

"Because there's no reason why it can't be solved."

"Except that it hasn't been."

"You cause more damage than you know."

"How?"

"You shouldn't be directly involved. You only cloud the situation with your vigilantism."

He didn't even know it was a word. Vigilantism. Like something you get from using a dirty poolroom toilet. Hey, JoJo, you got a serious case of vigilantism there, don't you fuckin' touch me.

Whitt said, "This situation has so much cloud cover that you people have done nothing for years except bounce into one another."

She wet her lips and nodded. "It's been mishandled. A case like this involving children is always so sensitive that departments tend to tread heavily. It gets such media attention that everyone is worried about how they'll look. It becomes a distraction and a liability. And you've kept the spotlight fixed on it. You've caused a lot of the confusion and digression yourself."

Whitt tried to hit the grin again but his face wouldn't work. It felt like an inch of spackling paste had been spread across his flesh and allowed to dry. He wasn't sure if he could get his mouth to work, but somehow the words fell from him. "Yeah, that's it. All my fault."

"No, of course not, Mr. Whitt. I'm not implying that—"

"You don't know what you're implying, Ms. Carver.

You've got yourself a roomful of files and no context. Your superiors set you loose on your course so you wouldn't embarrass them further, not because they believe you'll solve anything. Brunkowski thinks more highly of me as an investigator than he does you. And he thinks I'm a shithead."

"I know that. It's his mistake. I'm going to get to the bottom of this."

"Okay," Whitt said.

"Don't look at me like that," she told him.

"What?"

"You heard me. Stop looking at me like that."

"How do you mean?"

"You know exactly what I mean. Stop it or I'll slug you in the goddamn face and make you stop."

She was coiled and ready to do exactly that, but he wasn't sure if he could stop staring, the way he felt right now. It was the first real emotion she'd shown, and he liked seeing it. He tasted blood. You never knew what the hell was waiting for you around the next corner.

TWENTY-TWO

All this time Killjoy had been sending letters, and Whitt had never thought to send one back.

It took him twenty-seven tries before he finished the note. He went through nine pens and ruined the coffee table.

He could only write so much before the frenzy would rush down into his hands and he'd drive the pen through the paper until he was carving into the top of the table.

Spelling out FUCK FUCK FUCK FUCK FUCK MURDERING FUCK YOU BELONG TO ME. The pens shattering, the table legs finally giving out. Whitt found himself alternately sobbing and laughing, covered in ink while he tried to write. Drawing frownie faces all over the place.

He overturned the couch a dozen times. The landlord called because of complaints in the building. Two sets of cops showed up asking what the problem was, hands on their gun belts, checking him out. Surreptitiously searching the bedroom, peeking in closets. Looking at the mess and staring at the front of his shirt like he might be covered with dark blue blood. Both times he answered their questions as calmly as possible and had them call Brunkowski.

The second time they handed the phone to him and Brunk barked, "The hell are you doing?"

"Writing Killjoy a letter."

"What? Why?"

"See if he'll step into a trap."

The voice squeezed out the side of his mouth, around the cigar that wasn't there. "You sure that's a good idea?"

"I suppose you'll find out one way or another. I've been playing by his rules for five years. It's past time to change the game around."

"What kind of trap is this? What are you going to say?"

"That's between me and him."

"Don't give me that kind of shit. I want to know what you're planning."

"I'll tell you about it before it goes down. I haven't made much progress with my letter yet."

"Where you going to leave it?"

"My windshield, I think."

"I could have ten men surround the area, follow you around all day." Brunk sounded a little embarrassed even saying it. "If you want."

"He won't bite then."

"You don't know that."

"I know that, so do you."

"I'm still going to be watching."

"I figured."

"Be careful."

"He only kills children," Whitt said and hung up.

The cops stared at him like he was out of his mind, which was fine. They left him alone after that and, after five more attempts, he managed to finish the note.

He drove up the street to a strip mall with a copier center and made thirty copies. He put the letter under his windshield wiper. It asked Killjoy if he'd ever seen the Protts using another house. If he knew where Franklin was. Saying, *I need your help.*

He'd placed himself in the hands of his enemy because it might be the only way to actually ever get ahold of him.

Asking Killjoy to help him find Franklin so he could ask Franklin how to find Killjoy.

He left the note on his windshield everywhere he went for the next nine days. Every time it blew away he pulled another copy from the glove compartment.

He imagined Killjoy seeing the note and reading it from afar, through a telescope from a half mile away, safe on a rooftop someplace. The astonishing realization striking him in the chest, that Whitt was asking for help. The smile on his brutal face showing off every one of his perfect teeth. Whitt, the last holdout, the only one who didn't stab himself through the heart, breaking down at last. Needing his Killjoy, and that need being a form of love. Loving Killjoy.

Whitt's cell phone rang while he sat in rush-hour traffic, stuck on the Expressway. He'd been driving around Long Island for more than a week, parking for hours at a stretch, leaving the letter in plain sight.

He touched the phone and the world grew hot and white. The sun was arching over the horizon, the red light slashing across his eyes. He felt his hands leave him, then his limbs, and finally the top third of his head went floating off. The phone seemed to answer itself.

Testament of Ya'al.

Harlequenin.

His lips parted and somehow the words escaped from behind the cage of his teeth. "Hello there."

The voice, when it finally replied, was electronically disguised. Deepened, slowed, thickened. The humanity of it utterly eviscerated. The kind of voice you expected a death angel of God to sound like. Sent down from the desert mountains with a sword dipped in blood. The fierce voice of Michael, Gabriel, Raphael, Uriel, Sariel, Israfel, Azrawel, all the many seraphim of the black burning air. The murderer of his child, the quiet killer of infants.

"Hello, Whitt."

Whitt tried to speak the hated name, holy in its significance after all this time. In its arcane ability to touch every facet of a man's life. His family, friends, the earth itself, the baby he laid to rest. He tried again and this time, the name came free, sounding abysmally normal, underwhelming.

"Killjoy."

"*I'm so glad we're finally getting a chance to talk. I got your note.*"

On a stolen cell phone and traveling, no doubt. How he must be anxious as hell, stoked beyond belief, wanting Whitt to hear his true voice and name.

"Yes."

You change the pattern only when you're ready. Only after the trap is set.

So Killjoy was finally going to make another move.

"*But first, I wanted to say that I hope you'll forgive me for not performing my duties lately.*"

"Your duties."

"*It's so easy to become distracted, even misguided, by the lures of normalcy. Do you ever feel this, Whitt? When you forgo the hunt for me?*"

"I never forgo the hunt for you."

"*I know. That's what makes you even more insane than I am.*"

The shit you had to take. Listening to the guy who put a pillow over your daughter's face calling you names. You could laugh at something like that until your heart stopped.

"Don't take any more children, Killjoy."

"*We won't speak of that right now. I must ask, though, why are you so interested in this fool Franklin Prott?*"

"He murdered a ballerina."

That got a screech of static out of the voice-altering device, a squawk of laughter. *"You know she really wasn't."*

"I know."

"What are you planning, Whitt?"

"Oh, you know us insane guys. We do all sorts of nutty things."

"Are you trying to be funny with me? I'm surprised. Really, with me?"

"Sure," Whitt said.

"You don't care about the Prott family at all, do you? You're hoping they somehow lead you closer to me."

"They already have. We're chatting now."

"Yes, like old friends."

"Are we?"

"Are we what?"

"Old friends? Do I know you, Killjoy?"

The answer being the only one possible. *"Of course you do."*

Whitt asked, "What mask are you wearing, Harlequenin?"

"It's not much different than yours. We'll remove them eventually."

"You know, anytime you want to go out for a beer, I'm willing." The top of his skull rising off again. "You want to stop by tonight?"

"I'm afraid I have plans."

"Tomorrow?"

"*I wish I could take you up on that. You deserve a night of peace.*"

"You do too. That's why you chose me. So I could bring it to you."

"*I didn't choose you, Whitt, you chose me.*"

"How about if you lay off that double-talk shit, eh?"

"*You'll find Franklin Prott at One-twenty-one Broadhurst Park outside of Huntingville Station. Go alone. No police involvement.*"

"Why? What do you care about Prott getting busted?"

"*There should be rules to every undertaking, shouldn't there?*"

Whitt remembered what he'd told Mike about Killjoy not being cruel. How he lived through his own construct, seemingly nonsensical, but forming some kind of parameters for his madness. Defined borders for his psychosis. There were plenty of lines Killjoy wouldn't cross.

Whitt wondered if he had any himself anymore.

Broadhurst Park ran behind all the factories that stood across from the back parking lot of the police station. He and Diana Carver had stared out the second-floor window at the heavy street traffic just outside. Across the road was an area of brush that led off to a Little League field. You couldn't see farther than that from the window. Franklin had pretty much just run in a straight line after he'd escaped. A quarter mile from the cops and perfectly safe from them.

"There will be music. The most heartening, celestial symphony."

Killjoy would be there, watching.

Blunt, sweet madness filled him in a rush, a flood moving from the back of his floating head to the front, sweeping his brain aside. All his thoughts, his past, and every memory drowned in the red tide of rage. Whitt leaned forward and champed his teeth on the steering wheel, biting harder and harder as he reached out with one hand and clutched under the seat. He got hold of the metal track of the seat treads bolted into the car frame and pulled. Adrenaline raced through his muscles, the fury feeding on itself as he swallowed his moans, knowing he was talking to Killjoy, that Killjoy was talking to him, and Karen was locked up and Sarah was dead. The steering column screeched. The car groaned around him, and the seat began to buckle.

"Why are you eating your steering wheel, Whitt? That's very bad, you know. You're going to ruin your teeth that way."

The drivers of the cars around him stared and affected nervous gestures. The light changed and the blaring horns were muted as if coming from the bottom of the ocean.

That death-on-wings voice now humming to itself, no different than a choir of blood-soaked children. As sickening and impressive as the unforgiving word of Heaven.

Whitt couldn't bite down his scream anymore, but

there was nowhere for it to go but up inside his swimming head, FUCK FUCK FUCK FUCK FUCK MURDERING FUCK YOU BELONG TO ME, as he mewled through his cracking teeth, blood sluicing over his lips and the roar of his utterly exquisite, enduring, immutable, and celestial pain.

"*Can you hear the music already, Whitt? Does it lighten your soul? Tell me. Is it sliding into your belly?*"

PART III

INCISION

TWENTY-THREE

One-twenty-one Broadhurst Park turned out to be an abandoned five-story brick building. Whitt wasn't sure what to make of it. There was a huge gate in front of the main door, jerry-rigged to stay in place. Maybe this place had once been offices for the managers before the factories had started failing. Illegal loft housing. Maybe the Prott cult had been crashing here for a while. Franklin might not be alone.

The parking lot around the building was huge and desolate. About a dozen streetlights were supposed to illuminate the area, but seven of them were out. The darkness seemed like a heavy undergrowth he had to maneuver through.

It had taken him almost two hours to make it out of traffic and find a route through back roads. Shadows moved in thick segments as clouds pulsed over the three-quarter moon.

Whitt was starting to smile without fully realizing why. Maybe because his mouth hurt so much.

No, it was because he knew something was about to happen. Could feel it building around him. No matter how it turned out, it would be better than everything else over the last five years leading up to this minute.

He got out of the car, grabbed the remaining copies of the note he'd written Killjoy, and tossed them on the ground. A slight breeze stirred them, and one by one they began to skitter across the lot.

Killjoy was around here someplace, maybe waiting for Whitt and Franklin Prott to slug it out. What did Killjoy expect tonight? See Whitt get a little blood on his hands? Or did he expect Prott to soften him up, kick the shit out of him? Get him ready for Killjoy to swoop in at the last moment?

Whitt didn't really care how it played out because they were both here, right now, someplace.

He stepped to the door.

Most of the windows were boarded up. He imagined illegal renters up there with nothing to cook on but a hot plate. One bathroom per floor. Maybe only every other floor. There was no sign of life anywhere. Tire tracks and shoe prints punctuated the mud and gravel in the lot. Probably from kids using this as a shortcut to the field across the way. Large dunes of sand and asphalt flanked the block. Well-worn trails weaved across the tract. Teenagers used their dirt bikes here, racing all around the rubbish.

So you've got to ask yourself, can you get any more stupid?

Coming here to a blind maniac's lair and not even bringing a flashlight?

Didn't even leave your headlights on.

Whitt turned and sniffed the air.

He smelled rain on the breeze.

And beneath that—turpentine.

Franklin's breath, poisoned by his mother's herbal tea all these years.

Whitt spun. He reached into his belt to draw the .32 and realized he was too late. He'd missed his chance and botched it already. It was over and it hadn't even started yet.

Powerful hands came out of the dark, gripped him by the throat, and yanked him off the ground. It felt like his head was about to be torn clean off. The nerves at the base of his neck fired off at once and filled his skull with a blaze of unknown colors. Whitt let out a gurgle like a cat being strangled and tried bringing the gun around. But there was no way to complete the move before his windpipe was crushed. He let the .32 drop and reached up to try to pry the fingers from his throat. Franklin Prott laughed in his face.

Man, what the fuck was in that tea?

"Mama said you'd come back to me," Franklin whispered, pulling Whitt an inch higher so he could say it directly in his ear.

The guy was impossibly strong and he carried Whitt three steps toward the front of the building. Fingers like iron, you hear that shit all the time, but really, here it was. Fingers like iron, folded steel, trying to rip right through Whitt's larynx and shred it apart.

Franklin rolled his blank eyes up toward the moon and let out a vicious guffaw that didn't want to end. It billowed and coursed and echoed around the empty industrial complex. That sick laughter coming from down in his belly and the depths of his malice, consuming everything.

Terror engulfed Whitt. And he hadn't been expecting to be afraid *at all*. Panic threatened to overwhelm him while he hung there in Franklin's hands, still sputtering, ready to beg. Eyes bulging, no air in his lungs, thinking, Killjoy put his money on the wrong man.

Another second passed before he realized this was the kind of situation he'd been training for all this time.

Snapping his forearms up against Franklin's wrists as hard as he could, it took him four tries to break Franklin's hold on him. The blind man stumbled aside and dumped Whitt on his ass. It was a small victory under the circumstances. Beating on a blind guy. Franklin didn't even grunt, just let out another chuckle that ran into the night, low and immensely ugly.

Whitt scrambled backwards and rolled—finally that fucking roll was going to come in handy—and whipped back onto his feet, coughing like hell. The first drops of rain splashed against his forehead. His breath came in burning heaves, like hot sand shooting out his throat.

Already Franklin was charging, but moving gracefully, at perfect ease like he wasn't in any hurry. Acting that this was fun to him and that he knew the outcome and had known it for years. His massive hands opened and closed in perfect timing to Whitt's pulse.

He flung himself forward and made a grab for Whitt's neck again.

Whitt slid deeper inside himself to the place where he went when he was practicing his moves on the mats. He struck Franklin three times in the belly, then worked his punches up to the sternum, his blows fast and with all his weight behind them. Moving upwards to chop at Franklin's shoulders.

The guy let loose with that laugh again and attacked once more. Whitt slung himself low and swung for Franklin's solar plexus.

But Franklin caught him by the wrist and pulled him off-balance. Hogarth, Colby, Terminus, Dr. Dispensations, O'Mundanity, somebody was definitely helping this blind bastard out. Whitt yelped as he was torn off his feet again and lifted into the air.

"You have no aura," Franklin said calmly. "None at all."

Whitt had to speak through gritted teeth while he pulled at Franklin's fingers, trying to bend them back far enough to break them. Goddamn, it was like trying to twist metal piping. Whitt got the feeling like this had happened many times before, throughout the ages. Merwin's mellifluous, lulling words came back to him.

Sputtering, his voice so gravelly he didn't recognize it, Whitt said, "You are forever a slave of... Mucus-Thorn-In-Brain. Bound."

"No!"

"Chained to the rock."

"It's not true!"

Franklin held Whitt up off the ground with his left hand and started punching the hell out of him with his right. Whitt couldn't help it, he started to laugh. He knew he looked silly up in the air like this, his blood flying into the darkness. Here he was being throttled and all he could do was whimper gibberish, hoping it made a difference.

What else had Merwin told him?

"Transformation is..."

"Quiet, you!"

"...all in the Cosmic Knot."

"Shut up!"

"But you don't value it above all else."

Whitt tried to tear at Franklin's face. The guy kept his blind eyes wide open, like it didn't matter to him if anybody plucked them out. Jesus. You see something like that even in a death match and it'll make a shiver crawl up your ass.

The fists tightened and Whitt groaned. He struck Franklin under the ear at the hinge of his jaw, where a ganglia of nerves sat. You clip it right and it's supposed to make a man scream in utter agony. Franklin kept sneering. His blank gaze boring like a drill through Whitt's head, and on into the writhing shadows.

Whitt's voice barely sounded human anymore. It had deepened, slowed, thickened into the kind of voice you expected a death angel of God to have. The fierce voice of Uriel, Sariel, Israfel, Azrawel, all the many seraphim of the black burning air. "A seed has infected your vessel. It gave birth in its dying throes . . ."

"You lie! My mother lies!"

There. The hands loosened for an instant and Whitt kicked out, catching Franklin on the inside of his right knee. Not hard enough to crack the cap, but it made the blind madman squeak. It knocked him back another step. A pretty nice move, when you got down to it. Whitt was finally proud of himself.

The guy wasn't invulnerable, you could still get his attention.

Whitt readied himself for Franklin's next attack, choking and spitting but standing there in the perfect *kata,* a stance where he could launch himself forward. Drive his fist right through Franklin's head.

Would that do it?

Would that bring Killjoy down out of the sky, wherever he was hiding? Bloodstains on Whitt's hands?

Whatever it took.

But Franklin merely stood there in the dim light and grinned.

Whitt went to one knee, arms still out in front of

him ready to strike, but he couldn't get enough air. The rain heaved and coursed harder now, whipping across his face. He was panting and hissing like a dying steam engine. His chest hurt, working desperately to keep air flowing down his wrecked throat.

Franklin turned with no hesitation, no fear of walking into a wall, lifted the huge grille gate in front of the door, and entered the building.

So, it was going to be a hunt after all.

Gasping, Whitt found his gun. It took him five minutes to make it to his feet. He spit more blood and shards of his cracked back teeth, let out a groan that was supposed to be a laugh, and followed into further misery.

TWENTY-FOUR

A strange sense of calm descended over him as he leaned up against the gliding metal gate, something he'd never quite felt before. It had to do with the knowledge that Franklin was only a step toward a greater evil. Whitt felt fully in control of himself even though his breathing was so fucked that he couldn't get one good lungful of air.

Whatever pitfalls there might be in the shadows would fizzle, just as Franklin had failed with all that impossible strength in his hands.

Killjoy expected Whitt to survive the onslaught, and Whitt—despite all his fury and hate—had great faith in Killjoy. Killjoy believed in him, and that was an encouraging thought.

His cell phone rang.

You'd think this might be a bad time to answer the fucking thing, but you never knew which enemy or ghost might be trying to get through.

"Hello?"

"Hello, Mr. Whitt. He can hear your fear. It's an ambush."

"I know that, Mr. Whitt." He was doing damage to his ruined throat by talking, but you couldn't refuse a call from yourself. "Tell me . . . something I don't know."

"You're going to die soon."

"Like I said . . . tell me something—"

"You're never going to catch either of them at this rate."

"So, you're just another naysayer."

"You've only said 'naysayer' once before in your life."

"Yeah, I liked it . . . better the first time, actually."

"Go farther. You've still got to go farther."

"How?"

"Don't ask me, Mr. Whitt. I'm doing everything I can. I've got my own problems."

"Worse than mine, Mr. Whitt?"

"At the moment, I'm of the opinion no."

"Of the opinion no?"

"Yes, of the opinion no. You're currently more fucked."

"I thought that might be the case. So how do I get to . . . where he is?"

"You go inside even though it's a trap."

"Then what?"

"You know what."

Whitt paused.

The meeting of yourself is the meeting of a stranger.

The man you're becoming has less in common with the man you were.

"I would also like to talk to you about your daughter."

"Certainly. What is it you'd like to discuss about her?"

"I think she needs a dog to take her to school."

"Is that right . . . ?"

"It is. A large dog that she can ride. Like a Great Dane."

"But, Mr. Whitt, that's quite impossible."

"Why is that, Mr. Whitt?"

"Because my Sarah is dead, you prick."

He hung up, thinking, This is it, I'm going to kill someone tonight. His teeth hurt like hell from chewing up the steering wheel, from being slugged in the mouth, but he still managed to smile.

TWENTY-FIVE

The heavy grille gate had fallen shut behind Franklin. It made an incredible racket as Whitt slowly lifted it open. Moonlight filtered in along with him, pooling silver around his feet. He shoved open the door and dove inside, doing the roll again. Not nearly as pretty this time. The gate came down and the darkness began to drop over him again. If Franklin had any kind of a weapon besides those hands, he'd use it now. But there was nothing.

Whitt felt his way along the wall in the blackness, sidling inch by inch. A large pad of switches and breakers stood out at hand level. He tried several and was surprised to see the lights flickering on all around him in the wide spaces of the warehouse.

An insane amount of scuttling and scurrying sounded all over the building. Whitt slid his back up against the wall wondering if anything would brush across his ankles, come tearing at him.

Whitt imagined what was ahead of him now. Five

floors of converted factory, illegal apartments, ominous stairways. He saw exposed girders, stacks of old engine parts and machinery all over the place.

He moved, plunging forward. If Franklin was going to attack, he'd do it now, fast, coming in while Whitt was learning the layout. He'd been on the loose for nearly a month. What had he been doing all that time?

Would he have kept up his role as the killing arm of the cult even without his mother overseeing him? If so, there'd be bodies secreted all over the building. People in funny shoes with their toes sticking out of shallow graves. Stuffed in the backs of closets. Under bathroom tiles.

Whitt checked each of the shoddy, chaotic rooms as best he could. He didn't know the proper search pattern for how you stalked a killer through a building. The rooms were small, most of them stuffed with all kinds of junk, some storage areas doubling as living quarters. Empty cans of food lay nearby. Nests of blankets in corners served as beds. There were stacked car parts, piping, lighting systems, tires, broken air-conditioning units, rusted and dented garage machinery.

The interior walls were little more than Sheetrock hammered to a couple of two-by-fours and cross-beams. A lot of them were crumbling or had already come down. Looked like the plumbing had leaked for years. There was water damage all over. Wet plywood had swollen until the nails had popped loose and the partitions tumbled over. He walked around the entire ground floor and still had no idea what the hell this factory had once manufactured.

He came to the first staircase, checking behind him, checking ahead. From somewhere above, that wild laughter began to rumble free again. Rattling around and coming from low in the furnaces of Franklin's belly. Whitt was starting to like the sound for some reason.

He called out, "Hello, Franklin."

The harsh, guttural words echoed everywhere, snapping hard off the distant corners. "Why are you here?"

"A couple of...reasons." It was hard as hell talking, but he barely had to whisper for the sound to carry through the building. "First, because there's somebody else I'm hoping will show up tonight."

"He won't come for you tonight. He's left you to me."

"You've talked to him?"

"He talks to me."

"You scared of him too? Like Mama?"

"Yes," Franklin said.

"Christ. What'd he tell you?"

"That he loved you."

Whitt ground his teeth together and the agony shot through his brain like a boiling geyser, showing him the beauty of single-minded determination in the face of having lost any other reason to do the right thing.

FUCK MURDERING FUCK YOU BELONG
TO ME

"You said you had a couple of reasons for being
here."

Whitt moved a quarter of the way up the stairs,
swallowing his own blood, which seemed to coat and
soothe his throat. He still wasn't sure how many floors
Franklin was above him, if at all. The way this place
was laid out, he couldn't be certain. "Second . . . you've
been a bad little boy . . . and need to go back to jail."

"You want to kill me."

"Not me, Franklin. I'm a force for good. I'm a nice
guy . . . faced with an impossible situation. I'm Mister
Heartwarming. Even your ma is crazy for me."

"You're going to die for mocking me."

"She sent me, you know," Whitt said. "She wants
me . . . to bring you in."

"That's another lie."

"It's the truth. As true as the Testament of Ya'al."

"No." Click click, clicking coming from above, like a
chick with stiletto heels up there doing a tango. No no
no. No no.

"Sure. Mucus Desisting the Efforts of Knee. Failure
of Urethra."

"No!"

"Your mother sent me here to stab you thrice in the
heart, with the point of the blade aiming north."

"She did not!"

Whitt held the .32 out in front of him, but the more

he thought about it, the less he wanted to use it. All these other guys were just using their hands. A pillow-case. It made him feel weak, needing a gun.

"Then she wants me to cut your throat so the evil incantations will dribble to the floor. Instead of being raised to the cosmic masters. You're unpure."

"Stop saying such things! You don't even have a blade."

"Sure I do, it's in my sock. Merwin wants you to know that this is the transformation that must take place."

"My brother is an idiot!"

"They say your genitals must be removed or the seed may infect another vessel and give birth even in its dying throes."

"You won't do it."

"Sure I will." Whitt thought again about why he was here. It had nothing to do with being safe. He stopped hedging his bets and just rushed up the rest of the stairs. The lights on the second story were much dimmer than on the first floor. "Mama elected me King Cultist. I'm the chief. I'm . . . the Big Kahuna high priest of Mucus. I'm phlegm with legs."

The rooms up here were loaded with even more shit: old mattresses, disconnected sinks, and spun copper. Whitt saw empty tuna cans, beer and whiskey bottles. Squatters maybe. Was that who Franklin had been preying on until his mother sent him back into action?

Lying in wait for some poor homeless kid to come along and grab some shut-eye out of the rain?

Whitt sniffed but couldn't smell much besides the dust and that turpentine stink. Franklin Prott was either sweating it straight out of his pores or he'd been brewing that poison here in the building.

"You can't get out through the windows," Franklin said, laughing again. "They're too small. And there are bars."

"Who says I want to get out?"

"There's fear in your voice."

"In yours too. And you...have a thorn in your brain."

"You're going to die here. You're going to be number nineteen."

"You've been busy. The baby was supposed to be number fifteen."

Crazed guffawing circling all around, that stench getting worse. Scuttling feet rushing along the floorboards. Who else was loose in the dark? Maybe the troll Crowfield Crenshaw, baring his green fangs, running across the floor causing mayhem, squeaking with his green-flecked lips, *"Let's try that again!"*

"This is my dark."

"It's as much mine as yours, Franklin. You just stay right there, okay? I'll be over in just a second."

TWENTY-SIX

Whitt aimed the gun straight up and fired once. The blast was so loud he let out a grunt of pain. Plaster sprinkled down from above. The noise reverberated and things in the blackness began moving in a terrified scramble. The flash gave off enough illumination for Whitt to see a rippling carpet of activity along the many slumped walls.

Franklin, at home here, must be flexing his powerful hands. He would let Whitt walk around all he wanted until Whitt finally stumbled past him. Then those fists would come out of nowhere. That was obvious and there wasn't much Whitt could do about it, except hope he lasted through the next throttling, too.

He heard that guffaw overhead and knew the guy had his head eased back, eyes rolling like hell. Franklin Prott's hands opening and closing, keeping perfect time with Whitt's speeding pulse, his ragged breathing, his reckless thoughts.

"You know nothing," Franklin said. Sounded like he might be on the third floor now. Maybe not.

"Well, a few things," Whitt admitted.

"Nothing of importance."

"There's no need to be rude, man."

Whitt swung into one doorway after another, wandering around bumping into junk. Killjoy must be nearby with a pair of binoculars, just laughing himself sick.

"Mucus-Thorn-In-Brain guides my step."

Franklin had to be following. His voice was much closer now, or seemed to be.

"Yeah, well, you're gonna get your ass severely beat down when Mucus-Thorn-In-Heart is born!"

"Thorn-In-Heart shall never be born!"

"He's already on his way."

As if there just weren't enough psychotic sons'a bitches in the world already. No, they had to go out of their way to take a normal advertising exec from the suburbs and make sure there was nowhere left for him to go except over the big edge.

Whitt thought about firing a few random shots, seeing if he could tag Franklin like that, but he just didn't want to be *that guy*, the kind of shooter who fires away out of fear. Not after going through all those fucking bottles.

He took the next staircase two steps at a time, searched the third floor as best he could before moving up the stairway again. But when he got to the fourth floor—the stink, it had softened too much. He knew he'd passed Prott somehow. The guy had to be below him.

Whitt returned down the stairs, doing what he could to watch all the hallways at once, the broken doors, the holes in the walls. There was just enough light for him to know he wasn't seeing much at all.

He heard a low noise coming from every direction and realized he was hearing rats chewing through the Sheetrock all over the factory.

In all the black corners, eating, breeding.

He turned and saw, outlined in the dimness, the silhouette of a woman wearing a long coat.

He thought, Okay, so Franklin's gone Anthony Perkins on me here, he's completely out of his head.

So what the hell, he's got the right to put on panties.

Or maybe it was Killjoy.

Thinking that perhaps Killjoy was a transvestite, stealing his wife's dresses and going out to murder and kidnap children.

Then, Whitt's mind racing along a track it had never gone before, thinking, Oh Christ, is Killjoy a woman?

Is that why he needs the mechanical voice disguiser? He's a her? How did that turn everything around? Whitt's mind flared with more possibilities than he'd been offered in years.

Now who was he looking for?

An ex-girlfriend? Some chick he'd gotten pregnant

back in college who held it against him so badly that she needed to kill his kid?

But behind the woman, stepping out into what little light there was, was Franklin Prott, with his hand on her throat.

He said, "Number nineteen."

Now Whitt could see Diana Carver, standing on her tiptoes, black eyes blazing as that impossibly strong killing arm dragged her up off her feet and, angling her jaw unnaturally toward her shoulder, began to break her neck.

TWENTY - SEVEN

Whitt pointed the .32 and fired.

He aimed about two feet to the right of Franklin's head, close to his ear but wide enough not to hit Diana. Maybe it'd shake Franklin up, loosen that powerful grip.

But it didn't. Franklin didn't care that somebody was firing a gun at him.

Even as the blast echoed, Whitt shouted so loud that blood swelled up his throat and across the back of his tongue. "Do something, Diana!"

That's how they did it on the cop shows on television anyway. You yell and your partner is ready at the perfect moment. She does her thing and you do yours, exactly right, and you're both just so slick.

Diana was well trained, not some part-time bullshit vigilante lugging rocks around somebody's backyard. She drove her elbow back into Franklin Prott's solar plexus, knowing exactly where to strike, then balled her fist and slammed it down hard against his crotch.

Whitt was impressed as hell, and a little disappointed that his senseis never taught him that one. He fired twice more, aiming for the same spot as before, then rushed forward.

All of it rattled Franklin Prott enough to weaken his grip. He didn't let go of Diana but she was able to get her feet back under her before Whitt's charge brought him up close.

Whitt pressed the barrel of the revolver against Franklin's head, but before he could pull the trigger the blind maniac dropped Diana Carver and squeezed his hands around Whitt's throat again.

Oh, this wasn't much better. This was actually downright bad. Whitt let out a yelp of agony and, weak-wristed as a painted geisha boy, he fired into the wall. The flash illuminated Franklin Prott's empty eyes so that, for an instant, Whitt could see straight up into the guy's brain, and he didn't like a damn thing he saw there.

He felt his neck about to snap, and had to drop the gun for the second time.

He grabbed hold of those fingers and pulled and twisted, lashing out with his knees, aiming for joints, the soft sweet spots. It was like hitting the frame of a '57 Chevy, but there was nothing else to do. Mama must've sprinkled a hell of a lot of salt around this place, making such a solid, protective magic circle.

Diana Carver had scrambled to her feet and was now helping him, the two of them chopping at

Franklin Prott in the places it was supposed to count, the blind crazy prick's laughter leaking out of him like vomit. But he wouldn't let go of Whitt's throat.

Whitt said, Giggle away, you bastard, first you, then the other. Except he didn't say it. His throat seized up on the first syllable and nothing more came out except that weird gagging noise. He was scared he wouldn't be able to say what he had to say to Killjoy when they finally met, frownie face to frownie face. Even though Whitt had no idea what it was he wanted to tell him.

Whitt thought, You know, all those rocks, they really didn't do much to help out. He felt a vast sorrow over the wasting of his time, imagining all the other useless things he could've been doing that wouldn't have hurt nearly as much.

They hammered Prott back into the stairwell, and he dragged Whitt along with him. It was fucking ridiculous, really, how strong this guy was. If they could get Franklin to the edge of the steps, he might release Whitt, flip over the rail, go tumbling and break his goddamn neck. But if the guy didn't die or snap his spine, then he'd be below them, cutting off their exit out of the building.

Diana Carver was coming up with all kinds of cool war cries. They sounded like the shouts Whitt's senseis would give before breaking bricks. Savage, orgasmic, the kinds of things you always hoped to make a chick scream in bed.

"Fall, damn you!" she screamed.

It was getting even tougher for Whitt to focus. He knew he was going down, his lungs ready to explode. He had maybe one good strike left to make before his legs gave out. He aimed for Prott's chest, directly over the heart.

Whitt tightened his fist, drew his arm back, swung his hips in a perfect meeting of action and form even though he was being throttled. Only remotely wondering if there were any dark gods waiting to be born inside of Franklin's heart. If they might just pop out.

But Diana Carver got there first, brushing Franklin back maybe two inches out of reach. Whitt hyperextended, hit the wooden railing, and heard a sound like thunder. Franklin whirled off-balance and finally let go.

The scurrying feet, the whispering chittering cries, swelled in his ears as Diana shoved Prott hard and the guy dropped silently through the cracked banister into greater blackness below.

Somewhere along the way Whitt had fallen down. He tried to stand and fell down again, wheezing and seeing the world grow wider with color and living blotches of motion at the edges of his vision.

"You are a very stupid person," Diana said, kneeling beside him, touching his throat.

"...thanks..."

"Don't talk. You've got a severely bruised trachea."

He wanted to ask if she had any water with her, hidden in the deep pockets of her coat. Women always carried water with them, forever dieting, terrified about gaining an extra molecule chain. But he didn't have to say it. She drew out a ten-ounce bottle and angled the mouth of it to his lips.

"Careful," she said. Whitt tried to swallow a sip. It was like drinking molten lead. He gagged, the ferocious colors in his vision pulsing, but eventually he could breathe again. He tried another sip and managed to work it down. His windpipe didn't feel crushed anymore, just scoured.

"There."

"Don't talk."

"I'm okay."

"No, you're not. We need to get you to a hospital."

"You all right?"

"My neck hurts a little, but he never managed to get his hands on me for long."

Whitt looked around. "You didn't bring a . . . flashlight either?"

"No," she admitted.

"And you call me stupid." He sat up. "What are you doing here?"

"Let's get outside to my car. I need the radio."

"You don't have a cell phone?"

"No."

"Why not?"

"Is that pertinent, Mr. Whitt? You're not supposed to be talking."

"So you rushed in here after a perp...without calling for backup?"

"Yes."

"Why didn't you use the radio when you came onto the scene? Don't you people ever follow protocol?"

Even in the dim light he saw a flicker of regret in her eyes. He knew why she'd burst in the way she had.

"You thought I was Killjoy, right? That I came in here to do...what? Filch kids from an empty apartment house? To duke it out with Prott...see who wins the serial killer crown?"

"All right, I was wrong."

"Not necessarily," Whitt said. "Even if I am Killjoy, that doesn't alter the fact that Franklin wants us dead."

"You really go out of your way to make it difficult to like you."

"Next time someone thinks I'm an insane murderer I'll try to be more pleasant. Why the hell don't you have a cell phone?"

The weak yellow light backlit her so that her bangs looked like talons around her face. He started reaching for her, to brush her hair away, but his hand was much too slow and she tapped his wrist aside. He needed more time to recover.

"I threw it away after I broke up with my boyfriend."

"The married guy."

"I never got around to getting another one."

"Use mine," he said, patting his pocket, finding it gone.

"I tried already. You landed on it during your fight with Prott. It's behind you, in pieces."

"Where's your gun?" he asked.

"I dropped it when he attacked me. It's somewhere on the first floor. He carried me up the stairs like I was a Dresden doll."

"Mine's around here on the floor someplace. I thought he was up higher. I passed him somehow. He could've come up behind me anytime. There's no other way out except down past him."

"Maybe he's dead on the landing."

"We're not that lucky."

"No, we're not."

The way she said it, like they really were partners, who'd suffered together for years through the worst life had to offer, made him grin.

"Are you ready yet?" she asked.

"Sure," Whitt said. He climbed to his feet, staggered two steps, and fell down.

"What the hell happened to your mouth? Your lips are all bruised too."

"I came in second in a kissing contest," he said, trying to get up again.

"Stop moving. I'd probably like you more if you weren't always such a wiseass."

"No, you wouldn't. You dig my verve."

"Excuse me?"

He leaned against a wall and it nearly buckled under his weight. "Help me find my gun."

She searched for a minute among all the shadows and scrap heaps. "Where?"

"I don't know." He kept his head down, searching the floor. They were running out of time. His nerves were squirming, knees twitching. "Hey, you want to go dancing later?"

"Stop talking. Jesus, you sound awful. How about if we just focus on the situation at hand?"

"Sorry . . . I'm a little jazzed at the moment."

"You're in shock. Probably oxygen-deprived."

"Okay."

"What kind of a place is this?"

"I think it was a warehouse once. Don't ask me for what. Then they turned it into cheap apartments . . . for the factory workers, maybe. They didn't do much re-modeling though. There's also a front gate that locks from the outside. We're probably stuck in here."

"How could he lock us in if he's already inside with us?"

"Killjoy did it," Whitt said, and couldn't help chuckling.

"Don't laugh like that."

"Sorry."

"You're happy he's here."

"He'll be along soon. I'm going to finally get my

hands on him. By the way, get ready for more bad news."

"What?"

"He'll probably hit the fuse box. I turned the lights on when I walked in. One of them is going to shut them off. Find my gun before it happens."

"Shit."

He wondered if she was going to give him a lecture on how stupid he was, a civilian running around an abandoned warehouse with a .32 in hand, but she was smart enough to be worried. And she was starting to believe in him, even though he was dopey enough to talk about dancing when he should've warned her earlier about the lights.

"I can't find it."

"Grab a pipe or a piece of rebar, we need weapons."

"Where?"

"Look around!"

When the lights went out he dove against her. They had to stay in contact in the dark. He heard her soft gasp echo off the walls, coming back at him loudly, and damn sexy—Christ, the closer you were to death the closer you were to wanting to get in a final lay. To drape your tongue in the channels of her gorgeous scars. She shifted in his arms. The two of them isolated in their reasons for being here, but brought together in all kinds of sorrow. It was romantic, really.

He held her tightly in the darkness and she said, "Let me the fuck go."

* * *

"What's that noise?" she whispered in his ear.

"Music," Whitt told her.

"That's supposed to be music?"

"It is to that maniac."

"But what is it?"

"Rats."

It stopped her. "I thought, for a second—"

"Yeah, I know." The squeaks and coos and breathy murmurs. "Could've been babies."

"It's music to him?"

"Yeah, I guess he likes rats. It's music to Killjoy because he likes babies."

"My God."

"How's Franklin able to move through this junk all over the place when he can't even see?" she asked.

"Did you look at his eyes?"

"Yes. And you're right, he is blind."

"Yeah, but it's presumptuous to think he's weak. Some other Cosmic Knot cult members were probably staying here for a while. At first I thought the owner of the building had broken it up into illegal apartments. Maybe that's how it started. But eventually squatters and the Protts and their followers turned up."

"Jesus Christ, how many of them are there?"

"Who the hell knows? A bunch of loonies who just

happened to run into each other and decided to hang out together. You and Brunkowski should sift through all this shit. Maybe you can find names of their followers who you haven't nabbed yet."

"I know my job, don't tell me my job."

"And you say I'm not pleasant."

"Well, you're not."

"Listen, Little Miss Task Force, I'm here for a reason."

"I know your reason."

"I want to find the man who murdered my daughter. I'm not tailing Killjoy because I played footsies with my boss in Quantico."

"Why, you rotten son of a bitch!" she hissed in his ear. "Who the hell are you to talk to me like that?"

"I don't have to be amicable, I'm a crazy person."

"Give it a rest, will you. As it is, I might just book you anyway. Now stop talking. If you can't move soon, I'll have to do it alone."

"You'd miss me too much. Give me another minute." Whitt paused. "Listen, it's really been bugging the crap out of me..."

"Oh Christ."

"Are you an 'agent' or an 'officer' or a 'miss' or what?"

She wasn't surprised. She must get the question five times a day at the precinct. "I'm still 'agent' but I don't know how long that's going to last."

"Keep kicking up a stink. If you fold now, they'll just roll over you."

"Thanks for the advice."

"Don't sneer."

"It's pitch-black and you can't see my face."

"I can sense sneers. I get them a lot."

"You are a very strange person."

"Now," he said, "is that nice?"

"It's the truth."

"Well, yeah," he said. "But don't take your eye off the ball."

"Shh."

"Just remember, this isn't about Franklin Prott or his mother's dumb-ass mucus group. It's all about Killjoy."

"If Franklin Prott is the only torpedo for the cult, then he's possibly more dangerous than Killjoy. They pulled a lot of bodies out of the ground at the Prott homes."

"He said the ballerina, Grace Kinnick, was number fourteen. The baby would've been fifteen."

"I was going to be nineteen."

"So Killjoy is still the worse serial killer, if you go by stats like that."

"I don't, really, and we're not splitting hairs when counting corpses. I wouldn't want either of them over for a Fourth of July picnic."

"How about me?"

"You either."

"I'm only in this to get the man who murdered my daughter."

"I realize that."

"There's no way for me to make this sound hip, but if Killjoy shows, he's mine. Let's go."

She said nothing to that even as the sound of the squeaking and whimpering vermin everywhere around them grew much louder. As if thousands more had suddenly been let in, poured in, dredged up from city sewers, and somehow—it was true in the end, this symphony of scuttling madness, like a nursery full of newborns, it did lighten Whitt's soul.

TWENTY-EIGHT

The fever wanted to take Whitt but he fought it back, moving down the staircase while Diana trailed behind him, his head loud with a blitzkrieg of his own words and memories. He heard his daughter say, *"Oh think of the mess, how can we be bothered? Daddy, let us dance!"*

"What's the matter?" Diana asked.

"Nothing."

"You made a noise."

"It's nothing."

They had found short pieces of rebar stacked in one of the hallways, each about two feet in length. This was a better way to do it, but still not the best way. Whitt tapped the bar against the cracked banister. He knew Prott could sense them parting the deep blackness. Killjoy might be outside, beyond the locked front door. Or he might already have entered the building, to wait in the corner, ready to turn the lights back on and bear witness.

Diana kept a hand on his shoulder, not pulling any of this, I'm the cop, I'll go first crap. He appreciated it, whatever the reason she was doing it. Having her breath on his neck, her chest pressed against his back, made the fear go down easier.

They passed the area on the stairs where Prott's body should've been if he'd busted his neck from the fall. They'd been right. They weren't that lucky.

Whitt tapped the walls and floor softly with the re-bar, using it like a blind man's cane. The rats started scurrying loudly ahead of them. He kept shifting his stance by degrees, weaving a little this way and that, wondering from which direction Franklin Prott's hands might come. He kept his left fist up, protecting his throat.

"Stop that," she whispered.

"What?"

"You're laughing again."

"Sorry."

"We need to get you to a hospital."

Her warm breath worked into his shoulders. Her heat massaged its way into his muscles. Strengthening what was weak, shoring up a couple of cracks. Imagining how you win the day and get the girl. Except that the blade of guilt was always there, waiting to slice away your simple hopes of being attracted to anyone ever again. Whitt thought of Karen in her small, perfectly Ted-decorated apartment. Sarah's face hidden beneath a veil of roses.

Your mood lifted for a second, and then the heel of God came down on it again.

Whitt, in the dark, not wanting to dance anymore. Not tittering anymore.

"Franklin?" he called. "I know the Testament of Ya'al. I live it. I love it. I'll share it with the rest of the world. I have them all with me. Hogarth. Pedantry. Airsiez."

"You do not," Franklin said, his voice echoing close, like the guy was applauding himself right under Whitt's nose.

"Colby. Terminus. Insensate."

"They're dead."

"Your brother kept them bottled up afterwards, and he gave them to me."

"His games mean nothing."

"Ussel. Dr. Dispensations. Everybody's here. O'Mundanity. Kinnick. Grace Kinnick. The ballerina. She's with me now."

"That's not who that woman is."

"Of course it is. You failed . . . twice now to complete the mission set before you. That's why your mother sent me to take you out of the game. She drew a magic circle of salt around me, I'm safe. I'm protected. I'm absolved, man. Me and the Cosmic Knot? We're getting it on."

He and Diana turned the corner and slowly eased down the final staircase, back to the ground floor. Whitt had a fair sense of where they stood, of how far it would be for him to take a run for the lights. Slap them on and see Killjoy standing there, his voice disguiser pressed to his throat, frownie face tugging his mouth out of whack. The trouble would be in not tripping over all the crap.

Dim, ambient illumination from the streetlamps shone through the small, high windows and cast a strange glow across the place.

He moved out ahead of Diana and she tapped his shoulder with the rebar. Part warning, telling him to stay close. Part threat, don't get too far ahead. This might be how the detectives did it, the feebs, in this situation, but he was here for another reason.

The world is only as wide as you want it to be. With a great detachment he saw the roof caving in, the meager walls tightening, and all the remnants of the warehouse like the pieces of his life pushing back into him. Between his ribs, through his eyes, and back into his head. Franklin swept into his arms, and behind Prott, Killjoy. The only way to take control was to step off the bottom stair and move out to meet them.

Whitt tossed the rebar aside and listened to it clatter on the floor, rolling for a second before striking metal. It was a stupid weapon, as bad as the gun. Some questions could only be answered in bone and teeth.

Diana said, "Was that you?"

"Yeah."

"What did you do?"

"Come on."

He reached behind and touched her arm, moved along the curve of her elbow until he got her free hand and clasped it. He tugged her along toward the lights and she hissed, "Slow down."

"When it starts, just walk straight ahead and hit the breakers. Killjoy's here but he won't stop you."

"I said slow down."

"Franklin's behind us, can't you feel it?"

Repentance. A picnic basket. Value. Transformation. *Significum Harlequenin*. Incision. The words providing him with his own protection. Whitt stopped, sensing fingers coming for him again, nearly there... *nearly*... and then he shoved Diana Carver forward. Whitt spun, lifting his elbow to strike Prott on the point of his jaw. You do that right and you can kill a man, drive his jawbone up through his brain. Knowing the bastard was there, Whitt twirled through the air, nearly pirouetting, hitting nothing. Rats brushed against his ankles.

The lights burst on and Diana Carver stood there twenty feet away with her hand on the breaker, holding the rebar up, staring at him.

She started to speak but there was no need, sometimes you're on time and sometimes you're too late. You miss your chance but your chance doesn't miss you, no.

Franklin was directly behind Whitt, those hands coming around for his neck again. He let out that titter and Whitt somehow matched him. Diseased laughter all over the place.

"Still hear my fear, Franklin? I hear yours."

This was it, everybody had wasted enough time already. Whitt kicked out behind him, catching Franklin in his crotch but feeling nothing give beneath his heel. Maybe the Protts had already taken care of their own packages. He lashed out again, turning slightly, so the edge of his foot would strike Franklin's knee. The pop of cartilage snapping echoed like fireworks. Franklin laughed louder. There was no reason in this world why the guy should be able to take such punishment. He shouldn't be this tough. All of the hopped truck drivers that Whitt had stomped were bigger, rougher, meaner too. But the snarled karmic knot had its own reasons for tying people together, until you couldn't be sure if you were trying to beat the hell out of a blind guy or just out of yourself. You did the same amount of damage to both.

Diana Carver came up behind them and started slamming the rebar into Franklin's chest. He got his fists up and tagged her hard in the face, but she didn't go down. Whitt pummeled Franklin's ribs but it still wasn't enough, and he watched the maniac backhand her sharply. Blood gushed from her nose as she fell aside and rolled hard into a pile of rusted machinery.

A soothing whisper drifted up from the muddy bottom of his soul, telling him to go with it, that everything would be all right. That it was good, *so good, so right, it's what you've been waiting for*...

Whitt's last 1 percent.

He lunged at Prott and squeezed his hands around the blind man's throat.

All of his hate bundled into his chest, as he drew Franklin near and stared into those blank eyes. "Okay, strangler, let's see how many hours you put into... building up your Adam's apple."

Then Franklin's hands came up and the two of them throttled each other, giggling in each other's faces.

If you were going to kill, you ought to be certain enough about it to do it with a smile.

If you were going to die, you might as well go out laughing.

The frenzy consumed Whitt as he clutched tighter, realizing at last that Franklin's arms looked wrong, the guy's hands weren't around Whitt's neck anymore, he was trying to pull Whitt's fingers off his throat. They had both fallen to their knees but Whitt hadn't let go. He sniffed and didn't smell turpentine anymore. Instead, it was an odor he'd smelled only once before. In his car, in the garage with the motor running, as his brain began to seize. Not death but the arrival of our ultimate reasons for dying. The flowery scent of hopelessness. The stench of watery shit running down your leg seconds before you give yourself over to a lesser fear than life itself.

Prott fell sideways and Whitt hit the ground beside

him, hacking and sucking air through his mouth like a dying bass. His lips blew soft ripples in a small puddle of Diana Carver's blood.

A white foam filled his skull. Another few minutes of this and he thought he might be able to get a good night's sleep, with no dreams, finally.

And now:

Rising from behind a short stack of tires, unfurling inch by inch, just a few feet away. Capering forward.

Wearing, get this—

A pillowcase over his head with the eyes cut out.

The frown painted on it like the face of a sad harlequin.

The downturned mouth looming closer, like it wanted to kiss.

Whitt tried to stand.

He got his hands under him and some kind of yellow froth spilled across his chin. He gasped wildly, but the air wasn't getting to wherever it had to go.

He'd always known Killjoy would be waiting for him at his weakest moment.

That frown, gazing at him, the same way it had stared up from the pillow over Sarah's blue face. The rotten fuck—his clothes were black and plain—he seemed to have a gut. Whitt tried to note everything, but the black stars before his eyes were bursting, going nova. The baby . . . he was holding a baby . . .

The voice disguiser working just fine. *"Hello, Whitt."*

Whitt reached out and threw everything he had into one punch. It wasn't much and he had to be careful not to hit the kid. His knuckles barely tapped Killjoy's belly and it was like hitting a sack of laundry. What did he have on under there? Another set of clothes?

A rumble of thunder rolled through Whitt's chest. He coughed up blood. Sweat streamed into his eyes. The searing crimson swirls taking over his mind.

I've failed, it's all been for nothing.

Face to frownie face and he was helpless as . . .

Killjoy lowered the newborn into Whitt's arms.

"Don't give this one back, Whitt, or you'll make me angry."

He capered away.

Whitt, heading off to sleep or death, held the kid close and thought, Mine. She's mine, this is my girl.

TWENTY-NINE

A needle in the heart, that'll sure wake your dead ass up.

Adrenaline.

They were working on him, moving fast in the operating room. Nobody looking too happy. Machines buzzed and caterwauled, the kind of beeping you hear in a movie just as a bomb goes off.

A nurse said, "He's awake."

The doctor, a real champ, told her, "That's impossible. He can't hear us. Tape his eyes shut again, and this time do it right."

Whitt tried to ask about the baby, but his neck had been opened up, retractors peeling the flesh of his throat aside, the cartilage cracked. Tubes snaked up his nose and down into his lungs. He could discern their weight inside of him, veering to different parts of his body. He could feel the doctor's fingers in there doing something at the back of his throat, moving around. It was an oddly appealing sensation.

He thought, What if this is it? What if I'm paralyzed? I don't want to have to hold a laser in my teeth and point it at the coffeemaker, have the monkeys go make me double lattes. Fetch my slippers, boys, now go start up the hovercart.

He imagined his apartment covered with monkey turds, Mike Bowman walking in and watching all these little anthropoids on the couch, jerking off to late-night cable.

The nurse taped his eyes shut, pressing forcefully on the lids. Whitt waited a moment and then opened them again. The thin pieces of tape held for a second then popped loose. He glanced around and made eye contact with the doctor, mouthed, Where's my kid?

They scampered around yelling and turning knobs, everybody blaming somebody else, and soon he dropped off to sleep.

They talked a lot about drainage. All these pouches filled with blood, shit, piss, and pus hanging off the bed, everything coming from him. It was enough to make you start believing in original sin. All these disgusting fluids coursing around inside you.

He was wrapped in gauze and bandages, covered in stitches, but not as many as he would've expected.

The big shocker, of course, was that he had a tracheotomy tube sticking out of his throat.

Breathing felt weird as hell, like he had an extra nose

six inches below his other one. They promised it was only for a few days, to aid with his air intake during the healing process. They gave him a pad and pen and told him to write out his answers. He wrote, *Will I ever be able to talk again?*

The doctors and nurses, there was a revolving band of them, all assured him he'd be able to speak in whispers within a couple of weeks. They asked if he wanted an Electrolarynx. He didn't know what it was. Finally somebody brought one in and explained how it worked. You held the microphone up to your throat and it made your voice sound like a *death angel of God, sent down from the desert mountains with a sword dipped in blood—*

He wrote, *No thank you. I'll stick with the pen and paper.*

A dentist had been brought in at some point and had pulled a few of Whitt's cracked teeth, most of them too far in the back to affect his smile much. His tongue kept prodding and working away at the holes. It gave him something to do while the time drifted by.

Except for his throat, he felt pretty much okay. They put needles into his IV tubes a couple times a day for the pain, but he never felt sleepy or muddled. He kept asking about Prott, Killjoy, the baby, Diana Carver, but nobody would answer him. They kept saying that somebody would visit him soon to discuss all that with him. They spoke to him like he was a child. Being mute was like not being there at all. When you couldn't leave the bed and couldn't shout, it made it easy for them to ignore your ass, so long as they stayed out of arm's reach.

"Seventy-five seconds on the far side of the river," Brunkowski said. "And still you came back. Not too shabby."

Brunk's eyes were pretty bad and he had to peer at Whitt's notes for a second, trying hard to read them.

Why didn't you get here sooner?

"Docs wouldn't let me in any sooner. You were dead on the table for more than a minute. It's only been three days since they brought you in."

Whitt looked around, puzzled. It had felt much longer than that. Maybe he had been a little murky and hadn't realized it.

Prott?

"Dead. You throttled him pretty nicely. I want a full statement from you on what happened, starting with the minute you got a lead on where to find him. Sergeant Stensford will be up here a little later to take it."

OK.

"Your father-in-law was here yesterday while you were sleeping. He checked in on you, sat with you for a while. Oh, and some chubby guy stopped by too. He brought flowers and candy, but the nurse said you're not allowed to have either in the room. They're out at

her station. I figured, if you're not going to use them,
I'll take them home to my wife."

Feel free, you fuck.

"Thanks."

How's Agent Carver?

"She's going to be all right."

Good.

"They held her overnight because they wanted to
give her a CAT scan, make sure that knock on the
head didn't cause any serious damage. She's gotta wear
this protective metal shield on her face because of the
busted nose. Makes her look kinda sexy. Those eyes
glaring at everything, you know? But she filled us in
on what happened and she's taking some heat for
this whole thing. What you did was stupid, but she
should've followed protocol. Civilians are allowed to
be dumb, but feebs aren't. She comes down here because she says everybody else botched the case and
then she pulls a bush-league move like this that nearly
gets both of you killed."

My fault.

"Sure, but she still made a bunch of rookie mistakes.
You're lucky. If Prott had twisted your head around a
little more, you'd be paralyzed and hooked up to a res-
pirator."

Strong son of a bitch. Didn't seem to feel pain.

"You did good. Bare-handed too."

Where's my gun?

"Recovered at the scene. You'll get it back when you

leave the hospital. You got three shots off and missed all three?"

It was the circumstances. And we were in the dark.

"Right. Neither of you thought to bring a flashlight?"

He thought about it for a minute. *Fools rush in.* Whitt felt an odd tremor move through his stomach. He wrote: *The kid?*

Brunk broke down and just put his reading glasses on. They made him look like a constipated accountant. "She's doing fine. We'll talk more on that later. First... was he there?"

Y.

"You saw him?"

Y.

"You get a look at his face?"

N. He was hiding in that warehouse. But after the fight with Prott, K poked his head up and danced across the floor.

"Danced? Actually danced?"

Capered. Wearing a pillowcase on his head. Holding the baby.

"Clothes?"

I was suffocating. Didn't notice much except they were black.

"What aren't you telling me?" he said.

??

"There's something more. I got you in focus a while back. I know when you're lying to me."

Whitt didn't think he was holding anything back, but then again, maybe he was. The thing about trying to punch Killjoy in the stomach, and hitting—what? Fat? A pillow? He thought about Mary Laramore pretending to be pregnant. Was that Killjoy's game? Jesus. Did he run around pretending to be a pregnant woman? Imagine that being part of his construct, trying to breast-feed the babies with his hairy man-nipples.

Cops say that sort of thing because they hear it in a perp's voice. What? You can tell by my trembling script?

"You're one of those honest types. It works against your grain trying to bullshit somebody."

There's nothing.

Brunk pulled his tough guy face, tried to do the leaning over with his tight shirtsleeves gesture, but he couldn't plant his fists correctly on the hospital bed. "Still think you're in charge, smarter than everybody else. Gonna hold on to it, huh? You still haven't learned anything? You do that and it'll eat you alive from the inside."

How about if you fuck off, eh? Sitting up in bed, setting his teeth on edge and not feeling a couple of the molars anymore.

"You ain't gonna be happy until you swing at me, are you?"

Probably not!

"Anytime. As soon as you're out of the bed and ready."

Whitt shifted, the bags of sin bouncing all over as he brought his right arm around in the proper stance. The way he should've hit Prott but hadn't been able to at the time. He laid one into Brunkowski's gut.

Brunk staggered two steps backward and nearly went down. Doubled over, he rested his hands on his knees for a second, before he stood and wiped the back of his hand against his lips. "One is all you get for free."

Jesus, he'd just punched a cop. Can you really do jail time for that? No matter how big an asshole the flatfoot is? *It's all I needed. Sorry.*

"Don't be, you deserved it. You were right that day in my office. I've been using you from the beginning, because I had nothing else."

You still don't.

"Well, we've got one thing. He left you another note. It was pinned to the baby's diaper."

We are in need of equals. But we hate them.

We now come to the tale of Padmasahavablastaonspringbreaka and Llamallamagoldstein, called Po and Lo, twin brothers and Tibetan Buddhist monks following their scholarly pursuits in the Temple of Qing Zang Gaoyuan.

Nestled in Namzha Parwa mountain, where the headwaters of the Indus and Brahmaputra Rivers run and the landscape is desolate, barren, and rock-strewn, dappled with the occasional Dairy Queen and Buck's Bait Shop. There they practiced the martial arts and sciences. They were also missionaries who wandered during the summer months along the "Roof of the World" and helped develop an alphabet for the Tibetan language, initiating translations of the sacred religious texts, struggling against shamanism and black magic, and dissuading men with low sperm counts from wearing briefs made of yeti fur.

Unable to fully stamp out the shamanist principles, they modified their teachings of the Mahayana theistic school, with expansions of modified Shivaism and Catholic guilt.

Po, "born of the lotus blossom," and Lo, "gimme more opium smoka," spread the word of Buddhist worship, which consists mainly in reciting prayers and sacred texts and chanting hymns to the accompaniment of horns, trumpets, and drums. Po and Lo also fronted the famed Dalai Lama Garage Band, which had a brief #1 hit in 741 AD with "Stay Away from Runaround Ommanipadme, Bodhisattva Man (If You Know What's Good For You)."

For this worship, which takes place three times a day, the clergy are summoned by the tolling of a bell and are seated in rows according to their rank. Po and Lo being the highest except for the Dalai Lama, the Bogodo Lama, and the Hobilghans, who've undertaken various ethical and spiritual disciplines with a view to achieving complete enlightenment and priapism. These orders constitute the higher clergy.

The lower clergy has four orders: the novice, the assistant priest, the religious mendicant, and the teacher of phys ed. Followed by yet another suborder, that of the lunchroom ladies, the substitutes, and the assistant principals. The members of each order must take a vow of celibacy and an oath never to wrestle midgets. As we all know, most monks break their pledges and are sent back into the world, disgraced and outcast from the Little People bars.

But though Po and Lo were twin brothers, of the same status, equal in every way, still Po began to grow envious of Lo. Perhaps because, as he washed his face in the pool of edification, he did not see himself, but instead always saw the face of Lo.

And, knowing his own weaknesses of character and body and mind, assumed that his brother was the stronger in all these facets.

Still fearing his ties to the world, he performed his rituals with that much greater vigor, hoping that the esoteric mysticism of Tantra, yoga and mantra, the formulae of spirit, and the ancient shamanistic practices that he'd come to embrace would lighten his burden.

During the great Feast of Flowers the temples, shrines, and altars were decorated with symbolic offerings of milk, tea, flour, pancake, ox-tail soup, exfoliation cream, proven moisturizers, sensual body mist, spray-on glosser, fresh white musk parfums de coeur, and similar gifts brought by the worshipers. Though animal sacrifices were strictly forbidden, Po began to plan how the offering of his own brother to the Buddha might be the greatest concession he could make.

Under the pretense of giving up the life of his brother for

the greater enlightenment of all, Po slew Lo with a ceremonial bidet. Though the abbot and acolytes were fooled by the apparent selflessness in this murder, the Dalai Lama understood it for what it was—a hatred of self. The Dalai Lama, comprehending the misery that inspired Po's act of violence, forgave him his transgressions. He allowed Po to grow a Vandyke and cornrows so he would never again see his brother's face in the pools of edification. Po, learning self-love, lived to be one hundred and four years old, and upon his death was heard to say, "I really like myself." In his next reincarnation, Po returned to this world as both Eng and Chang, the original Siamese Twins who fathered twenty-one children between them, all named Lotus Blossom.

Though we hate them, we are in need of our equals.

Don't cross me, Whitt.

Bring the child home.

Watch her grow.

Find your wife.

Resolve your world.

Revert.

THIRTY

When he next awoke Diana Carver was sitting in a chair beside him, writing notes on a Palm Pilot. The blankets at the foot of the bed were covered with color-coded files, neatly labeled. Psychiatric Reports. Killjoy Letters. Interviews & Statements. Case #31454 (Edward Whitt).

She had her right arm in a lightweight half cast, an empty sling around her neck. One side of her face was covered with bandages, her nose protected by one of those metal shield face masks. Kind of made her look like a superhero. She glanced down at him and said, "Don't talk."

He grinned just far enough so that she couldn't see the holes in his smile. He was going to need a couple of bridges if he was ever going to give anybody the full pearly white wattage again. The trache was gone and so were a couple of bags of original sin. He started voice therapy at the end of the week.

Making any progress?

"Probably not, but it gives me something to do."

You look cool. Gonna have a few extra scars to take the edge off those looks.

"Take such an edge off I'll never get another date. How're you feeling?"

Has anyone told my wife?

"No, but I called and talked to the chief of staff there, and some guy named Ted. He said he was her 'assistant.' I didn't want to give out too much over the phone, not fully knowing the situation. I said you'd been hurt, but not seriously. I take it she hasn't called."

N.

"I'm sorry."

Don't be. Ted didn't give her the message.

"New boyfriend?"

In a way. Did you find my .32?

"Yes, it'll be returned to you later."

Now, please.

"I can't give you a weapon in a hospital. Be reasonable."

He thought, After what we just went through, she wants me to be reasonable.

Diana leaned back in her chair and gave him one of those casual, long looks that only cops can really give. Thoughtful, questioning, resolved, rough, and ultimately meaningless.

Her cast was clean. No signatures, no children's pictures on it. Bunnies, roses, hearts. The hell was up with this woman?

What are your kids' names?

She tensed, and the dark eyes started glittering. "Will and Maria. I miss them too much. It hurts, you . . . ?"

About to say, you know? Like he might not. Might've forgotten what it was like, missing your kid.

Are you a good mother?

"What kind of a question is that? How am I supposed to answer that?" Her top teeth caught her bottom lip for an instant. She almost called him Mr. Whitt again, but must've realized how formal it sounded. But she couldn't make herself say his first name.

Honestly.

She took her time, extending the moment while she put pages back into the files, tidied the folders up, bringing them together, a stack of worthless guesses. "Not that it's any of your business, but yes, I am. They're with my parents in Manhattan right now."

Your ex doesn't see them?

"He flies down on weekends. I'm usually not around. My parents still like him though, so it's not so bad. And the kids adore him. That's what's important. Why are you asking me these questions?"

Gives me something to do.

"You just relax and let me get back to doing my job."

We're in this together.

"No, we're not." Saying it petulantly, like a kid who acts spiteful just to get attention from her daddy. "You've got to get that through your head."

Yeah, that'll happen soon.

They stared at each other for a while. Calmly, sort of pensively. Peeling away whatever they could, making assumptions. Running reveries out to whatever end, and then reeling them back in. She cocked her head and drew back her chin sharply, as if some stray thought had just hit her and impacted badly. She suddenly thumped the files on the mattress and the bed rattled, his bags of sin shaking around him. A nurse came in and gave him a handful of pills which he swallowed with some difficulty. It felt like it would never get any easier, even though it already was.

After the nurse left, Diana Carver licked her lips and he thought, Okay, here it comes.

But she said nothing, and after another minute of silence his mind cooled and flattened, and he was thinking about Sarah in her coffin again, Karen fainting at the funeral.

Any info on the kid?

Her expression, what he could see of it under the mask, was sad. "Yes, her name is Amy Morgan. Just under a year old. She'd been missing for about twelve hours. Taken from here, this hospital, the pediatric wing. Family Services were already investigating the mother and her boyfriend. He's a small-time drug dealer, doesn't like crying babies disturbing his nod. He yells a lot, pushes her kids around. She's got four. Nothing too serious, but he did grab Amy too roughly. Bruised her up, cut the back of her head when she fell against a kitchen drawer. Local PD had been watching

him for a while anyway. He's just troublesome enough
that they want to bust him. Him and the girlfriend and
the three other kids all came in with Amy, and they
started fighting in the emergency room. Somebody
called the cops. The mother wanted him out of the
house, but she's got a drug problem herself. She's a
dancer at the Tender Trap."

Whitt nodded. He'd been there once before with his
buddies years ago, back when he'd had some.

"She turns tricks every once in a while. Been in and
out of rehab. She's a fighter, but she got sucked into the
cycle. When they brought Amy into the emergency
room, the staff checked the baby in for twenty-four-
hour observation. The cops were getting everybody's
story down, this close to arresting the boyfriend. Then
Amy disappeared. Killjoy snatched her right out from
under everybody's noses."

Is the mother here now?

"No, she took the baby home as soon as she was returned. A pair of cops escorted her and watched while
the boyfriend packed up and left the apartment. He
won't be back. He knows there's a lot of heat on him
now. Maybe she'll have a chance to get totally clean
without him around."

It was a break in the pattern. Why would Killjoy
take the kid from the hospital? What had he been doing here? It was sloppy. A knee-jerk reaction. Ballsy too,
slipping right past the police. Why?

"Could he be a doctor? A pediatrician?"

Whitt thought about it for a while. A doctor, with access to children, the healthy and the hurt, with all the files he'd ever need right there at the tips of his fingers. Press a key and up comes somebody's entire life, their address, their work hours. He remembered that the seventy-five-year-old Viennese profiler had suggested the possibility of Killjoy's being a pediatrician. Or a nurse. Or a janitor in a hospital. The feebs had checked at the time.

The FBI checked.

"I know, but we could run another."

Only lead you down the wrong track. N. Not a doctor. Not a teacher. Not a janitor. Not a school groundskeeper.

"Why do you say that?"

That's what you'd expect a child killer to be. He'd have been caught by now if it was the case. Killjoy is different. He's other.

She typed more notes into her Palm Pilot. He knew she was going to check again anyway. It was the way she'd been trained.

"Why you?" she said. "Why's he stay in contact with you?"

My natural charm?

"I suspect not."

Now you're being mean again.

She almost smiled, but not quite. Then, squinting, glaring at him but not at him, looking all the way through him again, she said, "You were there."

Where?

"At the beginning. At his inception. When he made up his mind to kill."

Sure.

"You knew that?"

Sure. But when and where?

"There's no way to tell from the outside. Maybe at your daughter's preschool? A playground? What drives him?"

Whitt sat up farther. *The things he loves and the things he hates.*

"Then he'll keep on doing this until when? Until his penance is up? Until he has a bad day and starts killing children again?"

You're never going to figure it out. Whitt pointed at her. He tapped the note again. Underlined the 'You're.' Then added, *I will.*

"Oh, and why is that?"

He's going to tell me who he is.

"When?"

When he removes his veil. He told me as much. He's cracking.

That surprised her, made her stick a foot up against the bed, push back in her chair. "Why?"

He's not used to happiness. It's driving him even crazier.

"And then what will happen?"

I have it on good authority he'll kill me.

"Whose authority?"

My own.

She grimaced again, gave him the brutal stare. "What?"

He was losing ground. *Forget it. It doesn't matter. Not so long as I get him first.*

"Wait, what are you saying, Mr. Whitt?"

Jesus, after all we've been through you're still calling me 'mister'?

"All right, Ed."

Eddie.

"You talk more with this damn notepaper than you did when you were speaking. Goddamn, Eddie, you need professional help!"

Doesn't everybody?

Giving the grin again, and getting about the same result.

"No. We've all got problems, but you . . . you're clearly on the verge of a nervous collapse. Spending years tracking this maniac and getting nowhere, making absolutely no progress. Alone, with your wife in a psychiatric facility. No job to ground you. Beating up truckers to let off steam. No woman at home. No social life at all. One close friend who's more than a little eccentric in his own right. You've given up everything. You've allowed Killjoy to win."

Maybe you're right.

"I am right."

But that's the price to get Killjoy. I told you we should've gone dancing.

"Stay in bed and rest and who knows? Maybe after you get out of here, we will."

It was a lure, he realized. Bait to keep him around. He didn't mind. She must have known from the way he looked at her that she had her hooks deep in him, through no fault of her own. Or his either, really.

You couldn't help who you fell for, or why. It should've been okay for the moment, but he couldn't stop thinking that things just weren't going to play out the right way. In another time it would've been heart-wrenching. Tragic, maybe. Or just funny. Just like it had been between him and Karen.

Do me a favor. I need my cell phone back.

Her arm must've started bothering her. She straightened the empty sling and, with her free hand, guided the cast back into it. "Your cell? It's trashed, remember? It was smashed in the fight. I tried calling for help from the warehouse."

Right. But I need a phone. With that same number.

"So Killjoy can reach you."

Right.

"We can try to tap in on it."

No. He's too smart. He won't call if there's a chance.

"He won't know."

He knows everything else.

"He's not God, Mr. Whitt."

He's as crazy as God, Agent Carver.

"The fuck does that mean?"

He was starting to realize that a lot of the stuff he

said just didn't have the same oomph on paper. He shook his head.

"I read his latest letter. There's never been such a blunt referencing to direct correlation between the two of you."

Not correlation. Reflection.

"Yes, but how so? Are you reflecting him or he you?"

Same thing to him. He thinks we're the same. Or have been the same. Or are becoming the same.

"Why?"

He moved his foot beneath the blankets and the action caused her paperwork to slide away from her. *Whatever it is, it's not in your files.*

"How do you know?"

You would've found it by now.

"Then it's in his letters."

Not there either. I would've found it by now.

"So where do you think it is?"

His head. And my past. Whitt's hand was starting to cramp, but he gunned the words out. *We met somewhere. It was important to him. But I don't remember it. Now he wants me to go back to the man I once was. To revert.* Whitt grinned, and it made her draw away from him. He tossed the pad onto the bed, directly in front of her. *He's scared. He knows I'm going to kill him.*

THIRTY - ONE

His first night back in his apartment, with the trache tube out and his voice sounding like UHF static, Whitt woke from the usual nightmares and answered his new cell phone. Freddy Fruggman said, "I had a dream where I was very small."

"You did?"

"It was fucking seriously eerie, man, staring out at such a huge world. Especially for me. I'm usually too goddamn big and fat for the regular world. By the way, I left candy and flowers. Did you get them, or did the nurses take 'em home?"

"I got them, thank you."

"You gotta watch that shit, they'll rob you blind. What they don't take themselves they toss in the garbage. They threw out my grandmother's dentures. She left them wrapped in tissue paper, the next morning, some nurse had flushed them."

"I feel sorry for your grandma. Who was there in your dream?"

"Christ, you sound like hell. What did he do to you?"

Whitt wandered naked into the living room, the chill air feeling good on his stitches. "Forget that."

"Okay, well . . . you and Karen and Sarah were there in this weird plastic house, and you needed an interior decorator badly, man. I mean, really, that place was ugly. You're gonna make nasty comments on my cabin and then live in a house like that? Sarah kept asking me to help her do homework. She was ten, man, already a heartbreaker. Karen made tea. Do real people drink tea or is it just the Brits? We sat around with this shiny, silver plastic tea set. I haven't dreamed of her in, well, it's been a while. I'm not sure how long. Does that make me an awful godfather?"

"No, Freddy, it doesn't."

"And you were feeding me really bad meat loaf, man. I can still taste it, stuck in my throat like sawdust. No, worse, more like splinters of plastic."

"Which Freddy is this?" Whitt asked.

"What the hell's that mean? Hey, is your voice going to get better or what?"

"Yes."

"Man, that's good."

"Which one are you?"

"What are you talking about, Eddie?"

"Just tell me which one you are!"

"Oh. I'm the one staring at you right now."

Whitt turned on the light and looked down at the

dollhouse and saw Freddy inside, waving to him through the bay window.

Why shouldn't he be there? Freddy was the only friend he had left. He'd also cried harder during the funeral than anyone else, harder than Whitt had ever seen anybody cry before. We're all joined through our love, our fear, our grief.

"I'm still having the dream, Eddie, but I'm telling you now, I am *not* finishing this fuckin' meat loaf, I don't care whose feelings I hurt. You use ketchup instead of tomato paste? The hell's the matter with you? And what kind of bread crumbs are these?"

"They're crushed cheese crackers. Sarah liked them."

"Holy Christ! You trying to poison me? Why the hell do you use crackers?"

"Gives it a little more zing."

"Zing? Did you actually say zing?"

"I said zing."

"Zing, my ass. Use bread crumbs with Italian spices in 'em. Why don't you get some real food down here?"

"Nothing's real in there, Freddy."

"Oh bullshit, I'm taking another bite of it right now, and that's it. Christ, it's awful. I'm not drinking this tea, either. Get some beer for your fridge, imported stuff, and nothing lite either. You telling me this isn't real? Let's see how you feel after I upchuck across your kitchen floor."

"Why don't you come over for dinner next Tuesday?"

"I'll be there if you have the beer."

"I will," Whitt said. "Is Karen or Sarah there?"

"Sarah's dead and Karen's in the Falls, Eddie," Freddy told him. "Stop talking crazy."

THIRTY-TWO

The same spot as before.

Fifteen miles outside of Garden Falls the rain came down hard, like the tires had hit a marker that started the whole process. If you believed in signs you had to believe in them all. Maybe the world really did want you to stay away from your own wife.

Whitt tapped the windshield wipers to high and held the steering wheel steady in his hands, feeling the indents of his own bite marks in the tough plastic beneath his fingers.

A pickup in the next lane matched his pace perfectly. He didn't have to look to know what he'd see. One of the gray-faced, white-eyed denizens of these mountain towns, carrying crates of night crawlers or chickens.

This place had held his wife for half a decade because Whitt wasn't strong enough to save her.

He whispered, "Goddamn you," and glared at the other driver, expecting a hunched skeleton to be grinning at him. Seeing instead a woman alone, scared to be driving in such torrential rain. She put her blinker on and pulled to the side of the road. The storm would clear in a minute. Whitt kept going, feeling he'd lost something else already.

He drove up to the guard booth and the same skinny guy reading a paperback just lifted the semaphore arm and waved him on. Whitt wanted to jump out and slap the fucker silly, scream at him, What if it was Killjoy? You'd let him in? You wouldn't notice somebody in a pillowcase with a frownie face drawn on it. Hey, what's the book about?

At the front desk of the main building Whitt gave his name, got his visitor's pass. A tiny Asian nurse with reams of black hair spilling from beneath her little hat—a different Asian nurse with different reams of spilling hair—told him to please take a seat and wait for Ted. No matter who you were, you had to wait for Ted.

Whitt sat and watched the rain throb against the windows, the same way he had the last time he'd been here.

Ted didn't pop around the corner this time. He sort of glided, inch by inch, into view—his angelic hair and bottled tan preceding his body, like a glow, by maybe a half second. The white teeth so intense that you had to turn your eyes away until you got used to the shine. Ted was still wearing all the colors of Southern California's citrus groves. Dazzling orange pants, lime-green shirt, yellow sneakers. He looked at Whitt and yanked his walkie-talkie off his belt, hissed into it, "He's here! The one I told you about! Mayday! Mayday! Code one oh one omega! Code one hundred one!"

Whitt kept staring at the rain, thinking, Christ.

Finally he stood and Ted, to his credit, didn't back off. He held his ground, bending in on himself like he had a hernia, still muttering into the walkie-talkie. "Is anybody there? Can you hear me? Shit!"

"Relax, Ted, I'm not here to cause trouble."

"My God," Ted said, looking over, appearing genuinely concerned. "What happened to your voice, Mr. Whitt?"

"I was recently in the hospital. Didn't Agent Carver call?"

"Yes, I think that was her name, but I wasn't told anything. I mean, she didn't say it was an emergency."

"Any chance you mentioned it to my wife?"

"Well, no, I didn't want to upset her."

You could go around and around with people until either you died of boredom or they did.

Whitt said, "You did the right thing, Ted."

"I did?"

"Yes. Thank you for looking out for Karen."

"It's my job. And I care for her. But I must tell you—she hasn't been doing well lately."

"What do you mean?"

"She's had a setback."

"What kind of setback? Why?"

"We've increased her medication. A few days ago . . .

well, she had to be contained. Tranquilized. Sequestered, you see."

Whitt framed the word, knowing the truth of it. Sequestered. Put in the rubber room. In a jacket.

"Why?" he asked. "What was the reason?"

"We don't know. The chief of staff and our resident medical doctor have been by to check up on her. She's been...nonresponsive."

"Comatose?"

"No no, not that. Not nonresponsive, I'm sorry. *Unresponsive*. She refuses to answer questions."

They walked together up the north wing hallways, passing no one else. When they arrived at Karen's door, Ted raised his fist and knocked a specific rappity-tap tune. It wasn't the same as before. They'd changed their code. Except for the last damning thump, the one that Whitt knew represented him. Ted still thought he should warn her. Whitt wasn't all that certain Ted was wrong.

"Ted, I don't want to be rude or crass, but I'd like to see my wife alone."

"I intend to escort you inside, Mr. Whitt. If Mrs. Whitt asks me to leave, then I will."

Sometimes you could ask for more, and sometimes you couldn't. Whitt decided to let it slide.

Karen opened the door. "Hello, Eddie."

"Hello," he said, and watched her lovely face wrench with concern. He couldn't help it. He liked seeing his wife worry about him.

"Eddie, what happened? Your voice. You sound terrible."

Her features softening, the muted cast in her eyes starting to plead with him now. She took his face in her hands and, softly drawing him forward, wrapped him in her arms. He fell against his wife and she hugged him tighter, whispering in his ear, "Baby, baby, what happened to you? What did they do to you?"

A sob welled in his chest but didn't break free. She lifted his shirt and reached up beneath it, laid the flat of her hand against his chest, where it hurt deepest. But he loved the feeling of her touching him again. She moved her lips to his throat and kissed him on his stitches and scabs. Whitt felt the overwhelming urge to drop to his knees, his strength draining away for an instant.

No matter how strong you were, you were never strong enough. You wait five years for your wife to come back to you, and now she's doing it because you were nearly strangled. And you never believed before that there could be a bright side to this sort of thing.

He saw she'd been biting the backs of her hands again. The scar tissue was torn, red swathes of flesh missing. They'd tried bandaging her but she kept ripping them away.

"My God, Karen—" He grabbed her by the wrists and raised her hands before his eyes. It was like she'd been flayed. He could see areas of bone poking through.

"Karen, why are you—"

"How's Sarah?" she asked.

"What are you doing to yourself? Why are you biting yourself again?"

"Eddie? Eddie, how's Sarah?"

The familiar despair would've filled him again, and again, and again even now, except it was always there anyway.

The words came to him much slower now. He had a much more difficult time saying them, as if the awful truth were somehow moving out of his grasp. "Sarah's dead."

"I know that," she said, because it was, after all, true. "I mean, I know the first one is dead. And you gave the second one away. But how's the new one?"

"There is no new Sarah."

"Yes, there is."

"How do you know that? Who told you that?"

She was always staring into his eyes, and it was him looking away. She still spoke with that detached quality, like he wasn't in the room, not quite real to her. It was difficult believing you were still alive when your wife spoke to you like that. "You know what I'm talking about."

A freezing wind began to blow through him. Whitt tried to suppress a shiver and failed, thinking, no. No. "What are you talking about, Karen?".

He looked around and suddenly wanted out. He had to take his wife on a picnic again, go off to the park, watch kids on swings, but the image of a playground covered with crows wouldn't leave his mind. "Ted, I want to take her out of here."

"Excuse me?"

"Someplace else on the grounds. A garden. You have gardens here in this shithole?"

"It's raining out," Ted said.

"I know, but it doesn't matter. She's got three Gucci raincoats in her closet, for Christ's sake."

"Why do you want to leave?"

"Because for five years I haven't seen her anywhere except in this little apartment, and I want a change of atmosphere."

"You can't," Ted said, bringing his fingers to his mouth, chewing his nails. "You will not take Mrs. Whitt off somewhere!"

No matter what, no matter how nicely you asked, you couldn't make headway in any direction at all. "I'm not taking her anywhere. I just want you to tell me how to get to a garden and then for you to go away."

"I refuse!"

"She's my wife, Ted."

"She is my responsibility!"

"Before God and man, she's mine. You may be her interior decorator but she's still wearing the ring I gave her, you understand?"

Whitt had to double-check though. He looked at the scratched and bitten left hand to see if her ring was still there, if her ring finger was still there. It was.

You had to give it to ole Ted though. He didn't stand for any guff. Ole Ted was not a guff-stander. He held his ground, refusing to get off the stage. Lifting his chin and turning his head aside, shutting his eyes like he expected to take a rap on the chin. Like everybody would say, look at his courage, look at that golden hair beautifully shaped into flips and angel wings, he was willing to sacrifice himself to protect his charge.

Then he went into action. Ted leaped between Karen and Whitt and shrieked, "Flee, Mrs. Whitt, flee! Save yourself!"

"Jesus Christ."

Ted sort of hugged Whitt, trying to tie him up. He held on tight, put a cheek to Whitt's chest, shut his eyes again, and let out a cry as if he expected to get backhanded. The kind of scream Juliet lets loose with when she awakens to find Romeo dead at her feet. Like the girls in Shea Stadium when the Beatles touched down in '65.

"Ted," Whitt said, "what the hell are you doing?"

"You brute!"

Whitt figured the guy must smell a lawsuit here. Get Whitt to punch him in the nose and sue Mike Bowman for 5 million bucks. "Listen, just give me ten minutes with her, all right? Forget about the garden. Just go wait out in the hallway. Seriously, I appreciate you being a friend to her through all of this."

"You think you have a perfect right to do anything to anyone, don't you? You're a horrible man!"

"You really need to start doing off-Broadway shows, man."

He shoved Ted aside and Karen came forward giggling. It was the first time he'd seen her laugh since she'd been here, and the moment was so perfect—forgetting the insanity and murder—that he took her in his arms and kissed her.

Her lips were hard as granite. She stared at him curiously and her mouth opened. He knew she was about to ask him how their daughter was, no not that one, or that one either, but the newest one.

Now Ted was slapping at his back, yelling, "Monster!"

Really, anybody who knew this guy, would they blame Whitt for popping him in the face? Probably not.

Karen touched Ted's elbow, turning him gently. "It's all right."

"It's not!"

"Please, let me talk with my husband."

That was all it took. Ted tried to swallow his bottom lip, frustrated in the extreme, so much so that the wings of his hair were folding across his eyes. He sniffed dramatically, hugged Karen to him like it might be for the last time. Like an angry housemother he threw a final warning glare at Whitt and retreated from the room.

Sometimes you thanked the sweet baby Jesus and sometimes you thanked the good fucking Christ.

Karen took him by the arm and drew him to the bedroom. Five years and he'd never seen it. She held his hand firmly and he thought of the excruciating pain she must be in, holding on to him so tightly with those tortured hands.

Thick mauve drapes covered the far wall. She worked the cord and opened them wide, exposing French doors. He'd had no idea they were there.

She opened them and escorted Whitt out into a small private yard filled with azaleas and chrysanthemums. In the center of it sat a marble-top stone table and two ornate metal chairs, protected from the rain by a copper overhang.

"You wanted a garden," she said.

"I wanted it for you. I didn't realize you already had one."

"I should've brought you here before."

They sat close together. She put her head on his shoulder and he put his arm around her. You could do a lot of things when the world called for it, you could even pretend, for a few heartbeats, that you were the same man you'd once been. That you could, in fact, revert. Whitt pressed his lips to Karen's forehead and closed his eyes and focused his will, imagining that the world could be undone. Layers of years might be stripped away. His heart began to pound and the pulse in his neck sped along until it felt like his stitches were pulling loose. It reminded him that he'd already been dead for seventy-five seconds, on the far side of the river. He wondered if he'd been happy over there. He had no idea why he'd come back, except to finish this one last ritual. He probably shouldn't have come back. He opened his eyes.

Karen said, "Why did you give the first girl back?"

"She wasn't mine to keep. She wasn't ours, no matter how much we might have wanted her."

"Killjoy allowed it."

"He doesn't have the right."

She turned to face him. "You were the first of them. The first father whose child was taken. The first to have a child returned. It made you special. And you sent her back. Do you realize what you've done, Eddie? Perhaps you've killed her. Did you ever think of that? He only took abused children."

"Not her," he said, back on edge where he belonged. Needing to explain, to convince a woman locked up in the bin that what he had done was rational and right, returning a newborn that wasn't his. "She wasn't abused at all."

"How do you know, Eddie? How?"

"I saw her again, not long ago. Her parents love her, like we loved Sarah."

"You don't know that for sure," Karen said, almost with a growl. She shot to her feet and crossed her arms, those scarred, infected hands looking like she'd thrust them into open flame. "You have no idea what trauma she's been put through. What horrors. What pain. You can't be certain she's not being harmed."

"I keep an eye on her, Karen. I watch her all the time."

"As if she was your own daughter."

Whitt had nothing to say to that.

"Why her? Why would he give her to you?"

"I don't know."

"There must be a reason."

"Not necessarily. Not with Killjoy."

"Even with him. With everyone. Don't you under-stand that?"

He stared into Karen's eyes, so much sharper and brighter than his own, and knew that, yes, the anguish had bent and mauled her, but she was smarter than him, so much sharper.

"He was here," she said.

"What?"

"I woke up one night and he was in the bedroom with me, sitting on the edge of the bed. He was crying. He asked me not to turn the light on and I didn't. I just held him there, in the dark."

"What?"

"He's so sorry for all the sins he's committed. I wanted to forgive him. He's so much like you."

"Don't you say that!"

Whitt jumped out of his chair, backing away step by step, a terrified child himself. She skirted back inside the apartment and returned holding a piece of paper with handwriting he recognized. Shoving it toward him as he slid farther and farther away, until he was backed up against the garden wall. She pressed it to his chest and said, "He left this for you. Almost a week ago. He said I should give it to you, but... I'm sorry, Eddie. I wanted it. I wanted to keep it. It helped me, his words."

"No."

"His tears. On my sheets. They soothed me."

On his twenty-first birthday, Killjoy spent the afternoon talking with a hanged boy. The kid was his new college roommate, who had taken his own life after failing a rather unimportant midterm exam. Sissy called and asked Killjoy, Are you planning on coming home for Thanksgiving? Killjoy, taking a moment to think about it, propped his legs against the wall, knocking at it so the vibrations got the hanged guy's body swaying a bit, said, I'm not sure, I'll have to get back to you on that.

Sissy, relentless, in uproar. Mom wants to know.

Mom will know in another day or two. I'll call then to confirm, one way or another.

Replacing of phone. Staring at dead kid, who didn't have a rope so instead knotted five pairs of gym socks together. Young man Killjoy realizing, with some disgust and a modicum of pride, that one of the pairs was his own. Dirty. Having been in the laundry basket at the foot of the bed. Dead kid wanting to do himself in so badly that he couldn't even wait for a fresh pair, if socks were the only way to go.

The staring, also inflexible. The dead kid's eyes were open, tongue unfurled. Not black, as we've been led to believe, not purple, not even swollen. Just pinkish, sluglike.

Other things differing from what we've been told. No shit in pants. No hard-on. Face rather slack and placid, especially the eyes, which didn't bulge.

Killjoy wondering, what to do with this body. Thinking it was too good to go to waste, some effort should be made with the corpse. Something kinky perhaps, something funny. Dress it up differently? In a clown costume? In leather and chains? As Little Bo Peep? Leave it in front of Omega Theta Theta Sorority House? Scare girls who refused to lay either Killjoy or (now defunct) roommate? That'll show the stuck up perky-titted bitches! Watch as they shriek. Watch as they dance in terror. Watch as they cry out for the fate of Little Bo Peep. Watch as they prance about the lawn searching for the sheep. The sheep! Where art the sheep! Watch as they (hopefully) perform lesbian rites of love as seen on the Internet.

Sissy, implacable, continuous uproar, calling anew. Dad says if you're flying back he needs to know now so he can book you a seat.

Killjoy, relenting, thumping the wall again, listening to the creak of the stretched dirty socks. Tell Dad yes, yes, yes, yes, yes. Mom also, yes, yes, yes, yes, yes, yes. I shall return. I shall give thanks.

Sissy, remembering. Oh, happy birthday. Did you get the card?

Yes yes yes yes yes yes yes yes yes yes yes yes yes yes.

Do you give thanks, Whitt?

You should thank your Lord God each morning, each night, for all you have found in me.

As I thank Him for you.

The you that you are.

The you that you were.

You.

And Karen.

And the Sarahs I have given you.

Yes yes yes yes yes yes yes yes yes yes yes yes yes yes.

"He wanted to make us a family again," Karen said. "To make us whole."

The fever tore at Whitt's forehead, burning inside every muscle. The sweat poured off him in gleaming rivulets. "He can't return what he's taken."

"You wouldn't let him!"

"What?"

"You denied him! And the Sarahs!"

"There are no Sarahs!"

She raised the back of her left hand to her mouth and started to chew. He tried to grab hold of her wrists but she struggled violently, wrenching out of his grip. She bit him and bit herself, until there was blood in her mouth. She showed him her teeth. His girl. His girl.

"You refused to let us heal! To give those girls homes! To let me be well again! *You never loved me! Never!*"

She pitched forward and fainted in his arms.

Whitt carried her inside and laid her on the bed. He found towels in her bathroom and tore them into strips so he could bind her wounds. He held her in his arms, murmuring loving words to her that he remembered but could barely understand anymore.

His new tortured voice made it sound like another man was trying to make love to his wife.

Her eyes opened and clouded instantly. She shook her head like she was seeing him for the first time, awakening from a daydream that had felt too real but not real enough.

Karen smiled happily and asked, "How's Sarah?"

"Fine," he said.

His girls were gone.

THIRTY-THREE

If you wanted to find a man you had to learn what he loves and what he hates, because you'd discover him there, moving from one to the other.

Killjoy had hated Whitt and Karen and Sarah, and now he loved them, or said he did.

A man who had once despised families had somehow learned to adore them. Who wanted, on some level, to be forgiven. Who cried on the bed of a woman he'd driven insane, and who perhaps truly did despise himself. Maybe down where it counted, maybe not.

Whitt stood on Mike Bowman's stoop and stared at his palms as the rain ran over his hands, trying to put the association together. Killjoy's belly. Like hitting a sack of laundry. Punching the guy in the gut and feeling other clothes under there. His Clark Kent suit on underneath, the identity of his alter ego.

Mike, who would've found Whitt's body if he'd canceled his own ticket back when he should have, stood in the doorway with his powerful presence and expression of irritation. "Eddie, you're drenched. How long have you been standing there?"

Whitt didn't know. He'd gotten to Mike's front door and raised his hand to the bell but had been unable to push the button. Maybe twenty minutes or more. He hadn't noticed the rain much. This was the wrong place to be, the home where his wife had grown up. She was no longer his, no longer even her own, so there was no reason to be here.

But when you're a boy you need your father, and when you're a man you need all of your fathers. Whichever ones you could find, whichever ones would've found you in the garage with the car running. So he was on Mike Bowman's doorstep.

"Eddie?"

"Hello, Mike."

"Don't stand there, come in."

Leave it to Mike, the only one who wouldn't say, Holy fuck, your voice. He'd seen a lot worse in his day, probably had to cut a few throats himself overseas. The inhuman voice of a burning seraphim wouldn't mean much to him.

You could always count on your father figures to be proud of you when you were at your worst. After all these years Mike was finally showing something else in his eyes. He had a little respect for Whitt now that he'd killed a guy and had blood on his hands, like a real man. Whitt wondered if Mike might—yeah, here it comes, Holy Christ—might put a hand on his shoulder, grip him gently there, and work it into a pat on the back. Accepting him now in a way he never had before.

Mike embraced him, making it the third time ever. First on his wedding day, then at Sarah's funeral, and now because he'd strangled his enemy. Hugging Whitt in those powerful arms. The love your father had always held back, giving it to you now.

They sat in the den across from one another, same as always. Mike poured two glasses of scotch from the server between them, then looked up. "Your throat, is it all right for you to drink alcohol?"

It wasn't, but Whitt said, "Yes."

No ice, no water. Mike handed the drink to Whitt and took the time to pat his shoulder again.

Actually saying it. "I'm proud of you."

"Last time I was here you thought I was getting reckless. Involving myself too directly in police matters."

"This was different."

"Why?"

"You accomplished something."

That intrigued Whitt. He wondered what it was Mike felt had been achieved. He started to ask, but Mike interrupted. "You took evil off the street."

Whitt wanted a cigarette so badly that he reached for the pack in his pocket, except his pocket had been empty for weeks. When had he given up smoking?

Mike watched him closely, sipping his scotch, appearing more content than Whitt had seen him in years. The man not even asking about Karen. Or Killjoy. None of this, Oh thank God you're all right.

Still, Whitt didn't have to worry about the usual anxieties around Mike anymore. How he sat, how quickly he drank, how he handled pain, how much beard stubble was on his chin. He'd vaulted the usual hurdles of masculinity and joined the inner circle of fathers.

"What is it, Eddie?"

Whitt kept silent another minute. The papers had held back the fact that Killjoy had been in the warehouse. He looked Mike in the eyes and said, "We came face-to-face. I saw him."

"Killjoy."

"Yes."

"Explain it to me."

Whitt did, going back a little further and starting with visiting Mama Prott, the ruckus in the prison, Diana Carver, the truckers in the diner—maybe he should've mentioned them sooner, because Mike nodded, almost happily. Then the appeal to the man who'd murdered his daughter, the phone call. Whitt had to stop several times until the pain in his throat settled down a bit. Somehow, the scotch was helping.

"Did you learn anything new about him, on the phone or in the warehouse?"

There was a subtle accusation in his tone that said, If the guy was right there, in your face, and you botched the job of killing him, you at least should've picked up a few clues. That was Mike, always believing he would've done better in the same situation, but never having to prove the point.

And now all that newfound respect was starting to slide away down the hill.

Whitt held back the fact that Killjoy had visited Karen, and wasn't completely sure why he did. Perhaps because it was another bit of evidence that Whitt couldn't protect those he loved, and in failing to protect them, deserved to lose them.

"I have the feeling he's coming to the end of his string," Whitt said. "He's going to stop soon."

Mike stared into his glass. He shut his eyes, took a five count, and opened them again. The huge throbbing veins on his forehead were turning black. "I don't know whether to be relieved or not."

"Don't be. If he quits, he'll fade away and we'll never get him."

"What makes you think he wants to quit?"

"He's always wanted to stop, but he was driven. Now his drive is depleted. He's been imploring me to understand his reasons. He likes to think we're two of a kind. I was the first he offered a child to. I'll be the last as well."

It's so easy to become distracted, even misguided, by the lures of normalcy. Do you ever feel this, Whitt?

"Are you sure?" Mike asked.

"Yes."

But Mike didn't want to hear the answer. "Eddie, are you sure?"

"Yes."

"Eddie—"

"How about if you don't keep asking me that, eh?"

Like last time, wind knocked at the windows upstairs, so it sounded like there were other people in the house. Karen on the second floor, getting ready for a date, while Whitt sweated before the death gaze of her father. When Whitt thought about it, he felt a very acute shock that he'd survived any of it.

A draft brought the scent of dust and mold into the room, like a corpse had walked by and lain down behind the couch.

"Why?" Mike said. "Why you?"

"I don't know. But he wants to be normal, have a regular life. That's been a part of his construct from the beginning."

Mike slugged the scotch down and wiped his mouth with the back of his hand, thinking about a murderer out there growing more normal because of his crimes. A nervous tic beat twice in Mike's cheek. He turned to glance at the empty wall, looking through time and space at the photos in the room beyond, retracing his own memories.

"What are you going to do now?" Mike asked, sounding a little childish himself. His hands shaking. It was happening again, the man growing smaller in his chair, with so little in his life now except the creaks and stink of decay. Soon he would have even less, when Whitt was dead.

"Our paths crossed at some point," Whitt said. "Killjoy's and mine. I'm going back to my beginning."

The rain stopped but the wind had risen.

Whitt went back to his own beginning. Karen, she used to fill the wicker basket with wine, cheese and crackers, and peanut butter sandwiches for Sarah. *A real picnic basket.* He'd once had a life where his wife had fed him on a large blanket laid out under the sun, while their child laughed and ran through the grass. This place, perhaps more than the home they'd shared, was the beginning of his life beyond himself.

He scoped the area and found the spot where he, Karen, and Sarah used to relax on the weekends. He thought, I'll come back here every day until I'm pointed to the next step. He sat on the wet roots of an oak and stared at the road. He nodded for a while, dreaming that Killjoy had already vanished into misguided normalcy. He awoke and sat there for another three hours, watching the light traffic drift past, thinking about the man he used to be. Whitt stood to leave and saw Killjoy drive by.

THIRTY-FOUR

That sound again, the enormous electrical buzzing of pain, working its way across his body inch by inch.

Reaching for the sides of the tree, Whitt grabbed hold and his body tightened and spasmed, shaking as he tried to scream but nothing like his own voice erupted from his ruined throat. Cool fluids, so much brisker than his own skin, ran down his neck from where the stitches had torn loose. He was smiling so wide that the edges of his mouth split and blood poured between his lips.

Whitt spent a half hour online searching down facts that out of context held no meaning. Thirty minutes and it all came together.

A task force of more than ten profilers, behaviorists, and specialists from London, Vienna, New York, Quantico, and nobody could crack the cryptogram, because there wasn't one. There was no puzzle or mystery. Everything was right out in the open.

No murdered mother or sister. No sister at all. The father owned a bookbinding and printing business. Textbooks mostly. History mostly.

Communication. Letters. The supposed philosophers and professors. Southern jargon coupled with faux European sophistication. Textbook sensibility taken to the farthest degree.

Grandfather provided no obvious addition to the construct.

Great-grandfather had been a dentist back when they used to yank teeth at the barbershop.

There it was.

Teeth.

It had always been about his obsession with teeth. Babies and old men. You never really had to go any further than that to find the core of his fabrication. How many times had he stared into a baby's mouth and run his pinky along the toothless gums? And then, months later, the little nubs of bone poking through?

Whitt called the hospital and mentioned Killjoy's real name, asked if he'd been there the same day Amy Morgan had been snatched. He didn't expect them to give him the information over the phone, but you couldn't underestimate the willingness of lackeys simply to answer questions when asked. It was easier than having to think or make a judgment call. He kept asking questions, more and more personal, and they kept checking their computer and giving him the answers. Nobody followed protocol.

Whitt called Killjoy and invited him to the apartment for a late lunch.

Killjoy, in his real voice, asked what had happened to Whitt? Why did he sound like that?

Then Killjoy said he'd be right over, give him a half hour or so.

Whitt checked the .32 and waited, but something didn't feel right. He was worried Killjoy might not bring along the harlequin's mask he'd been hiding behind. Whitt went to the bedroom, grabbed his pillow, and yanked the pillowcase off. In the junk drawer in the kitchen he found a magic marker and used it to draw a frownie face on the fabric.

It still felt a little wrong. This was endgame.

It should be the original pillowcase, the one placed over Sarah's nose and mouth. But this would have to do. He folded it up and tucked it in his belt beneath his gun holster at the small of his back, hidden beneath his shirt.

Finally he heard Killjoy's footsteps down below, coming up the stairs. Whitt called Brunkowski and told him, "You and Diana Carver get over here. It'll all be over in the next ten minutes. If I'm dead, thanks for everything you did to help."

He hung up and answered the door.

"Hello, Eddie," Killjoy said, holding out his hand.

"Come inside, Killjoy," Whitt told Russell Gunderson, grinning and drawing his .32.

THIRTY-FIVE

Even now, knowing what had happened and what was to come, Whitt still felt that flood of elation, the urge to make sure Lorrie was all right. He gestured for Gunderson to step forward. "Come on, let's go."

The relief in Gunderson's eyes was no different than, Whitt presumed, the relief showing in his own.

Now that the harlequin paint had been washed away, they could just stand here, face-to-face, the way it had always been meant to be.

Gunderson maintained the easy broad smile, looking casual and comfortable despite the gun trained on him.

"How's Lorrie?" Whitt asked.

"She's fine."

"So, it wasn't strep?"

"You already know it wasn't."

Whitt nodded.

He'd been stupid all right, but he couldn't drag himself over the coals too much for that. Everybody had been unbelievably dense. The FBI the cops, Brunk, Diana Carver. Even the Viennese specialist. All of them.

Killjoy was other.

He wasn't a doctor or dentist, wasn't a janitor or a school groundskeeper.

Whatever he had been before, now he was a father.

That's why he had been at the hospital. Because Lorrie had had trouble breathing the other morning, and Gunderson had brought her to the emergency room, fearing she had strep. They'd waited over an hour—not too bad for an emergency room—before one of the staff saw them and took a swab. Two more hours before they were given the all clear.

That's why he'd taken Amy Morgan and broken his pattern.

Any hospital where they were going to give a stranger information over the phone about a guy named Gunderson wasn't going to have the best security measures anyway. He'd been there with Lorrie and spotted the bruised newborn. Saw the commotion with the cops, the mother wanting to get rid of her drug-dealing boyfriend, her other kids all yelling. Knee-jerk reaction. He'd behaved the only way he could since his repentance. He'd waited for the right moment to make his move, while everybody was squabbling. He grabbed the infant, picked up his own kid, and simply walked away.

Tens of thousands of children disappear each year.

Killjoy wasn't much of a planner.

He just did whatever the hell he felt like.

Now Gunderson sat on the couch, looking more at home in Whitt's apartment than Whitt had ever felt. It seemed like he was waiting for Whitt to serve him a drink, maybe one of those enormous lattes.

"Where is she?" Whitt asked, a little surprised at his own calm, after so much screaming and thrashing over the last half decade.

"I dropped her off with my father."

"He doesn't work the print shop anymore?"

"He's retired."

Whitt thought, Here's where we talk. This is where he exposes his soul and I perform the duties of my righteous wrath, and in the end—what happens then?

"You're not going to ask me why, are you?" Gunderson said.

"No. I think I already know the answer to that."

"It's simple enough."

"Sure. That's why nobody could solve it."

The two of them sat across from one another, not much different than the way it was at Mike's place. You've come 10 million years from Cain and Abel, and still the blood feats of brotherhood were all the same.

"You're not going to shoot me, Eddie," Gunderson said. Not smiling or frowning. There was no emotion there at all, really, except the sorrow. It came off him in waves, now that the clown face was gone.

"Sure I am."

"If what you wanted was my death, you would've done it by now."

"I want more," Whitt said, "a lot more, but I guess I'll settle for your death."

Putting it into words only weakened the grandeur of your hatred.

You can't give voice to the fever and frenzy. There are some emotions you've felt that no other man, despite his torments and tragedy, has ever felt before in the history of the earth. You stand alone before God because your scars and rage are unique.

"You should've listened to me. You should've gone to your wife and reverted to the man you were."

"As if it was possible."

"It is," Gunderson told him, sounding so certain. "I know it is. It's possible to change. I've done it." His repentance was written into the lines and planes of his features, now that Whitt knew what to look for. Like he'd said about the Pollocks, You have to get up close to appreciate it.

Whitt waited to see what would happen, which one of them would blink, if either, ever again. The moment had to be much more immense.

"I should've known from the beginning," Whitt said. "Love. You wanted it and when you finally got it you changed your ways."

"It's the greatest healing force in the universe."

"I wouldn't know about that," Whitt said. "I subscribe to the *Testament of Ya'al.*"

"What?"

"You left a lot of clues. Putting Lorrie in the picnic basket when you left her at my doorstep. It should've told me right off that we'd crossed trails at the park. That you'd watched me there."

"I watched a lot of people there."

"Why was Sarah your first?"

"Someone had to be."

"But why her?"

"She wasn't," Gunderson said, matter-of-factly and genuine as pain. "You were."

That stopped him. "What?"

"I spotted you in the park one day, six years ago. You looked happy. I hated that more than you'll ever know, Eddie. I despised and envied your elation, your *mirth*. I wanted to kill you then, but I wasn't ready. I was in the midst of my own transformation, you see? Becoming what I had to become. What I was forced to become. You understand that now, don't you? I didn't go back to that park for months, but when I did, my God, you were there again, looking the same. With a beautiful wife and a gorgeous baby daughter. I followed you home and watched you through your back window. I wanted to steal your happiness. That was the beginning."

"All because I had what you didn't?"

Gunderson stood, unafraid, really believing he might get out of the apartment alive. "Yes."

No matter the injustice, the inhumanity, when you

boiled it all down you came up with the same petty hurts and motives. Money, love, jealousy, revenge, sex. No madman ever did anything for any other reason.

Whitt had asked himself the question while lying in Gunderson's backyard, watching the man with his wife and daughter, watching a kid's movie. *Did Killjoy hate because of jealousy? Is that why he stole this guy's baby?* He'd been staring at Killjoy the entire time. So close to the answer and just not being able to see it.

Killjoy's belly. He'd punched him in the gut and felt something else there, the alter ego beneath. Gunderson always wore his little papoose carrier, even while he capered around the warehouse wearing his pillowcase. That was the secret identity.

And Whitt, perhaps he'd known the entire time.

Killjoy was the perfect daddy.

Swallowing hard, his voice stretched even more, doing his best to control his trembling hands. "And you thought you'd balance out accounts by giving me your own daughter?"

"It was the right thing to do."

"Giving away your own baby? *What kind of father are you?*"

"I'm a good one."

"But you filed a missing child report."

"Anne and I did. It should have been a flag for you. You should have found me right then."

"Everything you did was a flag. You concealed your-self well behind them all. Face it, Killjoy, you didn't want to be caught. You're the kind of martyr who lets everybody else go to the stake first."

"Are you ready to see your girl again, Eddie? You go home to your wife and I'll go to mine."

"Sure, except mine is out of her tree," Whitt said, shifting his hips and driving his fist into Killjoy's mouth. "Because you killed her daughter."

Whitt picked him up and threw him across the room into the kitchen. Gunderson slammed into the cabinets so hard that every drawer slid open. Plates, cookie sheets, and utensils erupted and crashed to the floor. "You're still an intolerant little prick, Killjoy. That's why you went to see Karen. You wanted to look her in the face again, after five years, and see your destructive handiwork."

"No—"

Whitt spun hard and kicked Killjoy in the face. It swept him across the kitchen and against the fridge, splashing blood on the handle. "You're still jealous. You wanted to rouse yourself once more. See up close the love you murdered."

"No!"

Whitt chopped him twice in the collarbone but didn't hear that satisfying snap of bone. Killjoy sprawled forward on his belly and started to crawl.

"You still don't quite have the happiness you were hoping for. That's why you were willing to part with your own baby girl, you prick!"

"No, Eddie!"

"There's blood in your mouth, Killjoy."

"Stop calling me that. It's not who I am anymore."

"It's who you'll always be."

Whitt started forward again and Killjoy reached down and snatched Karen's butcher knife off the floor. He lunged with a shriek, but Whitt avoided him easily. Killjoy got to his feet and staggered forward, slashing the air. Whitt backed into the living room, thinking how easily he could break this bastard's neck.

Killjoy thrust the blade forward again. Whitt started to sidestep before he realized if he did that he'd kick over the dollhouse. He froze, began to raise the gun, but he wasn't quick enough to stop Killjoy's motion. He put his arm up to block but not in time as the blade entered his belly and just kept going.

Whitt let out a grunt but nothing more, as Killjoy twisted it and twisted it.

It was what Mary Laramore had told Whitt to do to Killjoy. Look at that, the way these things happen.

Incision.

The pain was tremendous but strangely bearable, as if Whitt had somehow grown much larger than the confines of his own body. He reached down with his left hand and gripped Killjoy's wrist to keep the knife from turning anymore. A weird, almost childlike sound of happiness escaped from one of them.

"*Let's try that again!*" Whitt said.

"Crowfield Crenshaw the troll," Killjoy said. "It's one of Lorrie's favorites."

"Sarah's too. Hope you've got good insurance to cover the kid's college tuition."

"I didn't bring a weapon here, Eddie! I didn't want to hurt you anymore. You wanted this, not me. You needed this! You can't kill me. You love me! As much as I love you."

"I'm going to kill you just for saying that," Whitt said, his teeth dripping.

He'd known all these blood sacrifices were going to come back and give him power when he needed it most.

He still had the pillowcase with the frownie face on it stuck in his belt. He knew how stupid it was to do what he was doing now, with the knife in his belly. But still, it was the right move to make.

Whitt let go of Killjoy's wrist as the blade began to turn again. Using his blood-smeared hand to pull the pillowcase free, he reached over and yanked it down over Killjoy's head, the frownie face settling directly over his own.

That's it, that's how it should be.

My girls are here with me now. Whitt felt an immense tearing inside himself as he held the pillowcase in place with one hand and raised his .32 with the other. He brought the gun up to the frownie face, Russell Gunderson's face, placed the barrel between the black unfriendly eyes, and blasted Killjoy's goddamn sick head apart.

THIRTY-SIX

Whitt realized, with a lessening sense of terror now, that even tremendous force of will might not keep you from dying when an eight-inch butcher knife was in your belly up to the handle.

Incision. Oh yeah.

Freddy got there first. Whitt had forgotten about him. It was Tuesday night. Whitt had told Freddy—one of the Freddys—to come over for dinner. Goddamn if the guy didn't always show for a meal.

"Sorry about the meat loaf," Whitt said.

Freddy knelt beside him, holding his hands out, not sure what to do with them. He fell apart pretty much instantly and said, "Jesus fuckin' Christ, Eddie. What? What happened? What do I do?" The tears were already coming. Then, looking over at Killjoy, asking, "That him?"

"Yeah."

"Good, you did it, you did it. Don't worry, you're going to be all right. Don't give in. What do I do?"

"I'm not going anywhere," Whitt said, surprised at how weak his brutal voice sounded already. "Towels."

"Towels?"

"Get me a few towels to try to stanch the bleeding."

"Oh Christ, yes, towels!" Freddy ran off into the bathroom, came back with two dirty towels that had been on the floor. He placed them around the blade in Whitt's belly, afraid to push too hard. The teeny head on the big body going, "You hold on."

"I intend to." You always had to be the rock in the storm, even now.

"Don't fall asleep."

"I won't."

"Christ, your voice. Don't let go."

"You're preaching to the choir."

"Eddie, you hang in there."

"Stop making me talk so much. Call for an ambulance."

Freddy fumbled his cell phone out, getting blood everywhere. His fat fingers were too slippery to hit the right number. He kept pressing buttons asking, "Hello? Hello? Is this 911? Is anybody there?" Finally reaching somebody and shouting hysterically now, getting the address of the building wrong, even the cross street.

The sirens sort of just burst onto the scene from up the block. None of this hearing them in the distance for five minutes getting louder and louder. They must've hit them as soon as they turned the corner.

Whitt had an acute moment of regret thinking

about Lorrie and Anne Gunderson. Leaving them to slog through life under the taint of Killjoy's stigma. No matter who he'd loved or what good he'd done, Killjoy could never be redeemed.

He heard footsteps on the stairs, people shouting.

Freddy called to them, "Help! In here!" He sounded terrified and Whitt wanted to say how sorry he was for putting his last friend through this sort of shit and not even feeding him a decent meat loaf.

Diana Carver leaned over him with those blazing eyes peering out from the steel superhero mask. Whitt thought, No big deal, she'll just fly me to the hospital. Brunk was there too now, yelling something at the two cops behind him, all three of them with their guns trained on Killjoy's corpse. You had to have priorities.

Darkness wallowed and lingered at the rim of his vision, lapping for a time, and beginning to tug. Whitt looked over into the dollhouse. What a dumb move, all that training and then he fouls up his footwork like that. Guess it had to be. He saw Sarah peering out the living room window, her hands pressed against the pane, sobbing and trying to smash the glass. She cried, Daddy, Daddy, and he groaned. Moving up behind her now came Karen, her face crimped with determination. She hurled herself against the front door but it wouldn't budge. Whitt tried it from the other side, putting his shoulder to it, two, three times, about to throw himself against it again when he heard the quiet click of the lock snapping open. Meat loaf was cooking in the kitcher maybe it wasn't too late to feed Freddy a good meal. Brunk kneeled and moved the red towels aside and put his hands into Whitt's wet guts, trying to apply more pressure. The weird tiny thatch of hair slowly going this way, that way, timed with Whitt's ragged breaths. Someone spoke the Unspeakable Ten Thousand Eight Names, and his own was among them. Diana Carver bent over him, her face close to his, her lips glazed, and wiped the sweaty curls from his forehead. A musky, raw scent wafted from her. Whitt thought, In that mask she's finally going to kiss me. Don't go, she said, don't. Hold on. Tilting his head back and propping his jaw open, sealing her mouth over his. Rapping him in the chest. Karen said something that made him turn his head. He stepped inside and they came to him, his wife and daughter. He was back with his girls, laughing as he held his arms open and took them in, hugging them tighter while they whispered implausible secrets, and he had, he truly had, with the darkness stretching into impossible distances, he'd finally made it back home.

ABOUT THE AUTHOR

TOM PICCIRILLI lives in Colorado where, besides writing, he spends an inordinate amount of time watching trash cult films and reading Gold Medal classic noir and hardboiled novels. He's a fan of Asian cinema, especially horror movies, pinky violence, and samurai flicks. He also likes walking his dogs around the neighborhood. Are you starting to get the hint that he doesn't have a particularly active social life? Well, to heck with you, buddy, yours isn't much better. Give him any static and he'll smack you in the mush, dig? Tom also enjoys making new friends. He's the author of fifteen novels including *The Dead Letters, Headstone City, November Mourns,* and *A Choir of Ill Children.* He's a four-time winner of the Bram Stoker Award and a final nominee for the World Fantasy Award. To learn more, check out his official website, Epitaphs, at www.tompiccirilli.com.

Don't miss
TOM PICCIRILLI's
next novel,

THE
MIDNIGHT
ROAD

coming from Bantam Books
in Summer 2007.

Read on for an exclusive sneak peek,
and pick up your copy at your
favorite bookseller.

THE MIDNIGHT ROAD

by Tom Piccirilli
On sale Summer 2007

Flynn remembered the night of his death more clearly than any other in his life. The black details of it drove him from the wild slopes of his dreams back to the beginning of his pitch through the ice, down into the hopelessly dark waters below and the midnight road beyond.

There'd been a moment's premonition as he drove up the long narrow curve of the Shepards' driveway to their mini-mansion. A faint whisper of what was to come. The storm had ended two hours earlier, but a cluster of icicles had been rattled out of the trees by a heavy burst of wind. They slammed down against his hood so hard and unexpectedly that he overreacted and jammed the brake, his dead brother's '66 Charger going into a lissome power slide. He eased off the pedal and turned the wheel into the spin, relaxed with the familiar motions of someone who'd done a lot of street racing in his youth. The positraction got the car straightened almost immediately. His tires hit a clear patch of brick and let out a squeal like an animal cry of fear.

His stomach tightened. It was the kind of bad vibe he'd learned to ignore. Before his death he'd been an even bigger idiot than he was now.

There were no streetlights in that ritzy area of the North Shore. Maybe it was a sign of wealth, having to wind your way through the night all on your own. It seemed to be the case in a lot of rich neighborhoods on Long Island.

He looked out the frosted driver's-side window.

From the moment when he saw the two pale figures wafting like white lace on the snow-filled front lawn, meeting and parting and joining again in the moonlight, he had fifty minutes left to live.

Flynn's headlights flashed across the terrain and immediately the grim nerve worked through his chest again, twitching under his heart. Late January, eight o'clock, already dark, and there was a girl and a dog prancing about in the frozen yard, no parents in sight. It wasn't a good sign but he didn't want to jump to conclusions.

Most anonymous tips to Child Protective Services could be tracked back to a neighbor on either side of the home in question. But the Shepards had no neighbors within view. Large lots of brush and woodland rose up around the huge house.

This time out Flynn had caught the call. Tipster said a child was in danger at this address. No other comment. There didn't need to be one. If somebody says a kid's welfare is at risk, you move. You catch the call, you take the ride.

The girl stopped traipsing and stood at attention in her white ski suit and snow boots, watching him. The dog was a French bulldog, all white except for a black ring around one eye, wearing a white sweater and little plastic booties. It sat at her heel with its chin up, head cocked, staring intently at Flynn as he stepped out of his car. The only color that night seeped out from the dual golden front lights and the twin bronzed lanterns bordering the home's two-car garage.

In the glow he saw that the girl was about seven. A swath of snow clung to her chin. Her breath blew white streamers that burst against his belly as he approached. The dog's breath broke across his legs.

He had to play it carefully. If he approached the kid and she got spooked, screamed, ran into daddy's arms, then Flynn introduced himself as an investigator for Suffolk County CPS and the guy wasn't abusing her, all kinds of hell could break loose. Fisticuffs, maybe worse. Nobody wanted to be called a child molester, not even the ones who were guilty.

That's why most investigators were women. A lady could woo the wife, seem less threatening to the hubby. Flynn still wasn't quite sure how he wound up on the job, but for him one of the big perks was when some bitter, middle-aged ex-high-school jock who liked working over his wife and kids decided to throw down. You took your action wherever you could.

It was late. He should've been here over two hours ago, but the storm had hit while he was stuck in traffic on the expressway. Nobody could get anywhere as the freezing rain came down and the slush on the road turned to ice. Within a half hour there had been a hundred fender benders as drivers tried to roll off to the median, park, and wait it out.

He didn't want to frighten the girl. She didn't really seem spookable, standing there looking at him, but he wanted to go easy. She took two steps through the snow, her blond hair squeezing out from around her hood, framing her cute face. "Who are you?" she asked.

"I'm Flynn."

"I'm Kelly. This is Zero. What are you doing here?"

"I'd like to speak with your parents."

"Okay."

"Aren't you cold out here this late, Kelly?"

"Yeah," she admitted. "I wanted to see the storm, but my mother wouldn't let me until it had stopped. We're about to go inside. I'd invite you in, but I'm not supposed to do that. How about if you stay right where you are until I get to the door, and then you can follow, all right?"

"Sure," Flynn said.

Smart kid. Practical, even. He always got thrown by smart kids. He'd be getting ready to talk baby talk and they'd suddenly start speaking like college grads.

More icicles clattered in the trees overhead. Flynn leaned back against the Charger watching the girl make her way to the house, the small dog fighting his way through the drifts.

There were strict codes on how investigations were supposed to proceed. He'd been with CPS for five years and neither his boss nor the Attorney General's office ever gave him any static. He was the best they had because he didn't have any social life to interfere, which sort of put the whole thing into a bleak perspective.

Flynn slipped twice just stepping up to the front door.

Mrs. Shepard answered before he got a chance to stomp the snow from his shoes. Kelly stood right behind her to the left, and the dog sat behind Kelly. Flynn got the feeling he was in a very orderly household. One of those intensely domestic homes that ran with military precision and generally creeped other people out.

Mrs. Shepard had a flaccid smile soldered in place. She stared at him through the storm door and said, "Yes? How can I help you? What's this about?"

There were rules. You had to be up front. You couldn't rope the parents into anything. Couldn't sneak in and snap pictures. You had to be given permission to look around the house. They could deny you. They could shriek about lawyers.

He told her his name, showed his identification, explained that an anonymous complaint had been registered. Mrs. Shepard nodded as if she knew all about it and let him inside. He explained his position and asked that he be allowed to check the house. While he spoke, he casually surveyed Kelly, who had shed her snowsuit. No bruises on her face or arms that he could see. She seemed like a regular, happy kid.

Flynn waited to register Mrs. Shepard's response, but there wasn't any. The lady just kept smiling and said nothing. The bulldog strolled past looking sort of humiliated to still be wearing the booties.

"Mrs. Shepard?"

Finally she said, "Yes? What is it you want? What do you think goes on here?"

"Mrs. Shepard, as I said—"

"I'm Christina."

She was all riptide intensity. Flynn could sense the conflicting tensions inside her but had no idea what they were or how they would affect him. Her smile appeared to be painful, scraped into her face by a fishing knife. Her teeth were drying out, their high gloss fading. The faint aroma of scotch trailed off her. She was maybe thirty, quite attractive, with burnished copper hair that fell in two wide, rippling currents. The glaze in her eyes kept him from getting any kind of a real bead on her.

So he waited.

"Would you like some tea?" she asked finally.

That was a first. No one had ever offered him tea before. "No thank you," he said.

"How do we proceed?"

"I'd appreciate a tour of your home."

"And what will that prove? If I'm beating my child to the point that a neighbor—the nearest of which lives several hundred yards away—can hear her screams, wouldn't she be battered? Are you looking for pools of blood?" The smile had downshifted into an almost amiable grin, except it was way too wide. The corners of her mouth were spread so far they almost touched her earlobes.

"I'm just doing an on-site evaluation. It's very standard."

"Not for me it isn't."

"I realize that. I'm very sorry, Christina, but once a complaint has been lodged we have to follow up."

"This late? It's almost Kelly's bedtime."

"The storm kept me. Again, I apologize for the intrusion."

She was given to dramatic movements. Swinging herself around and gesturing with her hands like she was scrawling in the air. Kelly and the dog intuited her motions and kept stepping along with her, keeping just behind her, just to the left. It was a weird kind of ballet he was watching, the three of them so gracefully maneuvering along in the front hallway.

"All right," Christina Shepard said, giving him that leering smile again. "Let's take a tour of my home."

She walked him through it, all three floors. She offered to open drawers even though he said it wasn't necessary. She opened them anyway. Her hostility came off her in waves, the way he expected. But there was something more there. Flynn couldn't figure out what it might be, and his curiosity was really starting to bang around inside him. He stared at the side of her face as she led him room to room, propping open armoires and dressers.

She put her hands on him only once, gripping him by the upper arm and steering him toward the master bathroom. This lady had some serious muscle. He felt her coiled strength and the furnace of her agitation. She opened the medicine cabinet, grabbed a handful of pill bottles, and started reading off labels. "Zyrtec, this is for allergies. Flexeril is a muscle relaxant for my husband Mark, who has a bad back. Zoloft is medication for depression. I suffer from it. Surely that's not a crime."

"No, it's not," he said.

"Thank God for that. Would you like to speak to my daughter? Ask her questions?" The mask slipped another notch as she called for Kelly. The girl and the dog paraded into the bedroom like Marines landing on a foreign beach. "Foul questions, no doubt. What kind of a man wheedles his way into working with children every day, Mr. Flynn? What thoughts go through your piggy mind?"

He let it slide. She had a head full of serpents herself, he'd decided. He'd heard a lot worse and Christina Shepard didn't seem angry with him so much as she appeared flush with clashing forces.

Flynn turned to the girl and said, "Kelly, I work for people who look after children just in case someone is hurting them. Maybe even a friend or someone in the family. It happens sometimes. Do you have anything you want to say to me?"

She peered at him like he was a puzzle with a few missing pieces. "Are you asking if my mother and father hit me, Mr. Flynn?"

"Yes."

She let out a titter and covered her mouth, and the bulldog did a little dance in his booties and barked happily. "Of course not. Why would you ask me something like that?"

"There, are you satisfied?" Christina said. "I'd like you to leave me and my family in peace now."

Flynn said, "Thank you for your cooperation, Mrs. Shepard."

"Fine. Just go."

She didn't follow him as he left the upstairs bedroom, but the bulldog did. It got in front of him and dropped a chew toy at his feet. A plastic hamburger. Flynn tossed it down the stairs and Zero shot off after it. The dog waited at the bottom of the stairs until Flynn got there, then dropped the burger at his feet again. Flynn bent to grab it one last time before he left, and the nerve twitched inside him again.

He didn't know why at first. It took a second to figure out. He looked left and right. He glanced back up the stairs. He was leaning over with his face near a heating vent.

He heard humming coming from somewhere deep in the house. A man softly murmuring a childish tune.

You didn't expect to hear a man sound like that. It wasn't a guy singing lullabies to his kids. There was more to it. The man *was* the kid. Flynn's stomach tightened at the tune and his scalp prickled.

He looked back over his shoulder. Christina and Kelly Shepard were still upstairs in the master bedroom. Zero was still waiting for Flynn to toss him the burger. Flynn did so and the dog went scampering. Then Flynn looked along the length of the walls and tried to track the vents in the direction he thought the sound might be coming from. He walked past the living room to the large kitchen. There were three doors there. One led to the garage. Another was a huge closet that was more like a storeroom, full of massive boxes and gigantic cans and enormous jugs, the kind of oversized packages you get at a cost-cutting warehouse.

The last door led to a cellar.

Flynn had twenty-seven minutes to live.

He didn't like the look of the door. There were two sets of locks, both open. His bad juju detector was already blaring. He pulled out his pocketknife and worked the hinge pins free and put them in his coat pocket. The way the door hung, it looked exactly the same, but nobody would be able to lock him down there.

He was playing it all wrong but something kept telling him this was the only way to play it. His brother's presence felt so strong around him now that he could imagine spinning around fast enough to catch sight of Danny. He didn't have enough for the cops, not even for his boss Sierra, who was already going to read him the riot act for the way he'd played this one. He'd be lucky if he stayed out of the pokey himself.

But some things you couldn't help. You decided on your course, and you saw it through.

He hit the light and descended the stairs.

It wasn't a cellar, but a damn nice basement turned into a guy pad. It was the kind of room that men without sons spent a lot of money on while awaiting the arrival of their first boy. A flat-screen high-definition television sat high against one wall. Shelves were packed with a huge DVD library. An ample L-shaped leather sofa made Flynn think this was the place where all Shepard's friends watched the Super Bowl and the World Series every year. There were sports collectibles in glass cases all around: signed photos, footballs, catcher's mitts, boxing gloves.

It would've been a hell of a nice place except for the guy in the cage in the middle of the room.

Flynn just stared for a second. Sometimes you needed an extra breath to help you decide where to go next.

The cage was pretty small, the size of a boarding kennel for a German shepherd. Bars were half-inch steel, and the frame had been welded together with precision. The door had been padlocked.

Inside sat a man with a misshapen head, as if someone had flung him against a cement wall when he was an infant. His slack lower jaw bent too far to one side and threads of drool slid down his chin. Thick, knotted scars and brandings cross-thatched his body, even his inner thighs. His left arm had been broken, poorly set, and now tilted slightly backwards at the elbow. He was still humming, and his gentle brown eyes that were about an inch too far apart kept watching Flynn.

"Hey, hello there," Flynn said, trying to make his

voice sound as natural as possible. He wasn't doing anywhere near a good job of it. "I'm your friend. I'm Flynn. Can you talk to me? Can you understand me?"

The man grinned, his gaze full of bewilderment and delight. Something started to crack in Flynn's chest. After all he'd been through, the guy was still glad to see another person, still singing. The nerve throbbed so painfully through Flynn that he had to put his hand against the cage to steady himself.

He checked the stairs thinking this could be it, this might be the night he got shoved over the line and he'd never be able to cross back again.

Zero appeared at Flynn's ankle with the plastic hamburger in his teeth. The booties did a good job of soundproofing his paws. The cellar door creaked and slipped off one of the hinges. Flynn heard a small cry of surprise. Zero circled and Kelly appeared on the stairway. She had a handful of cookies wrapped in a napkin.

She saw Flynn but showed no surprise, just a smidgen of irritation. "Did you break the door?"

"Sorry about that."

"You found Nuddin. He's my uncle." Bending to the cage, she handed him the cookies through the bars. Nuddin accepted them and chewed them down with joyous noises. He only ate half of each one, and offered each remaining half to Zero, who ate from his hand.

Nuddin?

Nothing?

"How long's he been here?" Flynn asked.

"Since before my last birthday."

"Okay. When's your birthday, Kelly?"

"June. June fifteenth. I was seven. I'm seven and a half now."

More than six months the man had been down here.

Flynn had seen it twice before, mentally challenged children locked up in back rooms, kept in chains, but that had been in the south Bronx. In areas that looked like they'd been invaded, blitzed, nuked, where the rules dried up and things got savage, and superstitions burned out of control. Roosters ran wild in the streets, where they were kept on hand for the Santeria rituals. Maybe it was Santeria. Maybe new religions were being born every day in the slums. Flynn had seen a lot in his time, but you just didn't expect a retarded man to be caged in the basement of a million-dollar house out on the North Shore.

"Kelly, where's the key?"

"My mother has it."

"We need to get him out of here."

"Why?"

"Because it's wrong to keep people locked up like this."

"I bring him cookies...and fudge...and cake sometimes. I gave him a big piece of my birthday cake, it even had a rose on it."

"You're very nice."

"It wasn't a real rose though, it was whipped cream."

Zero dropped the burger at Flynn's foot and started pawing at his shoe, trying to get him to play some more. Flynn started for the stairs, hoping he could get the drop on Christina Shepard, but she was already there, perched halfway down, holding a Smith & Wesson .38 trained on him. He was beginning to think that the rules about how he was supposed to handle his business were really very fucking stupid.